From Best to Bested

FROM BEST to Bested

MN BENNET

Paperback ISBN: 979-8-9901493-4-2
Ebook ISBN: 979-8-9901493-3-5

Edited by Charlie Knight (CKnightWrites.com)
Cover art by Dragana (graphicsoulart.com)

www.mnbennet.com/

Author's Note

This is the darkest story I've ever written, and every word poured onto the page came with a cathartic release. Writing and reading are definitely ways to explore thoughts, emotions, and everything in between. All the same, I usually shy away from anything too explicit. This story haunted me for years, always a fleeting image here or there in the back of my head, but I always told myself it was too disturbing to write.

Finally, I gave into a scene just to get it out of my head, then another, and before I knew it I had several chapters written, a functional outline, and a desperate clawing need to tell Roman's story. This isn't a story for everyone and that's okay. This was a story I needed to write and one I hope to share with interested readers. It's disturbing and dark. It's unapologetic. It's raw and vulnerable at times while being surreal and uncomfortably erotic in other areas.

From Best to Bested is a MM dark romance. This is a tale about defeat, surrender, and submission, then clawing a way back out. Please check content warnings at the beginning of the book.

CWs:

- CNC
- Dubcon
- Manipulation
- Gaslighting
- Coercion
- Humiliation
- Bullying
- Anxiety and paranoia
- Self-loathing
- Name calling (pet names that are not affectionate)
- Homophobia
- Toxic masculinity
- Power Imbalance
- Hazing
- Violence/fighting
- Physical assault
- Hospitalization
- Torture (physical and psychological—not in relation to sex)
- Toxic relationship
- Emotional assault
- Emotional submission
- Graphic deaths (off page but explicit)
- Graphic violence on page
- Death on page
- Blood
- Service-oriented submission
- Attempted SA (on page)

Extreme acts of sex: oral, face and throat fucking, total top who is rough/aggressive, anal, choking, spanking, face slapping, fingering, rimming, biting, public play, pain, cum swallowing/eating/playing, breath play, praise and degradation, vocal top, noisy sub, hands-free orgasm, voyeurism, power dynamics including extreme acts of submission, cock warming, tongue baths, somnophilia, gagging, spitting, breeding, conditioning (psychological)

Actions of SA told through flashback: Drugging and manipulation (leads to non con), group action, gangbang, throat fucking, anal, branding, breeding, humiliation, and violence beyond measure of consent.

- To be clear, these are explicit warnings and highlighted during the flashback recollection scene (some are more graphically recalled while others are alluded to based on the state of the character's appearance the following day).

Dedication

For those who wanted to see more than Icarus' fall when he flew too close to the sun. Here's the journey through Hell after the plummet.

Chapter One

"Our champion has done it again!" Warden Sadler announced as Roman brought down his second opponent for the night.

Both audiences roared as Roman strutted around the arena. Less an arena and more a pit. Not the actual Pit that Roman had heard rumors of, but the concrete floor was unforgiving to anyone unfortunate enough to fall. But as champion, Roman didn't fall. He learned very quickly if he wanted to survive in Marlow Penitentiary and survive well, then he could never falter.

He kept his head held high for a moment, brushing a bandaged hand along his sweaty brow and knocking aside his shaggy brown bangs. This let the audience in the balcony above bask in Roman's face, letting them see the pride he wore as their reigning champion. They were the wealthy elite who funded every corrupt machination at Marlow Penitentiary.

Inmates called them the Lawless Authority, an absurd name in Roman's mind, but quicker than "rich snobs who indulged in illegal fights to satiate their own lust for bloodshed and crime," which was basically the lawless component of their name. The authority came from the fact they dictated things in the arena, bankrolling winners, sponsoring events, paying to shut up anyone who annoyed them, and so much more Roman tried to avoid when it came to the audience in the balcony above.

The second audience was more of a crowd that circled him like vultures, held in check by the guards who attended the late-night rumbles. This group was honestly held more in check by Roman and his unrelenting show of dominance.

"You call that a challenge?" Roman roared, tightening the gauze on his right hand before pointing an indiscriminate finger at the crowd. "I thought you lot wanted to come for my title."

The crowd had nearly a hundred inmates surrounding Roman from all sides. He ran the length of the makeshift arena, strutting close to the inmates and demanding a new challenger with his gaze. When that didn't work, he taunted them again.

"Is this all you offer?" Roman pointed to his unconscious opponent. "Have you all really just given up?"

In order to maintain the role of champion, he needed to defend his title, and the authority above favored him when he won consecutive lineups during the Challenger's Chance, an open mic, so to speak, for opponents to face Roman Grayson.

Most of the inmates here had fought and lost against Roman at least once. Few came down here just to watch, though some prioritized the stakes of the winning pots over the combat itself. Roman didn't care about the profit. Yes, he savored every penny thrown into his commissary, and every dollar added to his off-the-books account controlled by the warden himself, but what Roman wanted when he stepped into the arena was the power that came with his title.

At twenty-two, he felt more powerful than anyone else here, but sometimes, he still remembered the frightened twenty-year-old college kid who'd nearly left the world of violence behind him. Roman thought about the years he spent at university, the fighting days he put behind him after he learned he'd never go pro, the illusion of a real future with a career in whatever he wanted, the chances of leaving shit like this behind him, and then remembered it only took one fucking mistake to ruin everything.

Champions didn't make mistakes. They couldn't afford it. He couldn't and wouldn't allow it.

That was why he never wavered as champion. A weak champion, one too afraid to face his foes, would be dealt with outside the arena in an empty corridor with a guard who turned the other way. A cocky champion, one too brazen with competition, would end up face-first on the concrete. It took everything Roman had to maintain some semblance of a balance. It kept inmates in line, kept them off his back, kept them away from as many of the young men, the elderly men, and generally anyone too weak or naïve or pathetic to protect themselves.

Roman didn't care to be a hero—not that folks lined up to call him such things—life had beaten that out of him years ago. But he didn't like cruelty for the sake of being vicious, and his reign as champion at least kept the worst of it out of Marlow Penitentiary. He didn't delude himself into thinking everyone wanted to hold hands and thank Roman for his valiant efforts, but he knew after breaking a few jaws and reminding the world he was the strongest motherfucker here that it helped others breathe a bit easier.

"Come on," Roman shouted, adding a taunting edge to his voice. "Is there anyone bold enough to step up during the Challenger's Chance?"

He ran the length of the audience, walking in circles, stepping close to inmates, daring them to strike. Sometimes, he could tease a member into a blitz attack. No one fought fair in life—a lesson Roman carried for years before he ended up incarcerated—so he encouraged the behavior when directed toward him. Roman could take it. Roman could take anything anyone threw at him. He could stand tall and beat down any threat. He could survive and hold his title because that was how Roman stayed safe.

"I will!"

Roman smirked, turning around to take in the sight of his final opponent for the night.

Maxwell fucking King.

"*They planned this well,*" Roman thought, taking a deep breath.

He'd pissed around overexerting himself during the first two matches of the night, and now the gangs had plucked Maxwell King to finish off the Challenger's Chance, which was open for anyone to compete and dare to take the champion's title. Maxwell was 6'8" and nearly a foot taller than Roman, who hovered an inch or two below 6'0" depending on how much leeway he gave himself on measurements. Maxwell also had biceps thicker than Roman's neck and was built like a fucking Mack truck.

The title of champion came with a double-edged sword. Everyone fell in line to obey Roman's will; it afforded protection in the form of fear to him and anyone he wanted to protect, but it also opened Roman up to enemies everywhere. Most were too frightened to make a move on him, in or out of the arena, but they all waited with bated breath for his defeat.

Until Roman Grayson arrived at Marlow Penitentiary, the role of champion had never lasted more than two months. Roman had held onto the title for over a year. Almost fifteen months now, and he accepted at least three challenges during the weekly events, sometimes adding a second or third fight night in a week depending on the season, and he never once lost.

As Roman squared up against the man more than a foot taller with easily a hundred fifty pounds on him, Roman reminded himself the only way to stay on top was to never fucking lose.

Roman had faced Maxwell before in the arena. Roman also had the misfortune of facing Maxwell once outside the arena. Maxwell didn't take his first loss well and tried to gut Roman inside the weight room, which also ended up being the solution to an armed blitz attack where Maxwell sought revenge. Roman had bashed Maxwell's face in with a twenty-pound dumbbell and knew Maxwell held bitter resentment for Roman ever since, along with a crooked nose, five missing teeth, and an indent from the piece of his cheek they couldn't restore.

But while Roman had exploited his surroundings during the attempted alleged assault—the warden's words, not Roman's—he didn't have that luxury in the arena. If Roman wanted to beat Maxwell again, he had to fight him the same way he had the first time they crossed paths.

The difference being that Maxwell only saw a plucky dumb kid who got lucky to land champion the last time they faced off. Now, Maxwell knew what to expect when stepping into the arena against Roman, and Roman knew the terrible disadvantage that put him at during this official rematch.

With the ring of the bell and the roar of the crowd, Roman got to work. Immediately, he moved in for light strikes anywhere not packed with a mountain of muscle. In order to beat Maxwell, Roman had to rely on bug bites over bulldozer blows. Keeping his stamina in check, Roman remembered his breathing and weaved around Maxwell. One hit, one real punch, would knock the breath from his chest, and Roman couldn't afford to give up any tiny edge he had. Maxwell would wear out first. As the man raged with powerful swings of his fists, Roman could already see the toll it took. Little by little, Roman let Maxwell whittle down his own reserves while Roman taunted him with futile strikes.

"I'm going to fucking kill you." Maxwell nearly clocked Roman, stepping in closer than Roman anticipated and locking him against the crowd.

Roman ducked and rolled away, scrambling to his feet as Maxwell stomped behind him, determined to beat Roman while he crawled to safety. Maxwell's boots slammed with loud bangs, the force of steel against concrete, and Roman realized the footwear had a bottom padding of metal to really ensure Maxwell would break Roman's face with one swift kick.

The crowd wasn't a safe place for Roman; they hated him as much as he hated them. He kept low to the ground, rolling away from Maxwell's strikes as much as he avoided the danger of the crowd.

Once, in a show of stealth, Roman allowed himself to fall back into the protection of the audience when in a two-on-one match-up. Biggest mistake of his life. He still carried three scars on his left hip from the shiv someone used to level the fight against his favor. The warden hadn't called things to an end during that match, and Roman knew he wouldn't consider Maxwell's boots an unfair advantage now.

Roman nearly made it to his feet when Maxwell knocked into him, and Roman rolled close to the crowd. Too close. Someone started kicking him in the ribs, knocking the breath out of his lungs. Roman didn't have time to look at the coward who'd dared. Pick a number with this fucking group. No, Roman had already lost precious seconds and needed to escape Maxwell's thunderous stomps.

He moved with such terrible force, Roman didn't see a way out, a way to win, a way to avoid the heavy footsteps that sought to stomp Roman into the ground.

Maybe he didn't have to avoid the inevitable. A terrible idea crossed Roman's mind, and he hated himself a little for it. Any pain he felt seemed a fitting reward for his reckless strategy.

Unable to dodge, unable to get to his feet, Roman slid forward and punched Maxwell in the balls. The man's boots weren't the only thing made of steel, though. Roman had tried this strategy once before, only to find out Maxwell didn't flinch, and just like last time, Maxwell smiled down at Roman's foolishness and smacked him across the face.

The backhanded slap was less lethal than a punch, but Roman registered the reasoning. Maxwell wanted to shame Roman more than pummel him. He also needed Roman on his back, not slumped over and semi-conscious from a few punches. No, Maxwell wanted Roman to be fully awake and aware for what came next.

Without delay, Maxwell slammed his foot down into Roman's chest and stole what little air he held onto. Roman screamed, unable to stifle the pain of the boot coming down on him. Again and again and again.

Maxwell put the full weight of his body into the crushing force of his foot. Roman didn't resist, allowing Maxwell to feel the pressure of Roman's chest, ready to collapse. His hands seemed like delicate things when gripped onto Maxwell's massive foot. The man had smug satisfaction, pinning Roman beneath his heel and preparing to end him. He wouldn't stop at Roman's surrender. No, he'd want Roman's submission; he'd want Roman to admit his weakness when faced with pure unstoppable dominance.

"You're almost as ugly as you are stupid." Roman winked.

With that, it sent rage coursing through Maxwell as Roman anticipated, and when the man lifted his foot to give one more terrible and mighty stomp, Roman slipped his hands where he needed. Using everything he had, Roman twisted Maxwell's foot and used his weight against him. Maxwell had been foolish, tipping his own balance when crushing Roman, and all Roman needed was to tilt the trajectory a little more.

Maxwell hit the concrete, and everything went silent for a moment. His fall created a literal quake as the towering giant had been felled.

Roman didn't stop twisting just because Maxwell had tumbled forward and crashed to the ground. No. Roman didn't stop twisting until something popped. When Maxwell screamed, Roman snatched off the man's metal boot and straddled his chest as Maxwell struggled to roll over.

Roman slipped his hand into the boot and punched Maxwell in the face. When Maxwell roared, Roman punched him a second time. When Maxwell went feral, Roman punched him a third time. When the crowd booed, Roman punched Maxwell a fourth time. When Maxwell passed out, Roman got up and stalked toward one of the guards holding a line for the crowd. Some phony effort to keep order during the chaos of combat.

Roman punched him with the metal boot still over his fist. He removed the boot and let it drop next to the bloody and wheezing guard with a loud clank.

Instigating fights against the people in charge of his life had never been something Roman wavered with before or after his incarceration. It didn't take long for Roman to learn which guards were good and which were on the take.

Roman knew which guards inmates could trust, he knew who would turn a blind eye during an assault, he knew who moved product, and he knew this guard had acquired the boots for Maxwell King.

"Enjoy your matching faces, you fucker." Roman took heavy breaths, soaking in the roar of the crowd.

They might've hated him most of the time, but when they showed him love, it sent a rush of adrenaline coursing through him. It hit Roman with a high unlike anything he'd experienced. Roman loved these fleeting seconds, the wave of victory, the chant of loyalty, the calm afterglow of combat. He lived for these moments; he clawed at them.

"What a splendid victory," Warden Sadler announced, either burying his resentment for Roman's antics or truly not giving a fuck about the guard's face. "What a glorious bout with the Challenger's Chance. Our reigning champion has once again cemented his place at the top. Be sure to come back and see who the champion declares for the winter semi-match lineup."

Roman took heavy breaths, still holding back his exhaustion and unwilling to let anyone here see how truly winded he was, but he studied the crowd. Part of being champion was having a hand in all the competitions, not only his own fights. Being champion meant taking on the responsibility of working closely with Warden Sadler, but Roman tired of that early on, finding the corrupt man a bigger headache than a champion should have to listen to.

"Is that really it?" someone shouted.

Only Roman heard it. Only Roman heard it because he always listened to the whispers between the roars, always prepared for the threats veiled beneath the cheers, always ready for any attack.

"You go a few rounds, and you're done," the person called out again.

This time, a few others heard, and this time, the crowd quieted some.

"Talk about staging the bullshit," he said again, the stranger whose voice became more and more grating as it grew louder, and the audience became quieter.

Roman turned to face this loudmouth.

"Anyone here take bets on the big one falling?" An unfamiliar face appeared from the crowd, and the young guy pushed his way to the front. "I could've made a racket if I realized you were just playing pretend."

"Nothing fake about this," someone argued—someone likely friends with Maxwell and offended by the implications.

"I'm just saying," the new guy continued. "Your champion set it up real good. Take out the biggest threat and then call it a night."

"*That's because no one else is here to challenge me,*" Roman thought, but he bit back his words, too exhausted for an argument or another fight.

"I'd like to step up." The guy stretched his arms wide with confidence, awaiting a cheering crowd that didn't follow. "I'll take the Challenger's Chance."

Roman shrugged off the cheap taunting, not impressed or intimidated. He'd just taken down Maxwell King, who wore literal steel boots. There was no one who'd fall for some no-name's feeble attempt at looking brave.

"Looks like we've got ourselves another contender," Warden Sadler announced, egging on the audience around Roman and the one who watched from above.

Masked figures studied Roman, and he sighed as the warden gave weight to this new face. As the champion, he could accept or decline any match-up. Too many rejections, and he'd look weak. Every part of Roman wanted to say no, but Warden Sadler kept applying pressure with his words, encouraging the audience to join in, and Roman felt the pressure.

Warden Sadler hated Roman and would honestly push Roman into a million back-to-back fights if he could swing it.

The warden used to force Roman to interact with the clientele on the balcony more frequently. They were the real authority in the arena. The inmates and guards might've hated Roman, and the warden might've despised Roman, but so long as Roman remained champion, he remained in favor of the money that kept everything here moving.

After shucking his responsibilities for far too long, Warden Sadler tried to force Roman to meet the authority above, private showings where they could fawn over the mighty inmate, the champion in the slums, the dirty fighter they would clean up.

Roman put an abrupt stop to those meetings. When Warden Sadler challenged him, Roman broke the man's nose. When the warden tossed Roman in solitary for three weeks, Roman didn't break. When Roman finally returned to the arena, both men came to an understanding.

The Lawless Authority loved Roman, and his sudden absence demanded an explanation. Warden Sadler couldn't touch Roman so long as he remained champion, but Roman knew one misstep would be his demise.

"Fuck it," Roman thought before he stepped into the center of the arena and waved over his foolish opponent.

If he could survive a rigged match against Maxwell King, he could hold his own against anyone else tonight. He wasn't foolish, arrogant perhaps, too arrogant to shrug off the taunting, but smart enough to know to end the match quickly.

"What's your name, buddy?" Roman asked with a cocky grin. "I like to know who I'm bending over."

The laughter of the crowd made Roman's insides twist with regret. Roman wouldn't be bending this guy over; he didn't bend anyone over. Prison rules mixed with hyper-masculinity didn't offer Roman many choices when it came to feeding the beast of trash talk, though. It took everything Roman had as champion to put a stop to as many of the rapes around here as his clout offered. He still never stopped the screwing. Not that he wanted to. Live and let live, he didn't give a fuck who anyone fucked. But he knew a pressured face lying to him when Roman would try to interject. Some men went so quietly and so willingly, Roman considered the ruling as champion a futile effort in a broken system. At least he tried more than the staff.

The young man stepped into the arena, taking off his shirt and shifting his stance to match Roman's. From how he carried himself and the build of his body, Roman gathered he wasn't a stranger to combat. He wasn't as muscular as Roman, a bit leaner by the looks of it, but taller by a few inches. The sides of his head were shaved short, but the rest of his black hair was thick and styled in a sloppy fauxhawk, considering there was limited access to proper products, but the raised hair added to his height.

"Ezra Delgado," his fourth opponent for the night responded. "But you can call me Champion."

His deep bronze complexion was covered in faded tattoos and small scars, an indicator he was not afraid of a little pain.

Roman's own pale skin lacked tattoos, but his fresh bruises for the night had an almost humorously matching pattern to Ezra's ink.

"Oh, I like you." Roman would keep an eye on Ezra after he knocked some sense into him tonight.

Young guys like him, ones that didn't walk in with an immediate bond to a gang or family behind bars, often found themselves at the mercy of the cruel. Roman knew from experience that mouthy motherfuckers had to defend themselves more often or learn to shut the fuck up.

Something about Ezra suggested he didn't quiet down just because a threat towered toward him. Roman respected that.

Warden Sadler announced the match, and Roman went to work evaluating Ezra. It didn't take long to figure out Ezra moved as quickly as Roman, something two quick jabs to the face taught him. He favored his left side, so Roman did his best to skirt around on Ezra's right. That tactic only offered Roman a few breaths between blows.

Eventually, Roman and Ezra found themselves in a steady back-and-forth. Roman let Ezra lead the fight, using the time to catch his breath and look for patterns. Once he got a good gauge for things, Roman moved in fast, faster than Ezra's eyes could track. Roman was exhausted, but he had more than enough stamina to hold out.

A few swift punches changed the direction of the match, and soon, it was Ezra intently backing away, falling short of escaping Roman's reach and trying to study the move sets. Roman learned long ago to never leave a trail to follow. He changed his tactics, pulling Ezra back into stalking forward. When Ezra resisted, Roman taunted with some well-placed and painful punches. Anger often gave way to strategy, and Roman used that to pull Ezra into his defeat.

"How long you been here?" Roman asked, taking a lucky shot from Ezra, but only so he could knock him squarely in the chest.

"First day." Ezra winced, regretting the back step as his footing stumbled.

"No way." Roman weaved around Ezra and punched him in the right side with enough force to knock the wind out of his lungs. "First day, and you managed to slip down here."

Roman baited Ezra with a few more questions, enjoying the conversation and noting how easy it was to feed off the guy's energy. The more Roman caught his second wind— well, more like his seventh wind at this point—the more Ezra struggled to keep up.

It didn't take much longer before Roman had knocked Ezra off his feet and sent him crashing into the concrete. Ezra struggled to move, his hands shaky on the ground. Roman leaned in, a bit to taunt his opponent, a bit to rile the last of the fight left in him. Ezra swiped, then faltered, and returned his hand to keep from collapsing entirely.

"Nice moves," Roman said mockingly, but he held genuine respect for the boldness.

Roman had waited nearly two months after his arrival at Marlow Penitentiary before daring to step down into the arena. He waited another month before stepping into his first match. It'd been nearly six months before he was bold enough to make for the Challenger's Chance and challenge the former champion.

"Catch your breath, kid," Roman said as if he were some sage old man.

Truthfully, he and Ezra looked about the same age. Hell, Ezra might've even had a year or two on him. Still, with the man stumbling and panting for desperate breaths as his entire body trembled, Roman couldn't help but feel he looked down at a desperate, young kid. Roman recalled being that young, that sloppy, years before his incarceration, years before he found his way out of the darkness of his life, not that he got very far considering where he stood now.

Ezra had great moves, natural skills, but he was sloppy. When this was finished, Roman would help train Ezra.

Roman turned to the crowd, raising his arms and demanding their cheers. The authority above applauded, and the inmates below shouted. Everyone wanted blood. Demanded it. Roman let them rage, let them roar, and he did his best to think of the best way to knock Ezra out so it'd make everyone's night without completely ruining Ezra's.

Roman turned to face Ezra one final time and found he'd vanished. Too quick and silent for someone in his winded condition.

A pain crashed against the back of Roman's head, and the realization of his hubris hit almost as hard as the fist.

The collapse had been a feint to catch Roman off guard, and he'd fallen for it too. He'd walked right into Ezra's trap, left himself exposed because of his own fucking ego.

Roman's eyes went wide, caught in the chokehold and unable to break loose. Everything he did to knock himself into Ezra, to pivot the weight, to shift their stance, didn't work. This didn't happen to Roman. He didn't move this carelessly. And if he did, if he found himself unable to breathe with an arm squeezing tight across his throat, he knew how to escape.

Every correct step failed him. It was as if Ezra predicted Roman's escape attempts, contorting his body to lean into Roman's failed efforts to break loose. Roman bucked against the pressure, against the growing weight of Ezra's body, as his footing finally gave way.

Roman landed face-first on the ground, and the rush of blood startled him awake as the tightening noose around his throat carried shadows across his vision.

Roman fought harder, taking what shreds of conserved strength remained, and worked to flip out of Ezra's grasp. A standing break would be easier. The ground worked against him, and Ezra seemed to team up with gravity to pin Roman in place. Instinct told Roman to flail, to scream, to panic as everything went red.

Red from fury. Red from blood. Red from fear-soaked shame.

It hurt, it nearly broke him, but Roman finally gained the tiniest bit of leverage and sucked in a desperate breath. He took a second breath to beat back the gnawing shadows that pulled him into the void of slumber. If he passed out, it was over. Roman had to properly break free.

Ezra slipped his thighs around Roman's waist during the scuffle, during the near escape on Roman's part. Once he had a solid grip, Ezra spun around, slammed on his own back so Roman was stuck on top, his stomach stretched tight as Ezra's legs held Roman's bottom half in place, and Ezra's arm squeezed tighter around Roman's throat. Ezra pulled so hard, Roman believed his head might pop off like a fucking doll.

Using his elbows, Roman tried to knock Ezra in the ribs, then his fists to punch Ezra in the face, but to no avail. Ezra used his legs to control the sway of their motions, both men looking like a turtle on its back. Roman's elbows beat into the concrete ground more than with their target, and his fists never landed enough force on Ezra's face to break his hold.

With his free hand, Ezra punched Roman in the ribcage. His strikes hit hard, the target completely unobstructed. The first punch radiated with pain, spreading across Roman's entire body. A desperate and exhausted body. The second punch knocked out what little precious air Roman clung to. The third punch put an end to Roman's elbowing. The fourth made Roman's legs give out entirely. The fifth made his arms surrender.

Roman wouldn't surrender, though. He shouted, feral and furious. He was a beast. He was the champion. He didn't surrender, he didn't submit, he didn't fucking lose.

The sixth, seventh, eighth, ninth, and tenth punches knocked the voice out of Roman.

Darkness came for him, but Roman pleaded and begged and fought against it. Even if his body betrayed him, even if the universe turned against him, Roman tried to move. He balled a fist. One fist. One fist, as if it'd do anything against the arm still strangling him, as if it'd do anything against the legs squeezing him tight, as if it'd do anything against the other fist still punching him again and again.

He'd lost track of the hits. The world turned hazy. The roar of the crowd became faint. Their cheers grew louder the weaker Roman became. He knew they cheered for his defeat. He knew they celebrated the champion's reign coming to an end. He knew they'd come for him now that he'd fallen. They'd come for everything he secured at Marlow Penitentiary.

As darkness squeezed the last bit of life out of him, he plummeted from the heavens and crashed into the earth. Roman dreamed of monsters chasing him from every direction. They cackled at his demise. They clawed at his flesh. They pinned him to the hard forest ground and demanded blood.

Chapter Two

Roman dwelled on his loss as champion for almost an entire week, hiding in his cell and sulking. The luxury of his cell came with the benefit of a real room, real walls, and a real door to close—even if the guards held the key for light's out. It still offered Roman privacy, unlike most of the barred cells on their block. Part of him wanted to attend the upcoming tournament and see what Ezra did as the new reigning champion; another part of him was relieved when the guard he asked said Roman lacked a proper invitation. It seemed it didn't take much to push Roman out of everyone's graces. Everyone except his cellmate, of course.

Levi Pierce strode into the room with an uncharacteristically deep frown. He'd given Roman time to mourn his loss as champion, staying silent during Roman's quiet days of sulking, but the frustration that ate away at

Levi's cheery disposition had become quite palpable. Levi rolled up the sleeves of his standard dark blue uniform, like it somehow offered a bit of breathing room to the stiff, cheap materials.

"Fuck being champion," Levi said with a flippant attitude. "You never needed it. You've always been a bad bitch. You don't need some basic bitch title to know that."

Levi did a hair flip. It was also out of character for him but certainly helped convey his sassy mood. Although, it nearly knocked his glasses off when he whipped his head back.

"Seriously." Levi brushed a hand through his shoulder-length, shaggy, chestnut brown hair. "Since the day you strutted in here all top dog and such, people have known not to mess with you or underestimate you. Don't let this get you down, man."

Roman chuckled, rolling his eyes in the process.

"What? It's true." Levi plopped onto the bunk beside Roman. "Why do you think I'm all buddy-buddy with you? From day one, I knew you'd be running this place."

"Shut up." Roman shoved Levi, always finding his ego boosts embarrassing with a twinge of humor.

Levi had been a frightened suburban rottweiler when Roman found him. A big, muscular guy who had several inches on Roman and easily thirty pounds of muscle. The fact was, Levi could've come into Marlow Penitentiary with a lot more clout if he knew how to capitalize on his intimidation, but he'd been raised to roll over and expose his belly far too much to ever be considered threatening.

Levi was soft and detoxing when Roman met him, and there was this genuine spirit about Levi that kept Roman's head afloat in the first few excruciating weeks of his sentence. They'd both arrived at the same time, and Roman had nothing to offer Levi except friendship. Levi hadn't wanted anything else from Roman. Even after he claimed his title, even after inmates and guards catered to Roman's whims, even after private funds helped make Roman's sentence bearable, Levi had never preyed on the opportunity.

He didn't turn down a gift, only a fool was too proud to accept assistance, but Levi never pressed, never suggested, never alluded in any manner to sway Roman one way or another. Levi seemed content just hanging out together, being friends, and surviving their mundane days behind bars together. That was what drew Roman to Levi.

"I said that guy is going places." Levi waggled his finger. "I better offer him a couple of blowies for the right protection."

"You fucking idiot." Roman burst into laughter, the shame of yesterday completely forgotten, washed away by Levi's continuing jokes, mocking the role of champion, flipping off everyone in this place, and generally just knowing the right words to distract Roman.

Jokes and conversation Roman sank into with ease.

Levi would occasionally tease about oral with Roman, but neither pressed the matter. Roman could never tell if it was some type of gay humor he was missing, light flirting on Levi's part, or just genuine prison rules surfacing despite Roman's desire to make Marlow anything but a haven for depravity.

Levi's open queerness had made him a quick target among inmates who knew he like sucking and taking dick, despite Levi's adamant 'top' status and his bold commentary about picking the dicks he sucked, finding the men here no more worth his time than a hot woman. So, when Levi would drop a joke that Roman was worth his time, it made Roman's head swell. Sometimes, it made both his heads grow. Not that he did anything about it or ever would.

Screwing because of captivity and lack of options made it seem like the feelings were never real. It was just his desperate horny mind giving way to a fantasy. Roman knew he only occasionally—more than once but totally less than a handful of times—jerked it to the idea of Levi sucking him off because of the jokes and the confinement. No matter the case, Roman never acted on the ideas, finding if he pursued that curiosity and regretted the feeling—realizing it really just was horny hormones seeking reprieve—he'd regret ruining the only real friendship he had.

"So, what are we doing tonight?" Levi retrieved his books, like he somehow planned on presenting them as a good distraction.

Roman didn't want distractions. He wanted to sulk.

"Everyone decent?" A gruff voice asked as a hand firmly slammed on the open door.

Warden Sadler came inside, eyed Levi up and down, and then turned an annoyed gaze toward Roman. The warden had a fat stomach from years of sitting at a desk, filing paperwork instead of keeping up with his fitness. Based on his massive biceps and sturdy frame, Roman suspected he was quite the heavy hitter when he was a guard. Roman also speculated Warden Sadler's ruthlessness for dirty business also extended to other facets of the man's life, and knocking heads in probably helped put the corrupt old man on this path of life.

"Need you to clear out your stuff," Warden Sadler said, not bothering to lead in with small talk or an explanation.

"The fuck?" Roman blurted. "No."

"It's not your room."

"The hell it isn't!"

"It's the champion's suite," Warden Sadler said, a look of pure smug satisfaction across his face. "It's for the champion."

He pretended to search the room, eyeing every corner and then resting his eyes on Roman again.

"Do you see any champions in here? I don't."

Fuck. Roman's own exploitations had finally come back to bite him in the ass. After all, this was technically his own fault. Prison came with the worst accommodations, designed to dehumanize and break someone just because they'd stumbled outside the lines of proper civil behaviors. Roman wanted more—Roman demanded more—as the champion. Warden Sadler shrugged him off until Roman did the impossible and maintained the title for three months, then four months, and on the fifth month, he refused to perform because of a crick in his back.

Suddenly, the champion's suite became available. Made from an old guard office, so slightly bigger than most cells and the sweet bit of privacy Roman had grown accustomed to. But the name itself meant it belonged to the champion, which was no longer Roman.

"Howdy." Ezra waltzed into the room, an empty box in hand, and scanned the lovely accommodations. "Thought I'd help with the big move. Damn, this is a rocking room."

"You expect me to fit all my stuff in here?" Roman scoffed, eyeing the warden.

"Almost everything here was procured by the champion, for the champion," he answered matter-of-factly, and Roman suspected that meant his earnings as champion would quickly dwindle away too.

He glared but went to work packing what he could. Levi scrambled to grab what he could and carry it in his arms. Roman took in what he could of the cell, the home away from home, the little piece of heaven he'd carved out with blood and sweat, and then he left, hoping he could forget how nice these tiny luxuries were.

"Whoa, whoa, whoa." Ezra intercepted Levi as he went to follow Roman out of the champion's suite. "Where you going?"

"Um, ugh, you know, like moving and such." Levi gulped. "Per the rules and stuff."

"Stick around, dude. I could definitely use a friendly roommate." Ezra looked up at Levi, smiling. "You wanna be my friend, big boy?"

"No, not really." Levi scrunched his face with obvious discomfort since he hated being rude, then he inched around Ezra and made for the door. Roman found Levi's large jock build paired with the awkward mousy nerd stature humorous most days, but now it did them a disservice.

"Stay." Warden Sadler blocked his path. "I'm not filling out a second change-of-room request form. I'm sure you'll like this boyfriend as much as your last one."

And with that, Roman had everything stripped away from the bulk of his possessions to his best friend. No title. No respect. No power.

He trudged through the cellblocks, following a guard from one locked-down area to the next, ignoring the jeers from inmates who mocked his situation, delighted in Roman's comeuppance.

When he finally reached his new cell, Roman miserably went to work settling in.

"Roman," a taunting voice called out to him as he entered the cellblock. "Roman, Roman, Roman, wherefore art thou Roman-O? More importantly, where is Roman's hole?"

Jake "the Snake" Finnegan. Roman glowered as contempt and disgust both fought for equal footing on Roman's face.

If there were a mascot for sadistic sociopaths who preyed on the vulnerable and fucked their way through victims like most people ate their way through a bag of potato chips, then it'd be a full-page banner of Jake Finnegan.

"Get the fuck away from me before I break your arms," Roman said slowly, firmly, and filled with rage. "Again."

Jake raised his hands in surrender, then brushed them through his short blond hair. He hung at the doorway as Roman unpacked what little of his possessions he'd been allowed to keep.

"I'm just being neighborly." Jake smirked, the lines on his face accentuated the scars that framed his face in the most bizarre way.

Something about Jake's injuries appeared self-inflicted to Roman. Even with their jagged cuts, they seemed so perfectly drawn out, highlighting his features. That made Roman recoil more since Jake didn't fear pain of any measure when it came to pursuing his desires.

Making Roman a conquest always ran high on Jake's goals. Now that Roman wasn't champion, he'd have to remind the Irish mob psycho that just because he didn't hold the title, it didn't mean his skills had lessened any.

"If you need help settling in, feel free to ask me anything," Jake said. "I'm only a few rooms down and be more than willing to help you adjust to this new position."

"Pass."

"Oh? You just wanna go in fast and rough?" Jake's smirk grew bigger. "I can respect that."

"Fuck off."

"I most certainly will." Jake turned around quite dramatically and walked away with a soldier's flair. "Be seeing you around, Roman-O."

The rest of the inmates in Roman's new cellblock weren't much better than Jake himself, who thankfully kept his distance. No, he was a true snake, so Roman understood even far away and seemingly disinterested with Roman's arrival, Jake plotted like a hungry viper. He'd strike when Roman least suspected, and with no one at his back, Roman worried the poison would overwhelm him.

It didn't help that half the men on this block were part of Jake's crew. The warden had dropped Roman in the most dangerous place ever. It made sleeping damn near impossible, afraid he'd wake up tied down to someone who jammed their door before light's out and popped the lock on Roman's cell.

He hadn't seen that done since his time in jail, back when he was on trial, awaiting sentencing, but popping the lock on a cell door was common practice there and allowed inmates bold enough to walk around without guard supervision, complete access to the block. They were the most dangerous sort. They'd find their way into some unwitting guy's room, and the screams and shock were unlike anything Roman had heard before. It still haunted his thoughts as he feared what

Jake might do if Roman closed his eyes for a little too long. Would he sound like a dying animal? A broken beast? A desperate and pleading shell of a person? All sounds Roman couldn't get out of his head, sounds he'd hoped to never hear again.

Each day presented a new threat that Roman had forgotten all about from his early days of arriving. No, Roman had never faced this level of scrutiny before. Before, he was just some no-name twenty-year-old guy, but now, he was the cocky champion who'd fallen from grace. Now, he dealt with verbal taunting and threats everywhere he went. Twice now, he'd been alone when confronted by men bold enough to pick a fight without an audience. And by no audience, Roman quickly realized that included the guards who turned away and busied themselves elsewhere while Roman defended himself.

As the champion, no one threatened him. Most accepted the beatdown he gave them, accepted the title he held, and stayed the fuck away. Now, no ranking meant no authority. The guards treated Roman like any other inmate, maybe a bit worse since they resented the hold he had over them. Warden Sadler might've hated Roman, but if he caught word that one of his guards wasn't giving the champion proper treatment, then that guard wouldn't be long for this world.

Did Roman exploit his authority? Abso-fucking-lutely. Did he use his powers for good? Meh. Debatable. Did he deserve to look over his shoulder every second of every day on the off chance someone would beat him, stab him, kill him, or worse? No one deserved to feel that way; no one deserved to live that way.

Roman couldn't find a way out unless he won back his title, won back some shred of respect.

His commissary funds ran dry after a few days, and his private funds as champion had magically disappeared after he lost his title. It meant Roman had to rely more heavily on the sustenance from the cafeteria to get by. If anyone could possibly mistake the slop they served for nutritious. Each meal cost about $0.35 to produce, which meant bulk supplies, half-rotten produce, flavorless bites, and expired meat—if they were lucky.

Roman stared at his plate, ignoring the jokes at his expense, the bold taunting from tables he walked past, the occasional threats from men who clearly hadn't watched Roman fight regularly. He might've lost one fight, but he wasn't some pushover. Part of him wanted to beat the shit out of every guy running their mouths, but even Roman knew he couldn't fight every single person here. What Roman needed was to remind these inmates of everything he could do. Without the arena, he needed a new venue to put on a show.

As he reached a near-empty table, Roman saw a guy shooting him daggers, so Roman took a chance and winked. He couldn't muster a cocky smile, but it turned out he didn't need one. The guy was up and over at Roman's table before he could take his seat.

"Sup, bitch." The man slapped Roman's tray out of his hands.

Roman had gotten used to the boldness, the arrogance, but knocking away his tray was a step too far. He really needed to do something about the brazen attitudes in Marlow Penitentiary before people deluded themselves into thinking they could walk all over him.

"You gonna pick that up?" Roman asked, expression neutral except for the fire in his eyes.

"Figured you'd bend over and grab it, bitch."

Roman rolled his eyes. This guy's intimidation efforts could use some serious work, but at least he didn't present much of a challenge to work with. The smugness on this guy's face would be the most satisfying thing to wipe away with a few punches, but Roman couldn't provoke a fight. He shouldn't. He needed to spin this quickly.

"You know what, you talk a lot, but I think you're a little too scared to actually do something about those words."

The guy kicked Roman's tray, knocking it into his foot.

Roman smiled, unfazed and glad to have found someone easier to provoke than himself. "Why don't you go over there, find your daddy, and ask if he'll help you swing a fist."

Roman nodded to the table of men where the inmate had been sitting a moment earlier.

"Ask him real nicely, and maybe some of your other boyfriends can help you start a fight." Roman stepped in closer, looking up at the guy with unflinching fury. "Because we both know you're too big of a pussy to do anything."

And with that, he swung a fist at Roman. A sloppy move that Roman avoided despite being practically pressed against the man. It didn't take long to knock the air out of the inmate's lungs and make him keel over, but Roman's real targets were approaching. Four men at the table had sprung up and charged for him.

Roman lifted his fists and braced for the chaos. He needed this, desperately hungered to unleash some of his anger. He hoped the added bonus of beating down a small group of men would help secure a bit of peace in the days to come.

Half of the men had dropped before the guards were organized enough to run toward the other side of the cafeteria. Roman wanted to drag this out, really savor the win, show the crowd of cheering men what he could do even when pressed by a group of assailants. More importantly, Roman needed to wrap up this conflict before the guards did. If they won in his stead, this bravado would be for nothing.

"What the fuck do you think you're doing?" a guard shouted, approaching Roman, who now stood alone with cowering crumbled men at his feet.

"It's all good." Roman raised his hands in surrender, taking heavy breaths as the altercation had left him more winded than expected. Perhaps the sleepless nights were catching up to him. "Just a disagreement—serious disagreement, obviously—but I think we've got it handled."

"You think?" The guard reached for his baton and cracked it against Roman's right forearm. "Who the fuck told you to start thinking, inmate?"

Roman nearly took a step forward, nearly lunged for the guard, nearly got himself into a world of trouble he couldn't backstep from. But guards weren't mouthy inmates. He couldn't provoke them. But he was also used to them knowing their place, understanding the hierarchy of things. Roman supposed, to some degree, they did understand how things ranked, seeing as Roman no longer held the authority he once did.

"You wanna start fights?" The guard belted Roman across the back of the head, then again in the shoulder. When he didn't drop to his knees or submit, another guard struck Roman in the back with several heavy lashes that knocked the wind out of his lungs. "You're not the champion anymore. No special treatment."

With that, they carted Roman off and showed him what happened to those who instigated fights, those who provoked violence by not simply submitting to the predators who flooded this institution.

They shoved Roman inside a small room and locked the door. Roman kicked and shouted and banged on the door of his solitary cell, unwilling to give up his rage for a second. Days would pass, and he'd scream until his voice was hoarse. Roman's furious temper seemed to be the only thing he had left.

When he got out, Roman would kill Ezra Delgado. He'd knock fear back into the inmates who'd grown bold and the guards who'd grown lax. Roman wouldn't surrender his title or authority without a fight.

Chapter Three

During his month of solitary, Roman dwelled on how he got here. It wasn't that different from his fall as champion, after all. It came down to Roman's arrogance getting the best of him; a blink of a moment and the lost footing changed the entire course of Roman's life.

He had always been a fighter long before he stepped into Marlow Penitentiary, but outside the prison, he used to be better at hiding his ruthlessness.

While Roman had presented himself as a preppy frat boy, he came from a much different background. Joining a fraternity wouldn't have been his first choice. Going to college, in general, had never been part of the plan. Not that his family made plans. No, they just survived, scrambled, and struggled against the tides of life. Somehow, Roman had found himself living a dream he didn't recall having. When

Stacy promised him the fraternity would always have his back, Roman almost started to believe her.

Stacy. That was a haunting name and one he tried not to fixate on as his mind reveled in memories of a former life he'd never claw his way back to.

He fell fast and hard for the silly rituals, the constant comradery, the surreal parties. But that all disappeared when Roman got arrested. Sometimes, someone would reach out. Nothing big, nothing life-changing, but a call or a card or a twenty tossed into his commissary helped remind Roman he hadn't been completely forgotten by the outside world.

The quarterly contact from a brotherhood official felt more like a checklist than true care. Not that Roman wanted to be remembered by the outside world. After what he'd done, Roman wanted to disappear most days. He just hoped that in the darkness, he wouldn't have to fade away. He wouldn't have to suffer any more than he already did, but the universe seemed content.

Flashes of red and rage reminded him of what brought Roman here, how his unchecked temper had cost him everything in his life yet served as the only life jacket to keep him afloat here at Marlow Penitentiary.

One drunk night out on the town, a mouthy guy on the streets of a busy downtown while bar hopping, and Roman in a mood to show off a bit of the darkness he carried before dressing in khaki slacks and silly polos. He'd hit the man too fast, too hard, and once the violence began, Roman couldn't stop himself. He raged against the man, slamming him onto the pavement. He'd seen blood, and he was hungry for more. Punch after punch, and nothing seemed to satiate his thirst.

The cheers of his brothers fueled him for a moment, but their concern did little to temper his rage. None were bold enough to pull him off, to stop Roman in his tracks, and he relished that power, that authority he carried in a blink.

"Stop," Stacy had snatched Roman by the arm, a pleading look on her face rivaled with the constant calm she carried everywhere she went.

Roman loved that about Stacy. She was an enigma. Everything she did put her in the center of friends, of parties, or people in general, but no one really knew Stacy unless she allowed it. Roman had been allowed to know her, truly know her behind the veil she wore for the audience of life, and he loved the unmasked Stacy. But in that moment, it wasn't Roman and Stacy and his daydreams about finally having a real relationship with her. No, right then, Roman's rage won out, and he shoved her away.

Roman wouldn't be contained, but he didn't want to hit her, to hurt her, even though he wanted to continue fighting.

He still thought about how fast the truck hit Stacy. He still thought about how much blood there was, how much of Stacy's insides were littered across the ground. Littered because they were useless to her now. There wasn't a goddamn thing Roman could do to temper back the night. Stacy had died on impact, and the worst part was that he hadn't stopped fighting. Anger had consumed him, and while a flicker of Roman's vision caught sight of the horrible events his shove had caused, most of him still wanted to break the man beneath him.

Now, he wanted to break the man even more, toss the blame onto him. Blame him for everything wrong in Roman's life. It seemed so easy to pour out that fury through his fists. It took everything to pull Roman off the half-dead drunk, and Roman still fought, still raged against the police.

He didn't rage during the trial, though. No, all his anger had been knocked out of him the first time the police showed Roman a collage of Stacy Anderson's corpse.

"I hope you die in there," Stacy's mom had hissed.

That wounded Roman. His apologies to the court meant nothing to her. The years he spent as Stacy's friend—as Stacy's anything-but-a-boyfriend because she had goals to check off in life first. The years he joked with Stacy's mom, singing a song she'd endured a billion times before Roman, but still managed to sing along with him every now and then. He credited his cute face; she claimed he had a good voice.

None of it mattered anymore. Roman had lost that life the minute he faced charges. He tried to push Stacy out of his mind, a difficult task since she haunted him most days.

Roman's release from solitary didn't come as a comfort. Yes, he could finally have engagement with other humans again, but the taunting comments had only gotten worse in his absence. Inmates practically lined up to pick a fight with him, provoke him again, get him another month of solitary, or worse. He had no friends, no allies, and no relief from the barrage of enemies. Roman needed to put a quick end to this situation.

Patience had never been a virtue Roman mastered or respected, finding it more imperative to lunge for an opportunity instead of waiting for the earth beneath his feet to settle. Roman bolted for the cafeteria. Early or not, he didn't care. He silently waited for the lunch crowd to arrive, and once they had, Roman approached Ezra and his new flock of followers. In the month since he'd seen Ezra, the only thing that'd changed about him was the stubble on his face, which hid the boyish features he had when they first met, and there was this air of well-trained arrogance that oozed off him waves.

Levi, however, appeared hollowed out and exhausted. It pained Roman to avert his gaze from his friend, but right now, he couldn't chance eye contact. He was furious and ready to fight, but seeing Levi truly evaluating him would steal his anger and replace it with sadness.

"I want a rematch," Roman demanded.

"And I want another appeal." Ezra shrugged, licking pudding off his spoon. "Wants don't mean a fucking thing."

"You got lucky before," Roman said, placing his hands on the table, unyielding to the group sitting around Ezra. "But when the Challenger's Chance comes up, I want you to know I'll be there. I want you to see me coming, a courtesy you didn't offer, but now I know your tricks."

"Tricks?" Ezra tsked, still fixated on his dessert over Roman. "Tricks are what sad people call talent. They don't understand it, so it must be deceit."

Ezra was warping things, goading Roman, which he realized and did his best to ignore the bait. It had been a trick, a cunning and calculated one, especially for a man who professed to have only just arrived at Marlow Penitentiary that day.

The last time they fought, Roman went easy, Roman was tired, and Roman fell for an obvious ploy. It wouldn't happen again.

"Just be ready to hand that title back over."

Ezra chuckled. "You assume I would accept your challenge for a rematch."

Roman scowled. "Are you too big of a coward to face me again, to face me head-on?"

"You have nothing I want," Ezra said, finishing his pudding and reaching for Levi's. "Yet, I seem to have everything you crave."

Roman's eyes finally flitted to Levi. A shell of his former self. He sat silently next to Ezra, surrounded by the other men at the table, and didn't look up from his own tray. He'd gone ghostly white since the last time Roman saw him. His shoulder-length hair seemed stragglier, and despite being a lighter brown, it held a haunting darkness to it, adding to Levi's empty blue eyes and vacant expression.

"There's no challenge to dethroning you again," Ezra said, pulling Roman's attention back. "Might add to the humiliation, but I'm no monster. I don't wanna see you suffer just because you're arrogant."

One flick of his gaze back to Levi said that was an utter lie.

"How about this." Ezra cleared his throat, commanding the already captive attention of his table. "You come to me with a real offer, something worth my time, and I'll entertain your rematch. I'll give you a chance to lose to me again. Fair and square. Sound good, friend?"

Ezra extended a hand like they'd shake on it, shake on some unspoken wager Roman would have to set the terms to, and hope Ezra would accept. He slapped away Ezra's friendly hand. When a man at the table rose in defense, Roman glared, daring him to step up.

Part of Roman wanted to end this here and now. Fight Ezra, fight all eight men at the table, fight the guards who'd sweep in to break things up, fight every other inmate who'd cheer at his defeat. But Roman wasn't that arrogant. He knew even he had limits, and damn if that wasn't humbling.

Ezra snapped his fingers, and everyone at the table stood, not to fight but to follow as Ezra took his leave. It was at this moment that Levi looked up to steal a look at his friend. Roman wanted to speak, to ask what had happened to Levi this last month, but he had ideas. Terrible, terrible ideas. Ezra whistled, and Levi's head snapped back to his tray, where he quickly shoveled something in his mouth, anything for sustenance, and then got up to trail behind Ezra like a fucking pet.

It infuriated Roman, fueling him to find a solution. Roman left the cafeteria in search of something he could offer to convince Ezra to accept a rematch.

The day didn't offer Roman any solutions, just more reminders of his new place in life. Dinner had been scarce since someone decided to throw a bit of extra protein into his meal in the form of dead bugs. A few more men instigated things, attempting to provoke Roman, to make him swing first. Not that it really mattered in the grand scheme. The guards turned their attention elsewhere when someone taunted Roman, but he knew the second he fought back or even defended himself, if one inmate were brazen enough to raise a fist, it'd be Roman who would end up back in solitary.

That night, Roman managed to convince a guard to add him to the arena attendance.

"Fine," he said. "But only because the champion is feeling charitable."

Roman clenched his teeth at that, biting back a snarl. Ezra did him favors, let him watch a bout he couldn't participate in. Not unless Roman had something to stake.

He'd hoped the event would spark some further insight into his predicament. Some of the fights were entertaining, at the very least, but nothing helped him. Maybe when Ezra finally stepped up after the preliminary matches, Roman would see something, learn something he could exploit.

The Challenger's Chance had finally arrived, but Roman didn't have anything to offer, anything to convince Ezra to accept his rematch. Roman considered taunting him, baiting the crowd into an effort to call Ezra a coward, but decided against it. They seemed to like his reign so much more than Roman's. He didn't set expectations for anyone except to leave him alone. They could be as cruel and spiteful as they wanted. They could abuse other inmates uncontested. They could give into their vices without reprimand.

Levi approached Roman, seemingly taking advantage of Ezra's pending battle and torn attention.

"You came?" Levi asked, poorly attempting small talk.

"I did." Roman sighed. "I'm trying to figure out how to get Ezra to agree to a rematch. Don't suppose you have ideas?"

Levi shook his head.

"Just think about it," Roman insisted. "You probably know more about him than anyone else, bunking together."

Levi clenched his jaw and shook his head harder, not wanting to betray Ezra's confidence, which deeply saddened Roman.

"What's happened to you?"

"Ezra's a strict person." Levi didn't offer more than that, but Roman couldn't simply accept the standard by line.

"Has he…" Roman swallowed the words, the question he wanted to ask, the answer he knew in his heart but desperately wanted to hold out hope for.

"He hasn't forced himself on me," Levi answered, and the relief that hit Roman was almost enough to make him fly. "And I haven't accepted his friendship."

"What?"

"He wants me to accept his friendship," Levi explained. "To give myself willingly, to choose to submit."

That was a first. Levi had been approached by plenty of inmates over the years because of his open sexuality, and very few offered a choice when telling him what they wanted. Levi would politely explain he was a top, add to the fact he was quite picky about the cocks he shoved in his mouth, and then try to break the tension of a threat with the levity of humor.

It never worked in his favor. Levi would get his ass kicked, but thanks to Roman, he never got his ass fucked. Roman always stepped in, always fought Levi's battles because the worst of the men always seemed to come in droves for Levi, picking on some vulnerable, easy gay guy who needed a real man's attention.

When Roman became champion, no one bothered Levi ever again. Now, Roman sank into the horrible realization that Levi would have to fight for his life, his body, every day until Roman could offer him real protection. Roman couldn't even protect himself right now. Not really.

"What happens if you don't accept his friendship?" Roman asked, watching Ezra drop his first opponent and demand a second.

"He said his cell is for friends only, and maybe I could relocate somewhere I'd be happier." Levi's face began to crumble. He fought it so hard, willing the tears back, but Roman saw him about to collapse into devastating sadness. "He suggested the warden could transfer me to Finnegan's cell."

Roman's entire body froze. Jake "the Snake" Finnegan would destroy Levi. He'd break him and hollow out everything left of Levi until all that remained was a strung-out husk of a man, unable to think or speak, only serve the vicious crew that funneled drugs throughout Marlow Penitentiary.

"He's a fucking psycho," Roman snapped, balling his fists and fighting every urge in him not to walk into the arena mid-fight and deck Ezra.

"Yeah," Levi scoffed, more somber than angry. "Hence why I'm scared. Jake's been making comments, teasing. It's gonna fuck up my sobriety, and I don't know if I even care."

"Maybe you should be Ezra's friend." Roman gritted his teeth, hating himself for the suggestion but truly believing that if he couldn't protect Levi, then at the very least, Ezra could and would.

He'd make for the better option than Jake any day.

"Considered it," Levi admitted, guilt and shame making his face turn even more pitiful. "But I'm just a game piece to Ezra. He'd grow tired of me within a few days of my submission, a few weeks if I were lucky. Then I'd be exactly where I am now."

"What do you mean?"

"Everything he's doing, the way he talks when we're alone, is directed toward you." Levi turned his face, hiding behind his hair while admitting he talked about Roman behind his back, or at the very least allowed Ezra to talk while he listened. "He wants you, Roman. Wants to take everything you hold value for and destroy it."

Roman scowled.

"I think it's like his way of scorching the earth and saying your reign meant nothing." Levi weakly shrugged. "There's nothing he wants from you, just to see you miserable, so there's no way to make him accept a challenge."

Roman fumed, growing more and more furious with each passing second. He'd lost everything, but he damn well wouldn't lose his only true friend, the only person who had his back no matter what, the only person who didn't give a damn about the title of champion.

Roman bolted into the arena, unable to contain his anger anymore. Patience be damned. What the crowd thought meant nothing to him. Ezra would answer for this. Without hesitation, Roman swung Ezra's opponent around by the shoulder and decked him across the face.

A one-hit knockout was all it took, but Roman didn't credit himself too much. He'd seen Ezra toying with the guy, wearing him down until he could barely stand. Hell, Roman unleashing his rage on the guy would probably allow him to salvage a bit of his dignity when he came to. After all, Roman had used a cheap trick to blitz-attack him.

"This is your attempt at forcing a confrontation?" Ezra tsked, shaking his head at Roman like he'd caught him stealing from a cookie jar. "It's poorly calculated. You assume you're the only person here who will break the rules and overstep."

Ezra looked to the crowd, where some of his new allies pushed their way to the front lines and awaited a sign to jump Roman, to take him down before he could even land one hit on Ezra.

"I'm here to set terms for our rematch," Roman declared. "A wager, if you will, for the current champion."

Ezra smirked at that slight.

"Already told you, you've got nothing I want. Already took your crown. Took your stuff. Took your bestie. You got nothing left to offer me."

"I do."

There was a curious look on Ezra's smiling face, but his eyes, those haunting green eyes, held more rage in them than all of Roman's muscles, ready to lash out and attack.

"Oh? What's that?" Ezra asked, his cool and cunning voice only added to the anger Roman kept in check.

"You can have me."

Chapter Four

Ezra blinked, the anger in his eyes and joy on his face replaced by pure bewilderment. The crowd roared, disgusted, intrigued, and delighted by the turn of events.

"What makes you think I want you?" Ezra asked, eyes fixated on Roman but scanning the crowd as they curiously listened.

"Like you said, you already took everything from me." Roman shrugged, downplaying the massive wager he'd thrown out for all to hear. "My title, my cell, my best friend. I'm thinking there's one more thing of mine you want."

His pride. It was the ultimate thing to offer in prison, the last thing an inmate would want taken from them, stripped away.

"I graciously accept this wager." Jake cut in, smiling and menacing, feeding the already hungry audience the idea of bedding and breaking Roman.

It was a dream come true for Jake, so despite the incredible discomfort the entire scenario brought Roman, he took some small satisfaction in shutting down Jake.

"You've tried your hand at those terms without the wager," Roman replied, acknowledging when Jake and a few of his crew members found Roman alone and unprepared and tried to take him by force. "You lost then, too."

Jake had handled his loss as champion well enough, never caring for the demand of reigning and entertainment. No, he didn't care Roman had claimed the title, but he certainly wanted to claim Roman.

It'd been a grueling fight. Jake learned after walking away with two slings on his arms to never make an attempt on Roman again, with or without his crew at his side. He could and would taunt, nothing to be done there, but Jake knew no amount of his venomous nature would beat Roman.

"So, I beat you in a fight, and you bend over for me?" Ezra asked, dismissively shrugging while gesturing for additional clarification.

Roman couldn't discern if he was downplaying his piqued interest or truly bored at the potential. Maybe Roman should've bet someone like Jake. He shuttered at the idea. Not that Roman intended on being defeated again, but there were worse things than giving it up to a cocky guy strutting around with the new champion title.

The biggest problem was that if he made this bet, if he lost this bet, then it'd put an even bigger target on his head. There was a reason that men didn't offer up their ass freely. Even Levi understood the second an inmate submitted, for fun or for force, they lost the right to resist the advances of everyone else who sought a quick release.

"And all you want is your title and bestie back?" Ezra quirked a brow.

"Cell, too." Roman shrugged.

"Yeah, I'm gonna have to raise the stakes." Ezra sucked his teeth, expression contemplative. "If you win, you can have what you want, but I want more than a one-and-done fuck when I win."

Roman's chest tightened.

"I want you to offer yourself to me entirely." Ezra looked past Roman and at Levi. "I want you to be my friend, completely complicit and compliant to my will."

Roman had suspected this potential turn in the wager. That was the purpose, to spark intrigue and offer Roman an opening to get back his title, his authority, and his friend. Ezra had all but forced Levi to take the same deal. Levi refused because who wanted to offer themselves up as a full-time bitch to serve a man arrogant enough to put the revised terms of the wager on full display for all.

"You'll be an absolutely submissive and permanent fixture in my life." Ezra smiled wide. "Obedient, too."

Roman swallowed hard at the menacing stare but kept his face as neutral as he could muster.

"I'll even do you one better," Ezra added, gesturing for the crowd to quiet. "When you lose again—because you will lose again—I'll still make sure your buddy stays safe. That means no worrying about who he ends up rooming with, what cellblock he lands on, or what he is or isn't willing to do."

Roman studied Ezra's calm, calculated expression and the corner of a smile that grew on his face.

"Champion's word." Ezra placed a hand on his chest and raised the other in a pledge. "No one will touch Levi so long as you uphold your end of the deal."

"Boo," Jake the Snake shouted. "I was looking forward to getting to know that big dumb pretty boy."

Levi recoiled a bit, eyes wide and wary as he searched the crowd, likely searching for where Jake slithered. At least Roman suspected as much.

"Well?" Ezra asked. "Can you be a man of your honor?"

"Just take his ass now," someone shouted.

The cheer of the crowd infuriated Roman. He wanted to lunge out, silence them, turn and face Ezra, and wipe that smug smirk away.

"Now, now, now." Ezra quieted the crowd again. "That's tempting, and I did already beat him, so by rights, I should get to plow him."

Roman nearly spat when Ezra winked, fueling the crowd with his lewd bravado.

"I suppose asking him to submit wouldn't be outside the realm of what I'm due."

Roman bit back a snarl. Beat him? He got a lucky sucker punch and chokehold. That was it. Roman would be ready next time.

"But beating a man only puts him in his place. Besting a man, though." Ezra walked the length of the crowd, slowly circling Roman. "Besting a man shows him his place."

Ezra's hot breath hit Roman's ear, and he spun around, locking his eyes on the man he wanted to defeat more than anything.

"When I've bested you, you will drop to your knees and serve me." Ezra encouraged the roar of the crowd, the humorous laughter they had for Roman's plight, and when they settled, he continued. "I will be your every waking thought. My desires will be your desires. My needs will be your needs. My pleasure will be your pleasure. Your sole responsibility in life moving forward will be to serve me and bring me satisfaction. Nothing more. When you lose this next match, when I have defeated you yet again, you will give yourself to me entirely. No one-time stint. Bet it all, or don't bother challenging me ever again."

"Done," Roman said with unflinching certainty.

He wouldn't yield, couldn't yield. Not if he wanted to show everyone he had nothing to fear. Not if he wanted to believe it himself.

The crowd roared, and Ezra asked for someone in the Challenger's Chance to offer him an opportunity to really spar, someone who hadn't already been defeated by him.

"I know some guys are eager to offer up their asses to me, but are there any real men here who just want to talk with their fists?" Ezra shouted, his hateful green eyes locked on Roman as the crowd laughed at their former champion's expense.

The bet had been struck, and Roman slinked back into the crowd and away from the arena. It was a reckless gamble consuming his thoughts throughout the evening. Roman knew he could win in the rematch. He'd underestimated Ezra last time. He'd been exhausted after three matches already. He'd been cocky. With Levi on the line, Roman wouldn't make any of those mistakes again.

Roman tossed and turned in bed, fixated on the wager, the raised stakes, on the win he'd need to survive a mess already at his feet. Too many inmates had grown bold against him; too many guards had turned a blind eye to taunting jabs, literal threats, vicious attacks. Roman couldn't risk the hell he'd face if he lost the match. If Roman didn't reestablish his standing at Marlow Penitentiary soon, he'd end up with more than a few barbs and the occasional sucker punch.

Now the fear of losing had crept into his thoughts while he slept alone in his cell. If he lost, could he follow through with the barter? It would make him a target to everyone and anyone. Would Ezra force him to follow through? Would others see the weakness if he backed out? Vipers like Jake the Snake would certainly strike if Roman reneged. Jake always looked for weakness in the men he broke. That was why Roman never allowed even a fraction of fear or vulnerability to cross his face when around Jake or his crew. They were the biggest predators in Marlow.

The real worry of backing out came with how Levi would be punished. Ezra would keep him and take him and make him submit, despite pretending Levi had a choice. A lie and an illusion for certain. Or Levi would refuse the offer, Ezra would tire of the teasing, and Levi would be tossed to Jake as a present, forced to fend for himself.

Roman's worries haunted him for the next several days, making sleep and his days alone with no one to talk to incredibly exhausting.

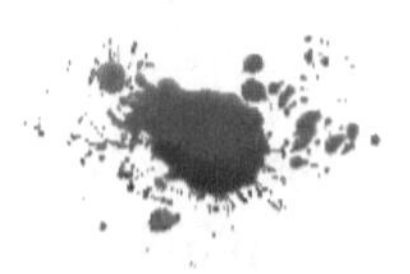

In the days that followed, inmates continued pressing Roman, picking fights or making threats. Some said they didn't need to wait until he lost another match to see what a noisy bitch he could be.

It turned out that defending himself against three men in the cafeteria hadn't reestablished his hold over his fellow inmates. It took taking down two more before the guards interfered. Thankfully, or much to his dismay, they decided not to throw him in solitary for starting another fight.

"Don't think this is a free pass," a guard said, shoving Roman toward the warden's office. "Just know I've got money on you getting your ass beat."

"In more ways than one." The second guard laughed, taunting smile, and hand on his baton. "My question is: are you jealous your boyfriend is sucking off the new champion, or are you hoping Ezra's dick is bigger than that faggot you're currently bending over for?"

Roman knew he shouldn't. He knew he already had too many enemies. He knew they'd brought him to the warden's so Sadler could ream him a new one and threaten him with solitary. He knew pissing off the guards without having the title of champion to force them off was a foolish, foolish thing. Still, nothing pissed him off more than when someone talked about Levi in a derogatory way.

Roman laughed with the oafish guard, then headbutted him until he keeled over. When the second guard went to reach for his weapon, Roman squared up and figured he could probably take these two before backup arrived and beat him to a pulp.

The door swung open and made the entire possibility moot. Ezra stood there, gaze fixed on the guards who left without a word or protest.

"Picking fights everywhere you go," Ezra said with a grin. "Figured you might try to get yourself locked up before our big rematch."

"Excuse me?" Roman snapped, offended at the accusation.

"Can't lose to me if you're in solitary, right?" Ezra batted his lashes. "But I've already had a word with our astute warden, and honestly, he'd probably let you set this place on fire and still keep the rematch scheduled."

Good alternative option. For a few seconds, Roman let his mind run wild with the fantasy of starting a fire and a riot and then just escaping Marlow Penitentiary. In his daydreams, he didn't have to worry about manhunts or predators or additional charges. Nope. For just a few seconds, he was sipping cocktails on an island that didn't extradite or cost more than a few pennies to live well. He sighed as his daydream fizzled out under the weight of reality.

Ezra ushered Roman into the warden's office, where the man sat at his desk, writing a report clearly marked for Roman's file.

"I was a bit disappointed to learn that Ezra agreed to the rematch," Warden Sadler said. "Honestly, the chance of you getting back your title makes me sick."

"Wishing you would've gotten rid of me while you had the chance?" Roman asked with a bit more bluster than he thought he could manage, but he refused to squirm in front of the warden.

He was quite shocked Warden Sadler hadn't made a move on him. Perhaps he expected Roman to be dealt with by the gangs who no longer feared him or the guards who no longer had to tolerate him. In either case, he considered himself fortunate that the warden hadn't swooped in with swift vengeance. And so long as Roman reclaimed his title, Warden Sadler would never be able to touch him.

"Personally, I rather like the bet you two have." Warden Sadler glanced between Roman and Ezra. "Maybe he'll fuck some manners into you."

Roman scowled, ready to lunge forward and break the warden's nose for a second time.

Ezra placed a hand on Roman's knee, steadying the tremble, likely confusing it for fear on Roman's part instead of an all-consuming rage held in check by little more than Roman's count backward from a hundred.

"That's the plan." Ezra smiled. "Give him a second chance, let him realize he never stood a chance, and then take him to bed since he's so desperate to get fucked."

Roman knocked away Ezra's hand.

"What?" Ezra's smile grew. "You're the one who came to me with the bet."

"Not surprising," Warden Sadler said with a scoff, having always considered Roman's friendship with Levi more than a friendship.

Roman knew that much, and he didn't care about the whispers. Levi was the only consistent thing in Roman's life since he arrived at Marlow Penitentiary. He was the only one who had Roman's back before he became the champion. Levi had taken beatings to protect Roman from crews like Jake

Finnegan's, people who saw a mouthy young man in need of some correctional justice correcting.

"I'm only here because of Levi," Roman said.

"Yeah, I caught that." Warden Sadler rolled his eyes.

"He's my friend, and I want to ensure that you uphold the deal." Roman glared. "I don't give a shit about the champion title, but you will leave Levi alone, keep Jake and Ezra and anyone else away from him."

"Just friends, huh?" Ezra chuckled. "The lady doth protest too much, methinks."

Roman turned his glare onto Ezra.

"Now, I see why you offered your ass up," Ezra said matter-of-factly, unfazed by Roman's rage. "Must be itching for a real man."

"Are we done here?" Roman stood.

"We are," Warden Sadler said. "You should consider yourself lucky you'll have the protection of champion no matter how this turns out."

A threat and a reminder that Warden Sadler wanted nothing more than to destroy Roman Grayson. He left the office with the weight of the world on his chest, making each breath more difficult. Between the gangs and guards who hated him, the dangers presented to Levi, the precarious war he waged with the warden, and the threat of Ezra beating him again, Roman couldn't focus.

"You pull a stunt like you did today at the cafeteria, and I won't toss you in solitary," Warden Sadler said, the edge in his voice turning hot and sharp. "I'll throw you in The Pit and leave you there to rot."

He had to win. He had to defeat Ezra. Reclaim his title. Hold onto any strength he could in this den of vipers. The next misstep would be Roman's death; he knew that more than anything. He'd spoken out too much, he'd crossed too many monsters, he'd left himself vulnerable from every direction.

The day of the fight, Roman couldn't stomach anything. Not that he wanted to eat the cafeteria food where spit in his mashed potatoes was a luxury seasoning compared to some of the things tossed in to mock him.

"You look terrible," Levi approached Roman outside of the cafeteria, eyes darting to see who watched his movements. It pained Roman that Levi and so many others had to watch their backs because Ezra didn't give a fuck about anybody but himself.

"Thanks?" Roman quirked a brow.

"My bad." Levi sighed. "Just worried. About you. Not about the situation. Not that I'm not worried about it. Not that I'm worried worried about it. Really, my only focus is on you and how not terrible you—"

"I didn't sleep well is all," Roman interjected to spare himself a ten-minute rant of Levi flailing about to dig himself out of a word hole he would only continue sinking further into. "It's all good."

"You look sick," Levi said. "Are you sick?"

"No," Roman insisted. "Nerves is all."

"Maybe you should reconsider." Levi had this pleading desperation on his face; all he could see was the worst.

That hurt more than the doubt itself. Doubt, Roman could handle. He had enough to spare. It was Levi's optimism crumbling away before him that really ached. Levi was such a beacon of positivity here, and the idea of losing that spark of joy infuriated Roman. The rage would be enough to push him through the competition no matter how hungry he was from missing meals, how worn down he was from watching his back, or how sleep-deprived the dread of this rematch had left him.

Roman would push through.

"Here." Levi offered Roman a bottle of water, clear and pricy and something he could no longer afford thanks to the warden cleaning out his commissary funds.

"Thank you."

"You look tired, dude."

"I'm fine." Roman took a swig. "I'll be fine. Everything will be fine."

Ezra whistled. Not the commanding dog call he'd used on Levi last time he dared talk to Roman. No, this whistle was flirty and encouraged others to add in their own mocking catcalls. Roman glowered, unwilling to fuel Ezra's blatant baiting.

"You ready to get beat down?" Ezra chuckled. "After the fight, I mean."

Levi swallowed his nerves, averting his gaze from Roman, and returned to Ezra, probably desperate to stay in the man's good graces just a few days longer. If Levi wanted Roman to backout or worried Roman would lose, then that meant Levi had already conceded his fate. Levi expected to get passed along soon enough.

Roman wouldn't let that happen. "See you tonight, Ezra."

With that, Roman left the cafeteria and returned to his cell, where he rested and ran moves until a guard arrived to escort him to the arena.

No other matches were set, no Challenger's Chance open to the crowd. All that awaited Roman as he walked into the cold basement arena was a rematch where he'd either regain his honor or lose what last shreds of dignity he had left. The authority above was bigger than it'd ever been. The crowd below had swelled twice in size, and it seemed guards who weren't even working late-night shifts had stayed to see the rematch.

"Here's to a spectacular evening," Warden Sadler announced, stirring the crowd. "The rematch no one asked for but the disgraced Roman Grayson begged for."

Booing from the crowd didn't surprise Roman, but the jeers from the authority, the wealthy founders, took him aback. They didn't seem so fickle.

"We all know what Grayson is willing to wager if he loses again," Warden Sadler continued. "One wonders what he offered just so our new champion would consider this fight worth his time."

Roman's entire expression twisted into fuming fury for the laughing crowd, the very direct assumptions they made for the warden's not-so-subtle accusation.

Ezra stood tall in the center, ready and taunting Roman to approach. Since Roman didn't care to build hype or delay the inevitable, he bulldozed past the crowd and went right for

Ezra. The first punch hit hard and served as the starting bell since both men ignored the ceremony of such things.

Ezra had allowed Roman an easy first strike, an act of gloating or pity, and one Roman would make the new champion regret. Roman came in faster than last time, not allowing Ezra an opportunity to recover, to pivot, to dodge. Blow after blow, Roman knocked Ezra back, keeping him close to the crowd but not daring to press in. He couldn't trust them not to help Ezra, not to hit Roman.

The last time they faced each other, Roman was exhausted and on his last reserves. This time, he knew his stamina would outlast Ezra. Still, his lungs clawed at him, and his muscles cramped. So much stress whittled away at him since his defeat, but Roman ignored the aches, ignored the pain. He continued pressing into Ezra, one successful strike after another.

Everything was going well until Ezra ducked and countered, landing his first punch of the night. Roman had readied himself the same way he had a thousand times before when an opponent came in to hit him. It would hurt, but Roman would be fine. He'd taken his fair share of punches to the face.

Something about this blow, though… The crowd gasped, adding to the ticking seconds of silence while Roman recovered. Blood painted his face, blurring the vision on his right side. Had Ezra been wearing brass knuckles? No, that was merely hope on Roman's part. He'd wanted Ezra to cheat, to pull something deceptive, anything to answer for why he struck so hard and now seemed to stand unfazed by the barrage of hits he'd taken.

Ezra stood tall and ready and not at all shaken. Roman, on the other hand, couldn't stop shaking. He couldn't remove the dread that ate away at his insides, he couldn't silence the taunting crowd, he couldn't even calm his erratic heartbeat that added to the panic. Ignoring his headwound at the very least, Roman swept in to continue, but Ezra was already finished with this fight. No longer interested in teasing out the last shreds of Roman's hope, Ezra spun around and kicked Roman across the head, sparking a terrible pain on the left side of his face.

When he hit the concrete ground, Roman didn't know if he'd crashed headfirst or if the two strikes had really taken that much out of him. He struggled to get up, struggled to ignore the laughing crowd, struggled to fight back the looming shadows.

Chapter Five

Roman awoke in the infirmary and lay silently wishing he could vanish from the face of the earth. The first defeat was devastating, filled with waves of embarrassment for his arrogance getting the best of him, but his second defeat was downright demoralizing. Shame crawled under his skin. Each breath he wheezed held a bitterness that ached his insides.

He'd lost a second challenge. He'd lost after declaring so much confidence. He'd lost after three hits. Maybe. That was all he could remember. The first one clocked hard and left him groggy. The second one, though… That hit knocked him off his feet. Was there a third strike? A blow that left him unconscious? Roman wanted to believe that. He wanted to hope there was some reason for his utter failure. He truly hoped he'd blacked out and would learn they'd gone more rounds, that Roman had put up a true fight, but that seemed more pathetic than wishful. Fixating on the fight itself almost drowned out the laughter in the arena. Mostly, he wanted to dwell on something, on anything other than the wager he'd made.

Much to his dismay, the nurse quickly discharged Roman and sent him on his way. He ignored the jokes at his expense and even the few men who walked up, instigating and ready to fight over any random perceived offense. Roman knew it was bluster, arrogance, and something that usually didn't come his way. Most people didn't bother him because they knew as the champion, he'd fucking obliterate them.

Without that title, people assumed he couldn't fight or hold his own anymore. Two failures and all his successes were washed away entirely. But Roman knew he could take anyone who actually challenged him. Right? He wondered that more and more as he walked through the cellblock. He'd known for certain he could win the fight, yet he'd been wrong about that, too.

It didn't take long for him to reach Ezra's cell, the champion's suite, Roman's former living quarters that he'd worked so hard to better. Until Roman came along, there was no need for a champion's suite. The longest reigning champion before Roman was Jake the Snake, and he'd barely held onto the title for two months before Roman knocked him off the pedestal. Maybe that was why Jake and the others could still hold their heads high. Their fall hadn't been nearly as far. Roman held the title for over a year. Countless bouts, continuous victories, challengers ripped to shreds when faced with him, and yet none of that meant a thing anymore.

Roman kept his head low as he knocked on the open cell door and stepped inside. He didn't want to see the nice wooden desk with functional drawers—something even most staff in the facility lacked. He didn't want to see his shameful reflection in the wall mirror. He didn't want to look at the plush cushioned chair in the corner opposite the bunkbeds. Most of all, Roman didn't want to be here.

"Damn." Ezra clapped his hands. "I had twenty on you not even showing. Guess we both lost a wager today."

Heat filled Roman's chest.

"You ready?" Ezra crossed the cell and closed the door, using his body to sort of push Roman deeper into the room.

"No." Roman ground his teeth.

"I guess I can try to set the mood," Ezra said with a little laugh. "What's the ambiance for 'deflower me, Daddy'?"

Roman shot Ezra such a sharp glare that if it'd been an actual swing, Ezra would have been knelt over and winded.

"I'm kidding," Ezra teased. "I mean, not entirely. I'm gonna fuck you, and I won't be gentle. I'm not gonna break you, but you'll be walking with a limp to the cafeteria tomorrow."

Roman couldn't speak. He couldn't risk saying something rude, flat out refusing Ezra, because it wasn't just him on the line. He'd done this to help Levi. If he backed out here and now, after failing, Levi would continue to suffer.

"You came to me with the deal, dude," Ezra said, stirring Roman from his thoughts. "I'm just here to *cum* and collect."

Roman gritted his teeth, which only masked part of his feral huff.

"If we're gonna be friends, you're gonna have to learn to take a joke." Ezra grinned, his entire expression light and carefree, except for his green eyes. There was malice in them, hidden behind the smile lines. "And learn to take dick. Lots of learning for you."

"We're not friends," Roman finally said. Declared. Announced. Willed himself to state without cursing Ezra in the process. "We won't be friends. I'll room here. You'll get me at night, whatever, but I'm my own person, and when we're not fucking, you don't speak to me."

Ezra sucked his teeth while taking a sharp inhale. "Yeah, that's not how this works. You offered yourself to me. I agreed because I want you. All of you. I get all of you. Friendship. Submission. Loyalty. Everything. Everything you do moving forward will revolve around me. Everything I do moving forward will ensure your protection and happiness. You will be mine in every sense of the word or not at all."

"No," Roman said flatly.

Ezra called it friendship, but it was just another word for being his full-time bitch, and Roman couldn't muster that. He couldn't stand here willing himself to be fucked. It was disgusting and degrading and demoralizing. Pride filled his chest with every breath, and he snarled at Ezra.

"The deal's off," Roman said. "Fuck you and fuck your friendship."

"Well, pretty sure you just said we wouldn't be doing that, but okay," Ezra said with a playful shrug as he walked away. There was a swagger in his hips, something an old western cowboy might do. "You want to renege on the deal you made, that's your choice."

Choice. Christ, how Roman hated that word. He'd heard it so many times in his life it rang hollow. It was his choice to go to a local state school so he could stay close to his family and support them or his choice to take the out-of-state scholarship opportunity. It was his choice to celebrate with his friends after finals or stay in and be a boring loser. It was his choice to take another shot or be the group bitch who couldn't handle his drinks. It was his choice to listen to some drunk trash-talk him or walk away. When he swung, when he struck the man down, he watched all his choices slowly disappear.

He failed to stop, making the wrong choice, and his violent actions knocked a friend into oncoming traffic. His deadbeat parents vanished when the charges came in, too busy taking care of the rest of the family, and since Roman couldn't afford to bail them out since he didn't even have enough money for his own bail, they didn't need him anymore. No one called. No one visited. No one sent cards.

He had the choice to accept the terrible plea deal presented or go to trial, where even his lawyer made it clear they'd eviscerate him.

He had the choice to keep his head down in Marlow Penitentiary or hold his head high and fight off anyone who dared.

None of his choices felt like choices. And now he had no one. No friends. No allies. No family.

"You can leave now," Ezra said, nodding to the door. "This bunk is reserved for my friend."

That was it? Roman had expected Ezra to fight him on it. To demand he follow through. Part of him secretly hoped for Ezra to make the push, take the option out of Roman's hand so he could preserve some semblance of his shredded dignity. If he didn't have a choice, really truly ended up forced into serving Ezra, Roman believed he could follow through. But this willful act of making Roman submit, to smile as he belittled himself, infuriated Roman.

"Goodbye." Ezra gave a dismissive wave. "I don't room with folks too good for my time."

Roman froze, knees locked and feet glued to the floor. Every part of him screamed not to go through with the deal he'd made, the foolish choice he'd agreed to, but another part whispered the harsh reality that faced him once he walked out of this cell, out of the champion's suite for good. Roman knew he wasn't the only one who would suffer if he stepped through that door. Levi depended on Roman, too. Levi had suffered at the hands of Ezra's taunts and looming predators ready to strike. Still, Roman couldn't will himself to submit, to surrender. He wasn't built for it.

Unable or unwilling to accept Ezra's choice, Roman bolted from the room. He barreled through the hallway, ignoring the jokes of other inmates, the bolstering, and he tried to think of what the warden would do to him.

Roman braced himself for landing in some slummy cellblock or roomed with predators so vicious he'd never get a full night's sleep again, but he took a deep breath and walked into the waiting area outside the warden's office.

He didn't speak to Roman, didn't see him, merely smiled from behind the glass panel of his door when news of Roman's rejection reached his ears. Guards escorted Roman to a place he'd never seen. Not that he'd been permitted in all the cellblocks, but they mostly looked alike. Not this place.

A guard pushed him inside a damp, stone room the size of a closet with a bucket that took up a quarter of his living space. There was no bed here. There was nothing.

Roman had been tossed in solitary twice for getting mouthy. This wasn't the same. Solitary had a toilet, a bed, padded walls, but this place…. This place was something he'd only heard rumors about.

He sank to the floor, terror weighing him down as he realized he'd die down here in The Pit.

Chapter Six

Every day of isolation gnawed at Roman. He couldn't see the time of day, and even for the ten minutes of freedom they came to offer when dragging him out for a quick shower, he never saw a window. He couldn't even be certain it was ten minutes a day. He wanted to believe that. He wanted to hope The Pit held some type of a schedule, a routine, but the longer he spent here with irregular meals in the form of cafeteria scraps, the more it dawned on him how forgotten he'd become.

After what felt infinitely long, a guard came to retrieve him for his ten minutes of freedom. He jolted up, wanting to make use of every ticking second, convinced he might be able to squeeze in a long enough shower for the water to actually run warm. But when the guard pulled him by the hair and shoved a hood over his face, then slapped cuffs over his hands, Roman panicked.

"Where are we going?" Roman asked, slowing his pace only for a baton to hit the back of his calves and force his next steps. "Where are you taking me?"

No one answered. No one cared to acknowledge Roman.

His heart pounded in his chest, ready to burst any second. This was it. This was his march to death. The warden had finally taken his revenge and decided to walk Roman to a silent end.

The hood over his head had eye holes, which perplexed Roman. When he finally reached a well-lit place, Roman could almost make out the setting of a makeshift arena. It wasn't anything like the arena he was used to, but there was still a balcony and a cheering crowd.

Roman rubbed his raw wrists from the cuffs slapped on far too tightly.

"Ladies and gentlemen, let's give a big howl for the Lone Wolf!" Warden Sadler announced.

Every rumor Roman had ever heard jigsawed in his thoughts as he took in the loud cheers and long howls of the audience.

The lights were too bright, and the filtered eye holes made it difficult to see much of anything.

The Lone Wolf was the champion of The Pit, or so Roman had heard whispers of. An undefeated feral beast of a man who cannibalized so many people the state prayed he'd disappear from the face of the earth, and so the warden, being benevolent and adventitious, created The Pit and sent inmates to face off against the beastly man. The stakes were high, but the rewards were great.

Roman saw through the smokescreen of lies wrapped around truths. Perhaps the Lone Wolf was a real inmate at one point; perhaps he was even a deranged cannibal. But he wasn't an undefeated mythical monster of a man. Roman had been given the new title of Lone Wolf, likely replacing the former inmate who died from a fatal injury or in his tiny stone cell from deprivation and isolation.

The warden had won. He'd watched Roman falter and sprung a fate so cruel he'd never crawl his way out again. Roman would wear this mask until he died, nameless and faceless to the authority above. He'd gain no fame, no chance of salvation, no freedom with victories. Roman would be forgotten here in the darkness of The Pit.

When the fight began, no one made an announcement. Roman simply winced at the sharp cut of a blade. A shiv that nearly dug into his forearm. He turned, dodging a second swipe, and nearly fell into the trap of two other men. Here he stood, handcuffed and surrounded by three men, each armed and ready to end his life with an audience cheering for his execution.

"Kill the wolf! Kill the wolf! Kill the wolf!"

How he survived the fight, he didn't know. It all blurred into a bloody, sticky mess. He had lots of shallow cuts and bruises covering his body, but he panted heavy and feral and victorious for tonight. Roman didn't know if he'd killed the men he fought or simply injured them beyond recovery. He clenched his fists. He didn't care.

Everything whirled from then on. Countless hours in his cell. Cheering crowds. Booing crowds. Angry armed inmates. Blood. Rage. Pain. Sleepless nights on cold stone floors. Hunger pangs that stretched on infinitely.

Roman wanted it to end, but he was too afraid to end it himself. Every time they tossed a mask over his head and dragged him to the arena, he prayed this would be the night he willed himself to move a little slower, make a sloppy mistake, barrel headlong into the sharp edge of some blade. But Roman continued fighting and wishing for death because he didn't know how to surrender. Even having been defeated so much already, Roman couldn't settle the fire that burned in his chest. He wanted to survive. He wanted to escape. He wanted a second chance, any chance to escape this hell.

Roman's door opened, and he fully expected to be hauled out for his ten minutes of freedom to stretch and shower, hoping for a chatty guard on shift. Instead, he found himself looking up at the last person in the world he ever wanted to see again.

"Don't you look like absolute shit?" Ezra knelt to meet Roman's gaze, then scrunched his nose, obviously realizing Roman smelled about as good as he looked and felt.

"How are you down here?" Roman asked, his voice hoarse since most days he had to rely on his brief shower for a chance at real drinking water.

"My reign as champion has earned me more respect than it ever offered you." Ezra nodded to the empty hallway, the lack of guards and the obvious control he'd gained over this prison.

Roman scoffed. He'd become a champion again. His own new type of champion, one without respect or reward, but a feral edge for violence that made the anger he held for Ezra all the more palpable.

"Geez, you really do look rough, man." Ezra eyed Roman's dirty clothes, then scratched at his own face stubble to indicate the unkempt beard Roman had.

Roman merely glowered, incapable of mustering much else.

"You're not the only one who's been struggling these past three months." Ezra pulled out a Polaroid picture and tossed it onto the floor of the cell.

Three months. Christ, had it already been three months of solitary? Worse. Had it only been three months of solitary? Roman didn't know which reality was worse. Time lost itself here, and he started to believe he'd never find it again. He looked at the photo, not sure what to expect, but had a sickly expression when he saw Levi alone in some candid cafeteria shot.

His expression had turned ghostly, his face filled with fear as his eyes seemed to look in every direction. Even with one single photo, Roman could see the fear etched in Levi's expression, the paranoia, the exhaustion.

Roman was lost and alone in here, but his best friend was lost and alone out there. When he rejected the offer and refused the wager, he suspected Levi might end up as collateral damage, but he hoped… But hope was foolish, and Roman knew nothing ever came from it.

"Come to gloat?"

"Come to help," Ezra replied. "I'd like to make you an offer one more time."

"Make Levi the offer." Roman tossed the picture at him. "He's not a bottom, from what he claims, but you've got a better shot with him than me."

Roman wanted to be strong, wanted to prove he'd made the right decision, but most of all, he hoped Ezra didn't simply shrug and walk away. Roman wasn't ready to close the door on this deal, even if he knew he should.

"Even if I wanted to be Levi's friend, he still doesn't wanna be mine." Ezra picked up the picture and turned it to face Roman. "Some deluded loyalty to you. The guy's survival instincts are seriously lacking. With your stubborn behavior, life has been hard on Levi. I imagine it could get a lot easier if the world knew he was in my good graces."

"Tell him to let me go, to be your friend," Roman said. "Hell, bring him here, and I'll tell him."

"Even if I could swing that, I don't want his friendship." Ezra stared Roman down, stared through him, stared deep inside his soul. "I want yours. I want you."

Roman stayed quiet.

"Uphold our original deal, and I'll do the same," Ezra explained. "I'll keep everyone off Levi. I'll keep everyone off you."

"Except for you," Roman said with a bit more snark than he thought he had left in him. "You'd very much be on me, inside me, controlling me every which way, right?"

"That was the wager, wasn't it?" Ezra asked, no mocking tone in his voice, but it still stung Roman's ears. "This is the last time I will offer my friendship. My clout is powerful, and it affords me favors, but even I only have so much sway."

"Just win a few more matches." Roman sarcastically punched a fist in the air. "The bigger the champion, the more loyalty you earn. Trust me on that."

Ezra gave Roman a dark look. "When this door closes, you're on your own."

"I'm used to it."

"The next time they open your cell, it'll either be to lead you to my cell or back to The Pit, where you'll huff and puff and fight until you fall down. Forever."

It was a definitive statement, not one of speculation. Ezra had the warden's ear and favor, and he likely understood the old bastard had grown tired of Roman clawing at victories and fighting to live one more pathetic day.

Roman almost considered accepting that harsh fate. Dying didn't seem like the absolute worst thing. He considered it a quiet ignoble death and far better than living longer only to suffer. He no longer had anyone in his corner, in his life…but then he considered the single friend he had. A true friend, not some façade of play pretend that Ezra painted.

"Levi would have a chance?" he asked more to himself than seeking further clarification from Ezra.

Roman's cowardice had already cost Levi and put him in danger. At least with this ultimatum, at least by upholding his deal, he might make some of it right. And if Roman were fortunate—which he truly believed he never would be again—he might even salvage some vestiges of his own life.

"All right," Roman forced himself to speak, every word scrapping against his tongue with an unyielding desire to continue fighting, continue resisting. But he was so tired. "I'll be your friend. I'll keep my end of the wager. I'll fuck you."

"To be clear, you won't be doing the fucking," Ezra said with a smirk. "You're okay with this arrangement? Absolutely certain?"

"Yep," Roman conceded.

"Perfect." Ezra's cadence was kind, his smile friendly, but even so, the wicked glint in his green eyes unnerved Roman. It was enough to make him want to crawl back into his solitary cell and hide. "I love to take care of my friends."

Chapter Seven

Roman was escorted from The Pit and taken to the showers, where he was given an opportunity to clean off. After three months in isolation, he had the two-minute ritual engrained in his head and quickly scrubbed down his body while shivering in the cold water. The quick wash never afforded much time to clean his cuts, and the harsh water often made them burn, but he did what he could with the time offered. Roman stepped back, prepared for the guard to turn off the nozzle and rush him out, but she seemed more fixated on some game she played on her phone.

Roman took advantage of the extra allotment and went back to scrubbing himself, actually getting the dirt out from under his nails, having a chance to properly rinse his hair, and being able to clean away the grime caked on his skin. He even shaved away all the mangled facial hair he'd been forced to sport in The Pit. Warm water finally funneled out after five minutes. It wasn't hot, lukewarm at best, but Roman soaked under the stream in utter bliss.

Once he'd finished, he was brought to his cell. Correction, his former cell. The champion's suite, which really hadn't changed all that much since he'd roomed in it before. The mirror mounted on the wall showed there wasn't anyone at the far-off end in either bunk. Still, he grimaced and paused at the door, hesitating about his next encounter with Ezra.

The correctional officer shoved him inside and complained about him dawdling. Roman was stalling, debating if he could go through with this, debating if he could give all this up again, too. It seemed Ezra not only kept all the items Roman had acquired during his time as reigning champion, but Ezra hadn't made any additional updates. He kept the cell fairly the same except for the bunk beds.

Roman sat on the bottom bunk and immediately sank into the stiff mattress. Not much to be done about the beds, but damn if the silk sheets didn't make a world of difference. The top bunk was standard and itchy and looked like they'd been slept in, whereas the bottom bunk was in perfect condition. Roman didn't know why Ezra passed on the better bedding, but he couldn't complain. Not this minute, anyway.

Lights out came around soon after, but there was still no sign of Ezra. It didn't take long for Roman's mind to piece together the reason. It'd been three months since he was champion, since he'd faced off in the arena, but those who competed always did so in the dead of night. Occasionally, there'd be an early evening competition, but those were mostly just leadups to the bigger bouts for the nighttime entertainment.

Roman shivered in the bed, anticipating Ezra's return. He feared it. He feared Ezra returning victorious and collecting on the promise Roman had made to a wager he'd already broken his word on once before. He feared Ezra returning with his head held low, having been dethroned from his title and holding no power or sway. If that happened, the warden would most certainly drag Roman back to The Pit.

The conflicting dread made Roman's heart race.

"You look peaceful," Ezra's voice broke the silence and pulled Roman's attention away from the heavy thrum of his heart.

"Looks can be deceiving," Roman said.

Ezra had a gash on his forehead with a few stitches closing it up but no bandage. He looked a bit winded, with a sheen of sweat running down his neck and to his partially exposed chest, keeping two buttons open and no undershirt. Despite that, Ezra carried himself well, not like that of someone who walked away from a loss.

"Rough night?" Roman nodded to the cut.

"Jake the fucking Snake got that lucky hit during the Challenger's Chance," Ezra explained. "Dude has come for my title three times. You'd think he'd realize."

"He's persistent," Roman said, thinking of how many times he'd fought off Jake in and out of the arena, how many other men in this prison were just as bad or worse than Jake. He didn't know if he was lucky to have caught Ezra's attention, sparked his fascination, or if he was about to walk headfirst into a whole new form of Hell.

Ezra stepped into the center of the room and waved Roman to join him.

"Are you ready to commit?"

Roman scoffed. "Don't you mean submit?"

That was what this was, after all, and Roman refused to look at it any other way. Still, Ezra continued framing this as a possibility for friendship.

"We're not friends, we won't be friends," Roman snapped. "Just whip out your dick already so I can get this over with."

"There is no getting this over with." Ezra's smile fell away, and his expression turned stony. "If you commit to this friendship, to this willing submission, then you need to understand it will be ongoing. Your every breath will be for my satisfaction, and my every action will be for your protection. You will see to my needs and my needs alone. You will understand that your existence is purely for my pleasure. Any release you get when I fuck you will be a sign of you performing your role correctly."

Roman swallowed hard, biting back the sinking fear of this awful realization. He knew what to expect; he'd prepared himself long before going to The Pit and dwelled on the options while in isolation, and now, as he stood there, he questioned this decision once again. It was a choice he couldn't walk back from. Once he surrendered himself to Ezra, others would know. His fallen standing would never recover, and he'd be stuck at the bottom quite literally in this sense.

But Roman knew as much as he hated swallowing his pride, he didn't want Levi to suffer anymore, and he certainly didn't want to die alone in a hole wearing a wolf mask completely forgotten by the world.

"Are you willing to commit?" Ezra asked. "Are you ready to make this choice?"

"Like I have a choice."

"You do."

"This or back in a hole to die." Roman glared. "Not much of a choice."

"You won't go back there," Ezra said. "Not ever."

"What?"

"Even if you refuse me here and now for a second time, you will not be returned to The Pit."

"You're lying," Roman snapped.

"I'm not," Ezra said with a definitive shrug. "Even if you change your mind midway through or wake up tomorrow sore and regretting your decision. Walk away whenever it suits you, and I promise you'll be sent back to regular gen pop. Might be my wing, might be another cellblock. No sway there, but it won't be solitary, and it won't be that awful Pit. I'm not vindictive, Roman."

"You're fucking lying."

"That was the warden's game," Ezra admitted. "I didn't like that game, and I felt sick letting him play it. But I didn't have the clout to argue. Three months of continuous wins, coupled with a bit of flirting with the higher priority clientele—let's just say those Lawless Authority folks really do like getting their way, so it's wise to convince them my way is the path they wanna pursue—and now I have enough say to keep you off the warden's immediate hitlist."

Roman frowned. He'd nenver made an effort with authority who watched from the balcony. They were perverse in more ways than one, and standing in the same room with elite clientele made Roman's skin crawl. He wondered if he had offered a few more niceties their way if they would've opposed the warden making Roman disappear after his losses. If they would've helped rebuild Roman after he fell from the title of champion. He also wondered how much of his soul he would've lost having a single conversation with those vipers who thrived on pain and anguish and betting on the lives of people like fucking cattle.

"So, I can't guarantee you won't end up back on the warden's shitlist, and I can't offer you protection from anyone you've pissed off, but I can promise you will never return to that dank place."

Roman let those words sink in, and he considered. If he weren't so exhausted from months of isolation, if he weren't so sleep deprived, so hungry, so bruised and beaten from countless treks to and from The Pit arena, he might've walked right out of the champion's suite and taken his chances against anyone bold enough to cross him.

But Roman didn't believe he'd survive long on his own, not after everything, and if this was what Ezra could offer without friendship, then maybe he really could keep him safe if he willed himself to accept the deal.

"I'll be your friend, whatever." Roman shrugged like he wanted to knock the words away from himself. "Just don't expect anything from me."

"Except you," Ezra corrected. "I get you in every way I want."

"Yeah, you get to fuck me," Roman answered. "Let's just go then."

"It's more than that." Ezra stepped close, cupping his hands around Roman's face with a gentle but guiding touch. "Everything you do will be at my discretion, meant to meet my needs, my happiness. If you're absolutely certain you can accept this, will yourself to be the hole I need for pleasure, the friend I crave for conversation, and follow my lead in all things moving forward, then we can begin."

"Let's get started."

"Get undressed," Ezra said with a commanding growl.

Roman did as instructed, more annoyed than self-conscious, and watched Ezra take off his clothes, too. He'd seen him shirtless in the arena already, the lean muscles and scattered tattoos over Ezra's deep bronze skin, but he hadn't seen the man from the waist down yet.

When Ezra revealed his dick, Roman's jaw nearly dropped. Not that he thought his wide mouth could hold such a thing. He couldn't believe Ezra was already fully hard, and he definitely couldn't believe how hung the man was.

"Ten inches, and no, that's not a liberal measurement on my end," Ezra said with a smirk. "There's confident, and then there's assuredly confident."

Roman didn't often feel inadequate. He knew at seven inches, add a half if he was feeling braggy, he wasn't the biggest cock on the block, but he also knew he didn't need to be. Size wasn't everything, and his seven got done what Ezra's ten could do. Or so he assumed. He also assumed Ezra's ten inches took a lot more effort, and while he assured himself he could handle any physical pain or sensation about to hit him, doubt crept into his mind.

"I don't want you stroking yourself during our time together," Ezra explained. "Your focus needs to be on my needs only. My pleasure will become your pleasure. You will learn this and learn to love this."

Roman swallowed hard at that.

"But don't worry." Ezra held his hands at the sides of his dick, gesturing and bucking forward to wave his fully erect cock. "You'll cum for sure. I've never had a complaint."

"I'm not gay," Roman said. "Not bi, not curious."

Somehow, reiterating those words made this the tiniest bit more bearable, like he could hold a mirror up to Ezra and show him the so-called choices Roman made. He didn't know how much he believed in the words, but when it came to Ezra, they were entirely true. There was no curiosity creeping over Roman's skin, only anxiety.

"Like you do you," Roman continued, brave face and tense muscles. "But I'm not getting anything out of this."

"It's anatomy, bud," Ezra said with a hard thrust at the air. "When I'm pumping your ass, you'll be rock hard and begging for my dick even deeper in your hole."

Roman didn't know how to respond, what to say, or how to feel, so he stood silent.

"But before we have fun with you ass up and face down, we're gonna make use of that smart mouth of yours."

Ezra pointed to the floor at his feet, and Roman got down on his knees. Knelt beneath Ezra, the man seemed so much bigger. His dick seemed so much more insurmountable.

This was it. This was Roman's point of no return. He kept waiting for something to interfere, to prevent his lips from meeting Ezra's dick. He wouldn't reject the offer a second time, but as his heart pounded and his body burned with nervousness, Roman anxiously took in the hard cock in front of him.

"Well?" Ezra stared. "Get me off."

Roman opened his mouth mechanically, unsure of where to begin. He leaned in close, ready to bring the dick between his lips, but he froze.

He stared at the foreskin pulled back around the head of Ezra's cock, the dribble of precum at the slit of his dick, the veins around his massive cock, and the girth all around. He considered all the things he liked when it came to head, from teasing to going all the way down, but he didn't think he could willingly subject himself to doing either.

Roman couldn't start, but he also couldn't walk away. Not again.

"Just shove it in," Roman insisted. "Do whatever you want."

"I want you to work to bring me off." Ezra grabbed his dick at the base and waved it up and down, playfully taunting Roman.

Unsure of himself and hating himself a little bit more, Roman leaned in with his open mouth and hoped Ezra would take the hint.

Ezra smacked the head of his dick against Roman's tongue. He pushed his cock in just a bit, allowing the head to sit in Roman's mouth.

"Do something," he demanded.

Roman didn't know what to do, so he closed his mouth around the dick and just sort of held it there, considering rotating his tongue around the head, but his mouth already felt so crammed he felt awkward trying to move around the head of the dick.

"Come on now." Ezra grabbed Roman by his ruffled brown hair and pushed his head further down on the dick, shoving it against the roof of his mouth. "You know how you like it, right? Do that. Get me off."

Roman's head bobbed several times under Ezra's instruction, following the flow of motion from his controlling hands. Each time Ezra pushed his dick further into Roman's mouth, and when it hit the back of his throat, Roman nearly retched.

"Hold on," Roman said with a gasp, pulling away and breathing in deep.

"None of that," Ezra said, turning Roman back to face the massive cock.

Roman opened his mouth and accepted Ezra's dick, only this time there was no steady push a bit further each time. Ezra had instead pushed with as much force as he could while thrusting forward at the same time.

"Take it all," Ezra demanded. "All of it. Now. Take it. Fucking take it."

Roman choked and gurgled as spit spilled from his mouth and snot bubbled from his nose while he desperately forced in air, which seemed more impossible with each passing second.

"Hold it," Ezra demanded, keeping a firm grip on Roman's head while the entirety of his dick ached in Roman's throat.

He couldn't breathe, he couldn't think, he couldn't stop gagging over and over and over on Ezra's cock, which remained firmly in place. Ezra lightly smacked Roman's face and neck, commanding him to hold it, to be a good boy, a bitch, a toy. When Ezra groaned with satisfaction, his grip eased ever so, and Roman used that to pull back. He had nearly gotten Ezra's dick out of his mouth when Ezra interjected.

"Not yet," he insisted. With one hand still squeezing Roman's hair and the other wrapping underneath Roman's jaw, he shoved Roman back down onto his dick.

Roman moaned, coughing and choking, eyes welling up with so many tears, the room turned into a blurry mess.

"You're doing good," Ezra said as he bucked his hips forward. "So, so good."

Roman gurgled, gasping a bit as his jaw somehow stretched just wide enough to finally choke in a bit of air around the massive girth of Ezra's cock.

"Look at that pretty face." Ezra held Roman's head down, forcing his mouth all the way to the base and keeping him there. Roman's lips brushed the trimmed black hairs of Ezra's crotch. With his other hand, Ezra wiped away a few tears so Roman could clearly see his face, see the wild look in his eyes. "You ready for me to get started?"

Roman stared, petrified, completely uncertain of what he was expected to do. He couldn't speak in this state. And the bewilderment of Ezra's comment fully sank in. Roman couldn't believe this was what Ezra considered…what? A warmup to a blowjob?

"Answer me." Ezra slapped Roman's face, startling him from the comment and the light pelt. "You ready for me to wreck this pretty face of yours?"

Roman attempted to nod, but with Ezra's other hand firmly in place, all he could manage was to somehow push the cock deeper down his throat as his face got pushed in closer, and his nose was covered with black pubes.

"Answer me, bitch." Ezra slapped Roman's face a second time, this time prompting a sad response.

Roman gurgled and wheezed and attempted to say yes.

"Good boy." Ezra pulled his dick all the way out of Roman's mouth.

Roman nearly collapsed onto the floor to suck in desperate breaths, but Ezra held a tight grip on Roman's hair and kept his head in place while Roman coughed and choked up spit. So much spit, he could feel drool all over his chin, over his chest, and even dribbling on his bare thighs. Massive amounts of slobber covered Ezra's cock, too.

"Open."

Roman obeyed nervously and prepared himself. Ezra went to work fucking Roman's throat with merciless vigor. The more Roman gagged and flailed in place, the harder Ezra's hips slapped against Roman. Taking Ezra's cock was the most brutal and exhausting thing he'd ever experienced. Roman grabbed Ezra's thighs, using them to brace himself but finding it a futile effort as it seemed to only bring out more veracity from Ezra.

The ache in his knees helped distract him from the pain in his throat, both sore in very different ways, and Roman hoped for a reprieve.

After a grueling ten minutes of Ezra face fucking Roman, he finally bucked a bit erratically as he slammed his cock in at an odd angle. Roman believed Ezra had stretched his entire throat out already, but somehow, he managed to find some muscles still tight enough to please him.

Ezra squeezed Roman's hair, slamming his dick all the way down and holding Roman in place as he twitched. Ezra's toes curled, something Roman noticed from the sideway angle Ezra twisted his head to.

"Aaaahhhh," Ezra growled.

The spurt of warmth that hit the back of Roman's throat filled him with equal measures of shame and relief. He counted the seconds and the number of jetted streams that tickled the inside of his throat. After releasing everything he could down Roman's throat, Ezra's cock finally softened in Roman's mouth, and the tension in his tight jaw muscles eased. Ezra remained where he stood, looking up to the ceiling and playfully stroking Roman's sweaty hair.

Ezra released Roman and stepped away from him in favor of lounging on the unused bottom bunk of the bed, a bunk that now belonged to Roman since he'd agreed to room with Ezra. A bunk Ezra must've only plopped into because he wasn't finished for the evening. Roman knew he couldn't be that lucky. There was this look in Ezra's eyes, this excitement and intensity that kept Roman locked in place on the floor.

"Come on." Ezra patted the bed, encouraging Roman to join him.

Roman wobbled a bit, feeling lightheaded and drained after so much time on his knees. He stretched his jaw a few times as he made his way to the mattress corner. With Ezra sprawled out, he had little choice in where to sit.

"Look at you, feeling so excited." Ezra nodded, and Roman followed the motion to see that his own cock had gotten hard.

Roman blushed, his entire face burning, which wasn't difficult since the face fucking had already made his face red and tired. It didn't make any sense. This wasn't what he wanted. This wasn't something he enjoyed. He'd have almost understood if it had happened if Ezra were fucking him, recalling how Levi explained how the male prostate worked. But sucking cock shouldn't have aroused Roman.

"I don't understand…"

"The human body is a fascinating thing," Ezra said. "It reacts to things the mind doesn't always grasp. No worries. It's probably just a sign you were always meant to submit, to serve. Even if your brain thinks you're an alpha, your body knows you're an eager bitch."

Roman frowned at that comment, anger burning in his eyes.

"I'm kidding. Kind of." Ezra playfully kicked Roman's knee with his toes. "Eventually, your mind will learn to like it as much as the rest of you. You just have to let yourself be happy."

Roman's frown deepened. Allowing himself to feel happy by this arrangement seemed more like a threat than a reward. The fact his body would betray him over something he still couldn't wrap his thoughts around exhausted him.

"In the meantime, clean me up." Ezra gestured, but Roman wasn't sure where.

He stared at Ezra's naked body, the trickle of sweat on his brow and running over his chest. Roman scrunched his face and turned to look for a cloth, something to dab Ezra clean.

"What are you doing?"

"Looking for a towel," Roman answered.

"No, no, no, sweetheart," Ezra corrected. "You made the mess; you clean the mess."

"What mess?"

Ezra grabbed Roman by the back of the head and pulled him down toward his dick.

"Lick it clean."

"What?"

"Open your mouth, lick up the mess you made." Ezra smiled down at Roman's perplexed face. "I want you to spit-shine my cock."

Roman stayed still, a hand squeezing the back of his neck, and his lack of a response served as his request to please make him do something different. Ezra waited in the silence, keeping Roman pressed close to his flaccid dick.

Shamefully, Roman stuck out his tongue and went to work, listening to Ezra's guiding instruction on where to move his mouth next, where to run his tongue. There was something more humiliating about licking Ezra's dick, working over and over to clean every crevice of his groin, than having Ezra simply ram his cock down Roman's throat. He'd rather just suck his dick again and be done with it; instead, he continued debasing himself, cleaning Ezra's dick with a tongue bath.

Roman licked Ezra's flaccid cock clean of the slobber. It was repetitive, lapping at Ezra's dick again and again, leaving spit but collecting slobber, collecting spit and leaving a new sheen of slobber when Ezra would grab the back of Roman's head and shove him to the base. He'd choke on the soft cock, feeling it grow semi-erect each time Roman gagged on it. Ezra simply smiled and waited for Roman to get back to work, letting him lick his dick for what felt like an eternity. Five continuous minutes of this seemed like such an infinite stretch of time.

"Work on the head," Ezra instructed.

Roman sucked on the tip of Ezra's soft cock until the man added that Roman needed to pull back the foreskin.

"Really treat it special."

Roman obeyed, pushing back the foreskin of Ezra's cock and revealing the head, which Roman licked and kissed and played with to Ezra's satisfaction. Vocal pleasure in the way he praised Roman and physical pleasure in the way his cock grew as Roman worked.

"That's enough." Ezra pulled his dick up and away from Roman's mouth. "Lick my balls."

He spread his legs a bit more, letting the large set hang between his thighs. They were big, and the thick black hairs felt gross on Roman's tongue, but he found licking them again and again a bit less grueling than sucking on Ezra's cock. But Roman couldn't truly escape Ezra's cock. As Roman lapped at Ezra's ball sack, the man slapped Roman's face with his dick, taking pleasure in the spit and precum hitting Roman as he ignored it. He kept licking the balls until Ezra told him to take them into his mouth and suck.

Roman obeyed, finding them hard to hold at the same time, the funk of sweat and saltiness and hairiness made him want to retch, but he gargled them in his mouth, sucking on the ball sack to Ezra's satisfaction.

A satisfaction that made Ezra's cock swell back to the full ten inches with minimal stroking on his part. He smacked Roman in the face with his dick, laughing lightly every time Roman flinched when the dickhead hit his eye.

"All right, time for round two." Ezra pushed Roman up a bit and sat forward.

Roman slid off the bed and returned to his knees, almost ready to get the next grueling blow job over with.

"Look at you," Ezra said with a smile. "Eager little cocksucker so soon."

"I'd just as well get this over with." Roman ground his teeth, willing to hold onto a bit of his defiance. Ezra might've owned him, but he wouldn't let him break him. He could fuck Roman's throat until he lost his words, but he'd still be just as spiteful with his gaze.

"Oh, I really hope you're that cocky while I have you ass up and face down." Ezra patted the bed, calling Roman over.

Roman held his breath, nervous and almost letting the glower in his gaze give way, but he held onto it. He knew this was coming. He knew what he'd signed up for. He knew Ezra wanted him to willingly submit in every sense of the word. But while he couldn't refuse him without suffering a different cruel fate, one that would drag Levi into it too, one that would make his life miserable in so many different ways, he still wouldn't give Ezra the satisfaction of submitting in every sense.

He'd give him his body. But not his mind. Not his spirit. Not his willpower. Roman didn't know when he'd reclaim his strength, but he knew he wouldn't surrender it all tonight. He only hoped he could keep his conviction in the long term.

Christ, that realization nearly hollowed him out.

This wasn't a one-time submission. This wasn't a one-time humiliation. This would be ongoing and Roman had to hold strong to himself if he wanted to survive. He had to keep his convictions while letting Ezra brutally have his way with him. It made the choice of continuing that much more challenging. Roman suspected this was the real motivator behind offering choices.

Roman joined Ezra on the bed and let the man survey him. Those haunting green eyes held a chilling hatred that the sly smile on his face didn't cover.

"You sure you're willing to commit?" Ezra asked. "Once I start, I don't wanna stop because you have second thoughts, but obviously I wanna make sure you're—"

"Then don't stop." Roman glared, assured he could handle himself, believing getting fucked would merely be a moment of humiliation but not any more painful or challenging than what he'd faced in a fight.

"Again, I say: you must be willing to give yourself to me." Ezra pressed a hand to Roman's cheek, turning his face to meet his. "It's the only way this works."

"Why do you care?" Roman snapped, teeth practically ready to bite Ezra's hand. "You know it's not real. You know I wouldn't be here if I had any real choices."

"You do have real choices," Ezra said. "I can guarantee if you walk out of here, you will not return to solitary."

Roman still struggled to believe those words.

"Even so, I wouldn't be safe out there." Roman bit the inside of his cheek. "Not anymore."

Too many people hated him. Inmates. Guards. The warden. He couldn't be certain someone else wouldn't take him by force in the same way Ezra wanted him to willingly offer.

"Correct," Ezra said. "You wouldn't have my protection. I'm sorry about that. But I only offer my protection to my friends."

"And if I walked away, would Levi be your friend?" Roman debated whether he could save himself, if he could fight off threats from every angle. Maybe. Unlikely. But he knew with Levi in the mix, he most certainly couldn't. He'd lose him.

"He wouldn't," Ezra answered. "He rejected my friendship in favor of yours. But I will keep him safe for you so long as we have a civil arrangement. That's what friends do for each other."

The sick way Ezra warped the word, warped the term, confused Roman. The way Ezra used Roman's real friendship with Levi and compared it to the perverse connection he wanted messed with Roman's head.

"Just fuck me already." Roman dug his hands into the mattress, holding back all his rage and hate and desire to fight Ezra.

"I can't wait." Ezra stepped off the bed and walked over to his dresser. He retrieved a small bottle and walked back. "Stick your hand out, two fingers together."

Roman obeyed and watched Ezra squirt lube onto his fingers.

"Perks of being champion," he said with a small chuckle, gesturing for Roman to rotate his hand so he could further coat his fingers. "Trust me, way better than raw dogging. I wanna break you, but I don't wanna break you, you know?"

Roman grimaced.

"Stick them inside you."

"What?" Roman shook his head.

"Trust me," Ezra said, waving his half-erect dick. "If you want this splitting you open, then you're gonna want that rubbed all over inside."

Roman didn't want any of this, and he certainly didn't want to be split open. To avoid any more risk to his already precarious situation, Roman did as he was instructed and winced at the awkward discomfort that came with sticking his finger in his butt, the shame of Ezra watching him work.

"Both." Ezra watched and waited for Roman to obey. "Now, all the way."

Roman took his time and flinched at the feeling of pushing further, his face contorted at the bizarre feeling of jabbing and stretching his insides. When Ezra insisted Roman massage the hole, Roman only felt more discomfort, more shame in the ordeal.

"If you think it feels painful now." Ezra nodded to his own massive cock. "Just saying."

"It doesn't hurt." Roman scoffed, refusing to give Ezra any satisfaction aside from whatever pleasure he'd receive getting off. Roman wouldn't let him think this bothered him.

"All right." Ezra stepped closer, his dick almost touching Roman's nose. "Open your mouth and say oooooo."

Roman rolled his eyes and did as instructed, leaning forward in the process to meet Ezra's dick that he'd undoubtedly shove in his mouth anyway. To Roman's surprise, Ezra dribbled the lube into Roman's mouth and over his parted lips, spilling some down Roman's chin.

"Get me coated," Ezra demanded. "No deep-throating. I can see those hungry eyes ready to work, you eager cock slut. But we need to focus on lubing. Not that a bit of spit won't help, but I suspect you'll take it a lot easier if we grease this beast from tip to base."

"We?" Roman thought as he ran his slimy tongue against Ezra's cock and worked to cover it in lube. He puckered his lips, kissing the sides of Ezra's dick and rubbing the lube on as best he could. He gave sloppy kisses of lube over every inch of Ezra's massive cock. Between the clinical taste of the unflavored lube and the funk of Ezra's dick, Roman fought off the urge to gag multiple times as he worked.

"On the bed." Ezra pointed and helped position Roman once he sprawled out with his face buried in a pillow.

He lay there silently, letting Ezra push his legs forward some, shift his knees ever so, and spread his legs just the way he wanted. Once he'd done that, Ezra angled Roman's ass to a level he preferred and popped Roman on the back a few times.

Nothing hard, but enough to encourage Roman to arch a bit. Currently, he had his back curled up like a cat, ready to pounce off the bed the second Ezra's cock touched his ass.

"Almost there," Ezra said, giving one firm push with his hands to force Roman down a bit more.

He felt like he was popping his stomach out, but he supposed that, from Ezra's angle, it looked just right.

"None of that." Ezra reached over and knocked the pillows Roman had onto the floor. "I'm not interested in a pillow princess."

Roman furrowed his brow.

"I wanna hear you," Ezra continued. "I wanna hear how much pain and pleasure I bring. Don't hold back any of it."

Roman remained stoic when looking back at Ezra, even if his body betrayed him with trembling. Even if Ezra's playful slap of his ass roused something in the tension Roman clung to.

"Ready?"

Roman turned away and nodded.

Ezra smacked Roman's butt again, then bounced his dick between the crack of Roman's ass a few times. "I've been dreaming about this day, dude. Bet you're gonna be the best hole I'll ever break in."

With that, he pushed his cock into Roman, and the sensation sent an immediate pain through Roman. He sucked in a sharp breath and held back a muffled groan. Ezra continued pushing in slowly, but Roman felt every inch, believing somehow Ezra had shoved all ten inches into him.

"Relax." Ezra scratched at Roman's back, a massaging act that helped when he forced Roman's back into an arch again. He hadn't even realized his spine had tightened up. "It's just the tip. We'll let it—"

"What?" Roman interrupted, pained and ready to be done, impossibly stunned by the comment.

"Oh, yeah. We got a lot of meat left to fit in." Ezra laughed a little. "Don't worry, though. I'm gonna give you a chance to adjust. Let your hole stretch a bit. It'll make it easier when I start pounding you out."

True to his word, Ezra gave Roman another minute or two before he pushed further into him. Now that Roman realized all he had inside before was the head of Ezra's cock with another inch or so, he felt the distinct difference with every push.

His body quaked in Ezra's grasp, and he took swift, sharp breaths, hoping to ease the pain. It spread with a burn that consumed him entirely. He'd never felt anything so excruciating. His muscles tensed, and he clenched, resisting each push, knowing it worked against him.

"Relax yourself," Ezra said as he bucked his hips forward. "Let me in."

Roman winced, grinding his teeth and keeping his entire body tense as if flexing his muscles would somehow help. It didn't. It made every push more severe, it made it harder for Roman to bite back his grunts, and it made this whole ordeal so much more exhausting. Finally, he submitted and tried his best to relax his hole.

"Good job." Ezra raked his fingers over Roman's back and sides, eliciting a bizarre comfort in the mix of unending pain. "Now, let me hear you."

Roman groaned, unable to hold back the entirety of the noise but unwilling to comply with Ezra's demand.

"That's it." Ezra bucked his hips again, pushing more weight down onto Roman and letting gravity help him slip his dick deep into Roman's ass.

Roman whimpered, which only encouraged Ezra to heighten his pace once deep inside of him. While he felt himself being split open, he fought to remain calm, to lay there and take Ezra's dick again and again. Roman stifled the shout by biting the back of his wrist. As Ezra started thrusting in and out of Roman, it took everything he had to hold back the need to scream. It was brutal and burning and unbearable, yet somewhere between the slamming pain came this euphoric sensation. That was somehow worse. It calmed Roman a little, and he released his gnawing grip on his wrist until his voice betrayed him, and a wispy moan escaped his lips.

"That's it, baby. Let me hear you. Lemme hear all those sweet sounds of surrender." Ezra continued railing Roman, calling him affectionate names between the sound of slapping skin.

Roman wouldn't give him the satisfaction. He couldn't. He had to keep something for himself, some piece of his dignity. If there was anything left to salvage. To keep from shouting when Ezra's pounding turned painful again, Roman bit the back of his own hand to muffle himself. He squeezed his knuckles so tightly, they turned a blotchy white. When his own cock began to throb, he tried to push himself up some.

Between Ezra's swift thrusts and the friction of the silky sheets, Roman's dick was in paradise. He couldn't tell if he'd already cum or not, so he looked down to see his bulging dick flopping around, precum dripping. The head bounced against the sheets, rhythmically following the pace of Ezra's strokes. He'd never found himself this ready to burst. He'd never found himself in this type of pain. He couldn't figure it out, but he bit harder on his hand and hoped the pain there would take from the pleasure his dick found in the way Ezra fucked him.

It didn't.

Roman growled, almost letting out a feral noise when Ezra pulled his cock all the way back and rammed into him. His hips smacked Roman's ass with each powerful stroke as Ezra repeated the long dicking act over and over.

"None of that, baby." Ezra reached over and grabbed Roman's hands. He resisted at first, but when his gaze caught the glare of Ezra's eyes, he allowed the man to pull his arms back.

Roman lay there while Ezra pinned his arms behind his back and continued pounding into him. With nothing to stop him, Roman groaned with miserable pleasure. It was grueling and terrible, and he felt like he'd lost a battle to a war he never stood a chance in.

His entire body shook, and Roman let out an exasperated shout as he came. His dick twitched. Every time Ezra pounded into Roman, his cock shot a powerful jet of cum until, finally, he lay there gasping into the mattress, wishing he could hold back the noises he made.

"That's right, bitch." Ezra released Roman's hands and thrusted harder, eliciting louder moans and heavier grunts from Roman. "You fucking love it."

Roman didn't contest. Roman didn't know. He knew he hated so much of this and hated how much satisfaction Ezra got from it, but after a few more minutes of pounding, his dick started to throb again, and somehow, that helped take away from the shame consuming him. His arms lay useless at his sides. His entire body felt like jelly as he took Ezra's dick, unable to do anything. The intense pleasure, building again so suddenly, stripped away what little strength Roman had left.

"Fucking take it." Ezra gripped Roman's hips, holding them tightly as he rammed his dick in fast, short spurts.

Roman could feel Ezra on the verge of a climax. The way his body trembled over Roman's, the way his dick pulsed inside of Roman, the way he clawed at Roman's skin a moment away, a second away, a breath away, and then he came.

He released the happiest growl as he leaned forward with the full weight of his body atop Roman. His hips bucked futilely as he finished pouring his load inside of Roman. His teeth met the nape of Roman's neck; both men shivered for a beat, and then he bit down.

"You're mine," he growled. "You exist for me now. Only me."

Roman lay there completely silent, allowing Ezra to kiss his neck on all sides.

"Say it." Ezra's teeth grazed Roman's shoulder. "Who do you belong to?"

"You."

"No." Ezra bit down hard enough to elicit a stifled moan from Roman. "Tell me. Really tell me."

"I belong to you," Roman answered. "Only you. For you. To serve you."

"You're goddamn right, baby." Ezra licked Roman's shoulder affectionately, then kissed it gently before he slowly crawled off him.

With the deed done, at least for the first night, Roman wanted to fall asleep and hope that, eventually, this wouldn't feel like such a laborious arrangement. There were parts that felt good. Parts that weren't terrible. But all of that vanished the moment the shame returned. It filled Roman to the brim, consuming his thoughts and reminding him this was sadly the best choice he could've made.

The hoots and hollers from neighboring rooms confirmed that suspicion. Roman teared up a bit at the jabs, the cutting comments, and the declaration that he sounded like a truly fucked bitch. There was nothing he could do to argue it. Everyone on the cellblock heard his final fall into failure, and now, he really had no one except Ezra and the protection he offered.

"Bow chicka wow wow," a familiar voice called out. "I've always wondered how you'd sound with a dick up your ass. Music to my ears!"

Roman wanted to sink into the bed and die. Jake's taunting voice rallied others to join in a debate on whether or not this was Roman's first time being fucked. On the one hand, they argued he sounded like a weak bitch about it, but on the other hand, he moaned like a truly experienced fa—

"Shut up." Ezra's demand crackled across the cellblock and brought every voice to a halt and squashed Roman's anxious thoughts, even if only for a moment.

Ezra wrapped an arm around Roman's sweaty body and pulled him into an embrace.

"Don't let them get to you," he whispered. "No one can ever get to you. Not with me here."

Roman silently stared at Ezra. He didn't fully accept his choice, but he made a little room for it, at least tonight. He was exhausted and worn out and desperately needed sleep.

Ezra leaned in close and kissed Roman. He instinctively pulled away but then caught himself. If he could take Ezra's dick down his throat, surely, he could handle the man's tongue in his mouth. It was startling, surprising. Ezra seemed mostly content in breaking down Roman's walls and forcing him to submit, fucking him without mercy, yet now he wanted to hug and hold Roman, to offer him a gentle kiss before bed.

Roman lay awake most of the night, lost in his twisting thoughts and wrapped in Ezra's arms.

Chapter Eight

The first thing Ezra expected from Roman when they woke up the following morning was to assume the position. Roman rolled onto his stomach, turned so his head was close to the wall, and his ass was up and hanging out from the bed. Part of him considered his options, considered walking out of the cell this second, but he wondered how many men would be there waiting to laugh, waiting to pounce. Roman conceded with his thoughts and adjusted a bit more.

He was still sore but found his muscles, at the very least, didn't carry the weight of lead after a few hours of real sleep. Ezra slapped Roman's ass a few times, instructing him to properly position.

"Bitch pose, please," Ezra said with a demanding knuckle pop on the small of Roman's back.

It was paradoxical. Everything about Ezra was. He wouldn't force himself on Roman, willing him to be a consenting member of this arrangement, even though Roman would never willingly subject himself to this.

Accepting the instructions, Roman moved his knees slightly, keeping them at the edge of the bed. He pushed his butt up some and arched his back as much as he could bear. Once he'd done that, the lube bottle squirted a few times, Ezra spit on his hand, stroked himself hard, and unceremoniously rammed his cock into Roman.

When Roman yelped, Ezra chuckled and rutted faster into the man. Each thrust hit harder than last night, with Roman's hole so sore. Roman moved his hand, blindly searching for Ezra, who hammered away behind him, and with a gentle touch, Roman pressed against the man's lower abdomen, hoping to silently convey a need to ease. Ezra ignored the plea, wrapping his hand around Roman's wrist and twisting it behind his back.

"Gimme the other one," Ezra demanded, now holding both of Roman's arms behind him at the small of Roman's back as he took in all of Ezra. "Let me hear you, baby."

Roman's head hit the wall a few times, adding to the pained grunts he let out as Ezra pounded away at his rear.

"Clench," Ezra demanded, releasing Roman's wrists and palming at his ass instead.

Ezra squeezed Roman's cheeks and spread them to give himself a clearer show of Roman's hole. Roman felt the pace pick up once Ezra did that, believing he took some extra satisfaction in watching his cock bury from head to base inside Roman.

Doing as instructed, Roman clenched his hole and lucked out. Ezra didn't drag out the morning fuck like he had last night's first time, relishing Roman's groans and tightened hole. After five brutal minutes of fucking Roman's ass, Ezra growled. His legs flexed, and he slammed one fist into Roman's lower back, then he grabbed Roman's hair to yank his head back. The action demanded a deeper arch, which Roman offered. Finally, Ezra's hips twitched and bucked as he came inside Roman.

Roman lay there in position, feeling the cum drip from his sore hole. He didn't move because Ezra hadn't instructed him to do so, and whether he realized it or not, he'd quickly become obedient to the other man's demands. The worst part of sitting here, keeping his ass exposed while his body trembled from the morning sex, was how his own cock throbbed so close to climax but not quite there. Ezra wanted Roman to understand his pleasure wasn't a priority, and Roman quickly realized he needed to ensure Ezra achieved climax as soon as possible.

After Ezra finished what he was doing, he rushed up close behind Roman and stuck his hand on Roman's hole, which elicited a startled groan. He wiped his fingers on the goop dripping out and brought his hand close to Roman's mouth.

"Good source of protein. Eat up," he said. No. He demanded. Everything from Ezra was a demand. One Roman could reject. But he'd already seen where he'd go if he rejected Ezra's friendship. In order to save his own skin, to live and survive in this place, he needed Ezra's clout. It was bad enough Ezra had already stripped Roman of every shred of authority he had in this place, but now, without Ezra watching over him, others would come for Roman. The entire cellblock had quieted outside last night, eagerly listening to Roman get fucked. He could imagine a dozen men who'd easily try to bitch him out if he lost his protection, if he lost his friendship with Ezra.

"Thank you." Roman swallowed the salty load covering Ezra's fingers. He sucked on them, doing his best to savor the taste of Ezra's fingers over the taste of cum and ass.

"Yummy, right?" Ezra playfully winked and pulled his hand away.

"Yep."

"Glad you like it." Ezra jabbed his fingers into Roman's tender hole—eliciting a wince—and dug deeper than needed, unnecessarily so. He withdrew and brought a bit more of his load close to Roman's lips.

He rubbed his fingers along Roman's bottom lip, sticking them in the space between his gums. He stared silently at Roman the entire time, waiting for a reaction, or at least Roman suspected as much. There was a lot Roman couldn't do anymore now that he'd handed the reins of his life to Ezra, but he could control his reactions. When he wanted to shout or wail while Ezra fucked him, he did his best to muffle it to a grunt. When tears threatened to pool down his face, he resisted them with all his power and stayed strong. When he wanted to recoil at the taste in his mouth, he remained steady. Roman rotated his tongue over Ezra's fingers and licked at the cum.

Ezra smiled. "Such a good boy."

Roman sucked on Ezra's fingers until they were clean.

"Get dressed," Ezra said. Correction, demanded. "We have a long day ahead. You're with me while we move about.

Don't speak to anyone. Don't speak unless I tell you to. Don't step more than three feet from me. Always stay behind me but in my line of sight. Understand?"

Roman nodded.

"Such a good boy, indeed." Ezra playfully slapped Roman's face, cupping his hands around Roman's cheeks before sliding them down to his neck. "Hmmm. I think when I fuck you tonight, I'm gonna test how well-behaved you can be. Would you like that?"

Roman nodded.

"Yeah?" Ezra tightened his grip around Roman's throat. "You'd really let me do anything to you, huh?"

Roman nodded, his face turning red, but he fought to keep his expression blank and unchanging.

"Kiss me." Ezra's eyes locked onto Roman, waiting.

Roman moved closer, Ezra's hands still around his throat but allowing him to lean in. Without delay, he gave Ezra a light smack on the lips.

"Kiss me like you mean it." Ezra's grip tightened.

Roman kissed him again, this time parting his lips and letting his tongue rotate over Ezra's. The rough stubble on Ezra's face grazed Roman's.

"Kiss me like your life depended on it." Ezra squeezed just a bit more. "Like my lungs hold the air you crave, the breath you need, the love you lost."

Roman kissed Ezra again, forcing himself to invade all of Ezra's space. His teeth bit, his tongue licked, his lips smacked. Without second-guessing, Roman crashed into Ezra, straddling him, pressing his hands against Ezra's chest, and pinning him. He grinded against Ezra, every cell of his body almost as hungry as his mouth. Each second roused both men, each second tangled their bodies more, and each second swept Roman away a little more. Roman felt his own erection pressed to Ezra's stomach and a new rock-hard throb from Ezra against his exposed hole.

Finally, they parted just enough so Roman could await his next request, the next kiss Ezra would demand, the fuck he'd order.

"I love how quickly we've become best of friends," Ezra said, releasing his grip on Roman's neck before playfully palming Roman's butt. "Come on, I wanna grab a shower."

Roman obeyed and silently followed him out of the cell so they could begin their morning routine. Keeping quiet was easy. Shame stole the words from Roman's mouth every time he wanted to speak.

Too many people studied Roman as they walked naked into the showers. He could feel the judgment, could taste the smug satisfaction carried in the whispers about him, and he could hear the cutting asides about Roman being a bitch, a bottom, a fruitcake, and a lot uglier words he never would've tolerated as champion.

It used to only take one cutting glare from him to silence a room. Now, when his gaze locked onto someone for even a fleeting second, it brought smiles and laughter to faces. He was alone and broken, and everyone celebrated his defeat and devastating downfall.

Eyes shot from Ezra's lean, muscular frame and then to Roman's hollowed-out form. He still had muscles, still had strength, but his size had dwindled after three months of irregular and inconsistent meals in isolation. His mass had fallen after losing his workout routine and only ever exerting himself in an arena as a masked nobody who people cheered would die.

He also felt so much smaller now that Ezra had fucked him. He only stood two inches above Roman, yet Roman felt as if he had to look up to meet Ezra's gaze.

Water splashed against Ezra's tight abs, and he didn't even flinch at the rush of cold water. He stared at the empty shower beside him, his eyes instructing Roman to take the spot. Roman washed up, ignoring the stares of others when Ezra invaded his space and scrubbed his back.

"Gotta get all the spots nice and clean," Ezra said playfully, rubbing his hands over Roman's butt. He didn't stick his fingers inside him—he didn't have to, everyone already knew—but Roman nearly collapsed. Somehow, Ezra noticed this and gripped Roman's hips until he steadied. "I got you. I will always have your back."

"*Yeah, so you can fuck me into submission,*" Roman thought, shooting Ezra an angry glare as he recovered.

Ezra ignored the sour expression, which Roman was certain he noticed based on the cool pause on Ezra's face before it lit up with a big smile.

"You mind getting mine?" Ezra spun around, exposing himself to Roman and waiting for a thorough scrubbing.

Roman ran his soapy fingers over Ezra's muscular back, rubbing his deep bronze skin clean from top to bottom. When his hands moved to the small of Ezra's back, he thought back to how much force Ezra had single-handedly put into shoving Roman into a deeper arch. He wondered how easy it'd be to shove Ezra down and steal back a bit of his pride.

He'd never win. He couldn't beat Ezra at his best, and he certainly couldn't beat him now that he'd been bested. Roman swallowed the shameful thought, finding himself disgusting for considering a blitz attack, a cowardly advance to snatch a temporary victory.

When Ezra's hand reached back and tugged Roman's hands, they shook in the firm grasp. Ezra guided Roman's hands further down, and Roman washed Ezra's butt, cock, balls, and thighs before they each returned to their own bodies.

Roman kept his eyes fixed on Ezra, studying him, studying the body he'd spend his days pleasuring, doing his best to learn more about this man. He had several small scars similar to Roman, but unlike Roman, he had a lot of random tattoos. Nothing seemed too important, too meaningful, but he did have a random black bar across his butt.

"What's the deal with that?" Roman gestured to his own ass in the place of Ezra's tattoo.

"Oh, man, the things a pretty lady can talk you into are infinite." Ezra grinned ear to ear while recalling this woman, whoever she was. "I wonder what things you'll convince me to do, babes."

Roman bit back a snarl and glowered.

Ezra chuckled, puckering his lips at his *babes* before continuing. "I considered putting 'Total Regerts' over her name but figured there wouldn't be enough people seeing this fine ass to catch the joke."

No regerts, the ultimate juvenile humor of irony. It almost made Roman smirk. Almost.

"Guess I should've taken this into possibility." Ezra waved a hand, looping his finger in a circle as if to indicate the shower room of inmates who'd see his bare ass every day.

With that, they returned to their showers and finished up before stepping out into the line of men drying off.

"Someone's looking a bit humbled this morning." Jake the Snake strutted through the showers, letting his dick bounce.

Roman didn't look. He knew that was what Jake wanted. It was something he'd done countless times before, boldly standing in the nude, flaunting his tattoos and muscles, waving his cock around for all to see.

"Didn't realize you had so much art." Ezra nodded, checking out Jake's numerous tattoos. "Makes me itchy for some new ink, too."

"I know some folks here if you're serious." Jake smiled.

"What do you think?" Ezra asked, nodding to Jake's tattoos. It came with a silent demand to check out Jake's tattoos, pieces Roman had already seen on more than one occasion, but he found himself obediently obeying Ezra's request.

Jake's tattoos were colorful and bold and murderous across his skin, some of enraged beasts and others of bloody women and a few vulgar words scrawled in various fonts. All in all, Roman thought it made Jake look like an evil rainbow. It was the serpent tattoo that normally caught Roman's eye, so big and bold, slithering around Jake's back and abdomen, even over a few of the other tattoos. The snake didn't cover them, didn't replace them, merely obstructed viewing on a few as if the snake had a greater purpose. Unlike all the others, the snake was black and white, and the lack of color aside from deep shading created a stark contrast to the other tattoos.

Roman didn't know if Jake's nickname or the tattoo came first, but considering how often he bragged about having a big snake-sized dick, Roman figured he just leaned into snake imagery more over the years. The tail of the snake started the tattoo built into one of the V cuts of Jake's abs. It continued slithering around Jake's back, looping around his left arm, crossing down Jake's ribcage, and reaching past Jake's abdomen and to his left thigh.

Roman grimaced at the prominent fangs on the serpent's mouth, the way it looked ready to launch off Jake's skin and attack. He also found it bizarre how Jake picked that particular location, noticing Jake's cock hanging so close to the snake's open mouth.

When the thought of how awkward or uncomfortable it'd be to suck the cock of someone while staring at that tattoo the entire time crossed Roman's thoughts, he blanched. He'd turned ghostly white, face warped in confusion and obvious discomfort. Never. Never in his life had he wondered something so outlandish. And even though his mouth belonged to Ezra, the thought of sucking another man's cock, the idea of it, should never pass through his head. Not even as a fleeting horror.

"See something you like?" Jake asked, drawing Roman's eyes up and winking. Jake wasn't a mind reader, but Roman knew he made his discomfort obvious. He could feel it, surprised the words weren't spelled out across his face. "I'd be more than happy to give you a taste of the snake."

Roman didn't respond. He waited for Ezra to say something, but instead, he stepped away to grab towels.

"You wouldn't believe the strings I had to pull to arrange for front-row seats in your cellblock last night."

Roman ignored Jake's cutting comments, his lustful gaze, his menacing smirk, and his sadistic lilt of joy.

"You sounded so sweet when you were getting dicked down by the champion. I listened quite closely." Jake sounded like a serpent. Not with a hiss as he spoke, but his words had this subtle slither to them, how they slipped in and struck with a venomous surprise.

Roman knew he'd been quite vocal from the mix of pained pleasure from Ezra's brutal fuck. Ezra wanted him to be noisy, wanted to announce his deflowering for all. Roman knew everyone had listened and hollered with satisfaction at him getting railed out. But it still wounded him to be confronted, to be called out, to be looked down upon with no pity or kindness. The only thing Jake wanted was to make Roman relive last night and offer himself up as a new cock for Roman to serve.

"I wonder how good you'll sound with my dick inside you," Jake leaned close and whispered. "I can't wait until the day you choke on my cock."

Roman trembled. Part of him wanted to punch Jake, clock him right here, and beat him to a bloody pulp. Another part of him worried. Too many men here relished in Roman's downfall. Too many might interfere. Normally, Roman only had to worry about cheering or jeering when someone foolishly picked a fight with the champion. But now he had to worry about others stepping in, stepping up, smacking him down. Most of all, he didn't know if he had the strength to fight Jake off right here. He was exhausted and sleep-deprived, and the shame of where his life had spiraled weighed heavily on his shoulders. Roman wasn't sure he could even lift a fist in protest.

"I'm gonna enjoy breaking your holes when you're finally mine," Jake said with absolute certainty.

He'd never hid the fact that he wanted to bend Roman over. He'd gone through polite advances, smug come-ons, threatening, postering, scare tactics, and so much more over the years. Roman always managed to fight him off, to beat him back, to shrug off his diluted antics. But now Roman worried Jake would take him here and no one would stop him.

"That's not going to happen, buddy." Ezra slapped a hand on Roman's shoulder, snapping him away from his fear-spiraling thoughts and back to the reality of things. "I don't plan on sharing."

"Maybe a trade." Jake shrugged with non-committal indifference, but his eyes were hungry as they locked onto Roman's naked body.

"There's nothing you have that I want," Ezra said.

"I got a pretty nest egg, some connections, and honestly, the way I heard you wearing out that ass, you should probably trade him in for something better. Champions deserve the best." Jake winked at Roman. "I like my things a little worn for wear, anyway."

"I don't think you understand," Ezra continued with this almost perplexed expression. "Roman is my friend. I would never do something like that to my friend. Sorry, but as long as we're pals, there's not a thing in the world you have that I want."

It was a haunting comment. Ezra spoke so genuinely, so matter-of-factly, Roman almost believed the sincerity in the words. But they weren't sincere. Ezra's friendship was merely a ruse to veil the horrible things he did to Roman. Things Roman consented to, things he willingly allowed from Ezra. It was this warped manipulation that continued messing with Roman's head. The longer he dwelled on it, the more confused he got.

Ezra's strokes were brutal and filled with hate when he pumped into Roman last night, but there was a tenderness to how he kissed Roman, an affectionate desire in his tongue when it parted Roman's lips. It didn't make sense. But Ezra continued going late in the night after they'd dozed off once, asking how close Roman was, waiting for a response, then changing his strokes to bring Roman off a second time without Roman even needing to touch his own cock.

Roman wasn't curious—not when it came to Ezra—but he was so confused. Still, even if he were unknowingly gay, bi, something in the middle, he'd never willingly submit, never give someone that level of control over him. Yet he had. He had, and it felt nice. At least in the sense he could breathe easy again. He didn't have to fight every second of the day just to survive; he could give the reins to someone else and let them keep him safe and secure. He hated himself a little bit for thinking such things, for being weak, for failing.

"What's that dumb expression?" Roman thought. *"Caught between a rock and a hard cock."*

The silly musing almost brought a smile to his face, but he couldn't find the humor in anything anymore. He knew that wasn't the saying, but it was for him. The rock being The

Pit, an arena of death, and a farewell to Levi's safety. The hard cock being Ezra literally pounding Roman into his place, showing everyone his superiority as the new reigning champion of the arena and parading a phony friendship.

Roman had found himself so lost in his thoughts that he hadn't even noticed Jake take his leave. Ezra nudged Roman.

"Come on," he demanded as he did with all the things he said, though there was a kindness in his tone.

Roman couldn't and wouldn't make sense of Ezra. Right now, all he hoped to do was survive him.

Ignoring everyone else's comments, Roman followed Ezra to get dried and dressed and then through the cellblock until they arrived at the gym. Ezra strolled through to the private section reserved for the champion, a perk Roman had lost once he lost his title. He didn't know if Ezra wanted to actually workout for an upcoming match or if he simply wanted to gloat while Roman stood on the sidelines.

"Ready?" Ezra gestured at the treadmills.

The champion's gym wasn't anything noteworthy, but unlike the main gym, which mostly consisted of outdated weights and hazardous machines, the champion's gym had some nice equipment. It wasn't a lot of stuff, but enough to make the room cramped and easily allow for a small group to workout together.

When a small group entered, Roman flinched, worried they'd come to challenge Ezra, worried they'd come to challenge Roman. Everyone knew this place was off-limits.

"Howdy." Ezra waved them inside, allowing them to survey the area. "Come on in."

"What're you doing?" Roman hissed in a concerned aside.

"Returning some territory and making some allies," Ezra whispered, a friendly smile on his face for the arriving men but a cutting glare for Roman.

Technically, the champion's gym wasn't for the champion alone, but it had become that way once Roman took the title. After Jake and some of his crew ambushed Roman after a workout, he fought them off, broke a few noses, and put both of Jake's arms in slings. Once he'd fended off the threat, he marched into the warden's office and made the demand the gym belonged to him. It belonged to the champion. If other arena contenders wanted to train in there, they could gladly face off against Roman in the arena for the opportunity.

Roman sighed, recalling how much weight his voice used to hold, remembering the authority in his demands, the confidence in his walk, how tall he held himself.

When he stirred out of his depressing thoughts, he found Ezra locked in idle chitchat with the other men.

"Yeah, we're getting in some cardio to work on our stamina," Ezra playfully said, reaching out to grab Roman's waist. "This one's got a lot of energy."

When Roman tensed at the hold, Ezra strengthened his grip and pulled Roman closer. He bumped Roman's butt against his crotch and made a show of the action.

"I should probably focus on my next match-up, but gotta make sure my bestie is in top shape, too."

The other men nodded and went to go workout, eyeing Roman the entire time.

"We'll start with cardio, then something to keep those glutes in fan-*fuckable*-tastic form," Ezra whispered, then slapped Roman's butt and squeezed. "After that, you can join me for a sparring session. I got a match against Victor Fox this week. I've heard he's a wiry fucker."

He was, and Roman knew that. Victor wasn't particularly strong, but he was good at evading blows and holding out until his opponents tired out. Roman thought of all the ways Victor could best Ezra in the upcoming match. He ran on the treadmill and fantasized about Ezra's inevitable downfall, the joy he'd take seeing him knocked down from the pillar of strength he'd shoved Roman off of. A smile crept onto his face as he ran faster and faster, wondering who would come for Ezra on that day. Who would ruin him the same way he ruined Roman. Then, a realization struck him, and he nearly tumbled over.

If Ezra lost, if Ezra was bested, Roman lost his protection. He'd bound his lot in life to Ezra, surrendered himself to the man, and used the clout and respect he had as the new reigning champion to shield himself.

"You okay?" Ezra had stopped running, too, legs straddled on the edge of the fast-moving machine and eyes locked onto Roman's shaky stance as he did the same.

"Yeah, just thinking of ways you can exploit Victor during your next match-up."

Ezra smirked. "Look at you, looking out for me."

Roman shrugged and resumed his workout.

"We'll be best friends soon. Just you wait." With that, Ezra continued his workout, and Roman recoiled in his skin.

Friends didn't do what Ezra did. Friends didn't force someone into a compromised position. Friends didn't exploit vulnerabilities and manipulate consent. Friends didn't take satisfaction in the pain of their friend.

Roman knew all this. He hated Ezra with a passion. He was disgusted by how his sole responsibility in life had become pleasuring Ezra. Satisfying his cock. Willing himself to swallow Ezra's dick. Bearing through gritted teeth as Ezra railed him and filled Roman's insides.

All the same, every gentle touch clouded Roman's thoughts. Every kind word confused Roman. Every gesture, smile, and act meant to loll Roman into a false sense of security worked to slowly chip away at his willpower.

He knew nothing Ezra did was out of friendship, the statement a blatant and cutting lie. Still, terrible thoughts about what friendship really was crept into his mind. Friends protected each other, which Ezra did. Friends helped each other, which Ezra did. Friends took an interest in each other, and Ezra craved conversation with Roman.

Roman focused on his fitness and moved from cardio to weights. Ezra hadn't been lying about training his glutes. Roman worked on his arms a bit, but mainly just a few reps to keep the muscle tone there. Eventually, a routine like this would make Roman more lean, probably thinner than Ezra. While Ezra focused on adding muscle. Roman wondered if Ezra were that methodical, if he'd really considered their exercise routine for the day purely as a precursor to trading their physical stature.

All in all, while Roman worked on his squats, Ezra came up behind him and steadied his form.

"A few weeks of this and that beautiful bubble butt will look even better." Ezra winked. "If that's even possible."

Roman's stomach twisted. He didn't mind being ogled. He didn't even mind when other men would check him out at the gym. He used to find it flattering when gay dudes wanted a piece of him. But now that he'd given up that piece of himself, been used and worn out to the satisfaction of Ezra's needs, Roman couldn't help but recoil a bit. He hated being a cheap fuck toy for Ezra. He hated committing so diligently to a workout routine that'd only make Ezra happier. He hated knowing Ezra would rake his hands over his body again today and use him until he climaxed and then use him again and again and again. Most of all, Roman hated that he allowed this, that he committed to this proposition because he was too weak and frightened to walk away. Roman hated himself more than anything else.

They moved from the private gym to a small, spacious sparring room that was mostly bare except for the training mat. Ezra directed them right into training. They sparred for a while, and Roman studied Ezra's technique. He seemed so insurmountable after besting Roman twice in the arena, but during this training, nothing about Ezra's style appeared grand. Yes, he had a good form. Yes, he knew how to use his weight and the weight of opponents in his favor. Yes, he was quick and good at improvising. But none of that seemed outside the realm of Roman's own abilities. They seemed like equals more than anything, yet Roman found himself beneath.

"You mind doing me a favor?" Ezra asked.

"Aside from going easy on your sloppy right swipes." Roman froze, eyes wide and face frantic.

He hadn't meant to call Ezra out, hadn't meant to poke fun at his technique. It seemed like something friends did, but Roman and Ezra weren't friends, no matter how much Ezra continued to demand they were now that he had Roman.

"See, this is why you're gonna be so much help, buddy." Ezra grinned, unfazed by the jab. "I was hoping you could kind of slow down your defense. I wanna test out some moves, but you're probably not the right opponent for them. Like you can do basic maneuvers and such, but don't focus so much on your guard."

"You just want me to take it?" Roman asked, an edge of irritation threatening to escape.

"Come on," Ezra said with a happy lilt. "We both know you're good and just lying there and taking it."

Roman fumed, prepared to protest, and considered punching Ezra squarely in the throat, but he paused. No, he didn't pause. He hesitated. He froze. He slumped a bit, realizing how quickly and how far he'd fallen that he'd allow someone to speak to him in such a way.

"I'm just teasing. It's what friends do." Ezra poked Roman in the stomach, tickling Roman to provoke a response, but Roman simply glared. "I've had a lot of match-ups since you were in solitary. Most of the guys are good, but none are as quick with their guard as you are."

Roman almost smiled at that. Almost.

"I just wanna test a few moves." Ezra insisted, a gentle pleading in his voice.

Roman expected it to be a demand, a command, but even though Ezra spoke with absolute authority, he also always offered Roman a choice. It felt like a trap every single damn time.

"*Fuck it,*" Roman thought. "*How much worse can things get?*"

And with that, Roman agreed to slow down and allowed Ezra to try out some of his new moves. Three body slams in, Roman regretted the choice he'd made. Not all that different from any other choice he'd made in life. Ezra took full advantage of Roman's blanket permission and total submission on the sparring mat and pummeled his partner with a flurry of swift strikes.

Pain radiated like a web spread across Roman's muscles. He would have bruises everywhere by morning.

When Ezra kicked Roman in the chest one final time, the blow knocked Roman off his feet and knocked all the air out of his lungs. He lay on the mat, wheezing and doing his best not to curl into a ball from the pain.

Ezra stood over him with his legs straddled at Roman's sides. "You look absolutely fucked."

"Yeah," Roman hissed, biting back a wince. "That's what happens when you volunteer to be a punching bag."

"You look absolutely fuckable, too." Ezra stared with his hands in his pockets.

Roman eyed the bulge in Ezra's grey sweatpants, the sadistic look of excitement in Ezra's eyes, and the hunger in Ezra's sly smile.

Roman pushed himself up, checking the sparring room to make sure Ezra hadn't invited others in here, too, like he had with the rest of the champion's gym. Knowing he had little choice, he rolled onto his stomach and hoped Ezra would finish fast.

"Whoa, look at you. So eager to please." Ezra tugged at Roman's sweats but didn't pull them down as he lowered himself onto Roman, sitting with his boner pressed between

Roman's cheeks, the only thing separating the two of them being their sweaty clothes. "I love how committed you are, how willing and ready to meet my needs you are."

Roman ground his teeth. He wanted to tell him to fuck off or to just get it over with, but he knew whatever he said would only result in a longer, more grueling fuck.

"Wish we had the time." Ezra smacked Roman's butt. "No worries, though. I will take full advantage of your hungry holes later."

With that, Ezra hopped off Roman and actually helped Roman to his feet. Once they were both standing, he squared Roman's shoulders and looked him in the eyes.

"Just remember, you're mine now." Ezra held Roman's hand firmly, keeping him pulled close to his body so the sweat and heat practically melted the two men together. "You're my friend, and I will protect you at all costs. But I want you strong. I want you at your best."

Roman tsked. The idea of being anything seemed an impossibility.

"Just because I broke you," Ezra said, "and I know I did, doesn't mean I can't fix you, too."

"Why bother?"

"Maybe I like the idea of two champions standing tall together."

"As long as one knows his place and bends over for the other?"

"Exactly." Ezra smiled. "We'd be an unstoppable duo."

That reminded Roman of his plans for Levi, plans for his friend to join him in the arena and stand tall as a warrior, too. But it never panned out. Levi was always too gentle, too kind, too soft for fighting. Roman hoped he was okay. Hoped Ezra had been true to his word.

"Or maybe you wanna build me back up because you know the next fall would break me beyond repair."

"Hmmm." Ezra studied Roman. "That would be bad."

No amount of consideration gave Ezra's intentions away but instead left Roman with more theories and worries and paranoid delusions. All he really knew at the end of the day was that Ezra wanted Roman, and now he had him. How he wanted him, Roman was still unsure. Why he wanted him, Roman speculated on.

"Guess I'll have to hold tight and make sure you don't lose your balance." With that, Ezra slung an arm over Roman's shoulder, and the pair walked out of the gym toward the next appointment Ezra had planned.

Chapter Nine

The errand had been another effort to show off Roman, to primp and parade him. Roman silently seethed as he waited for his hair dye to set. The flamboyant inmate who'd put the strange concoction made with everything other than actual hair dye stood with a hand on his hip as he leaned into Ezra. The pair made small talk during the wait, Ezra showing no annoyance at the man's obvious flirting. Roman didn't know if the community hairstylist wanted protection or simply found Ezra cute. It didn't matter; Ezra only had eyes for Roman.

Every time the hairstylist joked, playfully touched Ezra's arm, teased blatant sexual innuendos, and so many other obvious attempts, it failed. Occasionally, Ezra's eyes would move to Roman, especially if the conversation drifted somewhere sexual. Ezra burrowed holes into Roman with his stare, and Roman could feel himself actually quake a bit with the recollection of their sex. He could feel Ezra's cock swelling in his throat, making it hard to breathe while he sat and waited. He could feel Ezra's cock pounding away behind him, hands running over his skin, muscles stretched over his body, dick buried deep inside him.

When the time finally came, the hairstylist took Roman over to the sink in his cell and did his best to rinse out his hair. It took a lot of extra effort, and Roman had to remain bent over for far too long because of the low water pressure in the cells. It made Roman uncomfortable, exposed, raw, and like Ezra would walk up any second and mount him.

Ezra did appear behind Roman, his crotch gliding across Roman's butt ever so slightly, but he didn't pull down Roman's pants. He didn't make a lewd joke. He didn't even playfully smack Roman's butt.

Instead, Ezra gushed with excitement, encouraging Roman to stand while he examined his hair. Roman wished this were his cell—correction, he wished this was the champion's cell—because then he could look into the full body mirror on the wall and take in his new appearance. He had no way of knowing what color Ezra had chosen, but based on his glee and the cutting comment the hairstylist had made before they began, Roman suspected it would be unappealing.

"Guess I won't be the fruitiest one strutting down these halls anymore." The hairstylist swayed with his hands raised in a dainty pose as he retrieved the small hand mirror available and carried it back. "What do you think, Romie?"

Roman glowered at the pet name.

"You look amazing!" Ezra insisted, commanded, his voice booming and drawing the attention of those nearby.

Roman ignored the snickers as he took in his appearance. His ruffled brown hair had been slightly trimmed to help frame his face, but it was no longer a dark brown. Instead, Ezra had dyed Roman's hair a bright bubblegum pink.

"You like it, right?" Ezra asked.

Roman stared at two men in the doorway, not even hiding their laughter at this point, and the words Roman considered failed him.

"Is there a fucking comedy show I missed?" Ezra turned quickly, finally acknowledging the pair. "Please, share the joke with me."

One of the men swallowed hard as Ezra approached.

"I would like to laugh." Ezra shrugged. "I love a strong laugh. Does the body good. Please, share your joke with me."

"It's nothing," one man said.

"Then you should take your nothing and go somewhere else." Ezra glared, using his eyes to direct their exit. "Before I leave you with nothing."

Without missing a beat, he then turned and smiled at Roman, unfazed by the exchange a moment ago.

"Do you like it?"

Roman didn't respond.

"I do hope you like it." Ezra made a pouty face.

"It wouldn't be my first choice," Roman admitted, handing the mirror off to the hairstylist. "But if it makes you happy, then I'm happy."

"Because my happiness is all you care about, right?" Ezra asked.

Roman didn't know what to say. Agreeing felt like admitting he'd fully surrendered, and he wasn't certain he was ready for that. Disagreeing felt like he opened himself up to more horrors, more tests of submission meant to break his spirits. Silence would fail him, though. Ezra's sweet expression had already begun to twist into something angry.

"What are best friends for, right?" Roman finally said, breathing easy when Ezra's green eyes lit up at the question and a half smile.

When they reached the cafeteria, Roman took his tray of food. Not that the champion title came with too many perks on the cheap food here, but he did notice the freshest fruit and extra candy snacks on Ezra's plate.

Roman stared at the mashed potatoes that were somehow flaky and soupy all at once. They tasted worse than they looked, but Roman's stomach begged for sustenance. All the time he'd spent in isolation taught him to stop looking down on the gross trays in favor of the expensive commissary snacks he no longer had access to anyway.

"Here." Ezra set his candy bar on Roman's tray.

"What?" Roman didn't know how to react.

"Something almost as sweet as you."

That made Roman's face twist with annoyance.

"No thanks." He slid the bar back.

"Take it," Ezra insisted. "We both know you're gonna earn it later. Might as well enjoy one thing today."

Roman's stomach sank, and he accepted the candy bar.

"Levi!" Ezra called out, and Roman's entire body trembled.

He turned to find Levi standing a few feet away, frozen as a group of guys continued, and gave a sheepish smile. Roman wanted to smile back, wanted to compliment the new haircut he sported. It framed his face well, unlike the longer, grungy style he'd committed to for far too long. Roman's face burned when he realized Levi could see his new hairstyle too, a style that screamed pet.

"How they treating you over at cellblock D?" Ezra asked. "No one hassling you about their D, right?"

Levi coughed, an uncomfortable thing he'd do when he wanted to laugh, but he knew he shouldn't. That almost brought a smile to Roman's face. He understood Levi's need to hide his happiness at the sight of his fallen friend, but it sent a thrill through Roman to know Levi had happiness to hide.

"It's been good," Levi answered. "Nice group, and yeah."

"You're welcome," Ezra said. "It's hard pulling strings. Everyone wants something, you know?"

Levi grimaced at Roman, an apologetic gaze in his eyes. Everyone did want something, and Levi knew all too well what Ezra wanted from Roman and the price he'd paid. Roman could feel every unsaid word between their stare-off, and his jaw tightened as he fought back the words he wanted to say. The words he couldn't say. Levi had protection in the form of Ezra declaring he was off limits. Roman found himself too ashamed to talk with Levi, too lost to find a way back to his friend. He was grateful Ezra kept his word and glad to see Levi didn't look roughed up or worn ragged like the last time he saw him.

Roman didn't think his life had much of a future, nothing worth crawling toward, but seeing Levi shine a bit and thrive in this hellscape gave him a bit of hope in his decision. Dying in the dark alone and forgotten with a wolf mask would've been an easy out, but Roman didn't wanna give up. Not yet, at least. He just didn't know how to find a light at the end of this tunnel.

After lunch, Ezra dragged Roman with him to the public bathroom outside the cafeteria. Unlike the toilet in their cell or the toilets in the shower room, these bathrooms had stalls. Someone had told Roman it was because they originally made them for the C.O.s, but Roman didn't know if that was true or just a rumor.

"Christ, I love your hair." Ezra ran his fingers through Roman's ruffled bubblegum pink locks and got a solid grip. "I just wanna play with it all day."

With that, he squeezed tighter, pulling Roman's head back as he pushed him into a stall.

"It just gets me so fucking hard," Ezra growled. "You wanna help me out with that?"

"What are friends for?" Roman asked rhetorically, not expecting an answer but awaiting Ezra's next command.

He really didn't want to get fucked in this bathroom, the idea of standing hunched over so Ezra could fuck him, the fact he knew how brutal each thrust would be so Ezra could elicit a moan, a noise, anything so any passerby would hear Roman getting bitched out. Most of all, his stomach felt a bit queasy after eating, and he worried he wouldn't have full control over how his body would react to Ezra's dick ramming his insides.

"Get on your fucking knees." Ezra gripped Roman's pink hair and pushed him down.

Roman dropped to his knees and fished out Ezra's cock. He hadn't been lying about being hard. His ten-inch dick was already throbbing by the time Roman released it from the elastic band on his boxers. Ezra didn't wait another second. Once his cock was out, he shoved it right into Roman's mouth. When Roman gurgled and choked on Ezra's dick, Ezra groaned with satisfaction and pulled his dick back before ramming it in a second time. This time, Roman felt the head hit the back of his throat, and he gagged in protest.

Ezra kept a firm grip on Roman's hair, holding his head in place every time he thrusted his cock in and out of Roman's mouth. All Roman did was stretch his jaw to its limit and hope Ezra finished soon. He teared up about a minute into the brutal face fucking. His head remained firmly in place, hitting the stall door as Ezra went faster and harder. To keep from outright crying at the gagged reactions, Roman rolled his eyes up, locking them onto Ezra.

His mind wandered in a hundred places while Ezra violently used his throat. Mostly, Roman thought back to Levi's new haircut and suddenly imagined Levi during this encounter, during this blowjob, and the bizarre fascination made Roman's dick throb almost as hard as Ezra's.

Levi wouldn't leer down at Roman like Ezra. Levi wouldn't steal the air without offering something else. Levi would stroke Roman in return, or at least allow him to stroke himself while his dick painfully throbbed, seeking reprieve. Roman didn't truly know what Levi would do, but the fantasy helped him commit to his current reality. His own dick leaked precum as he took in more of Ezra's cock, mind lost on Levi.

Ezra's face had turned vicious, covered in a glean of sweat, and had a ruthless unblinking glare the entire time he fucked Roman's face.

Roman wondered if Ezra looked this menacing every time he fucked Roman. It wasn't animalistic or primal. It was hatred. There was a dark glint, a dreadful satisfaction every time Roman wriggled, choked, gasped, or gagged on Ezra's cock. Eventually, Ezra moved his thumbs, still keeping a solid grip on Roman's hair but moving just enough so he could wipe the building well of tears in Roman's eyes. He fought against the urge to cry, not wanting to surrender that piece of himself, but every time Ezra rammed his dick further than Roman's gag reflex could handle, he found himself becoming a bit splotchy.

"You love this dick, don't you?" Ezra continued face fucking Roman, finally releasing one of his hands, but only long enough to smack Roman's face. "Say it."

Roman remained silent, taking Ezra's cock deep into his throat.

"Say it," Ezra demanded, holding his cock all the way inside. When Roman squirmed and tried to back away from the pressure of holding the entirety of Ezra in his mouth, Ezra kept Roman in place. "Say it."

Roman gurgled, attempting to answer, attempting to say anything, but none of it lessened Ezra's grip. Finally, Roman unintelligibly attempted to say the words.

"You're goddamn right you do." Ezra spat his words, hitting Roman's face in the process.

How Ezra understood Roman's poor effort at saying he loved Ezra's dick, Roman didn't understand, but he'd finally pulled out of Roman's throat and gave him a minute to suck in desperate and painful breaths.

Ezra lightly pelted Roman a few more times with his hand and then slapped him with his wet dick until the well of tears broke, and Roman found himself crying and drooling all over Ezra's cock, much to the other man's satisfaction. He grunted, fucking Roman's face harder and keeping the entirety of his cock buried in Roman's throat as he thrust violently. Finally, he roared as he shot his load. Two powerful jets hit Roman's throat, which he immediately swallowed, but as Ezra pulled his cock out, he managed a third jet on the tip of Roman's tongue and lips and a final spurt on Roman's face.

Roman swallowed the salty cum on his tongue and went to wipe his face and lips clean.

"Don't," Ezra demanded, rubbing the slobber of his flaccid dick onto Roman's face. "You look so pretty covered in my cum."

Roman shuttered, holding back his rage.

"I want everyone to see how pretty my pink princess is," Ezra said with a wicked smirk. "Besides, this way, everyone who sees you will know you're my pretty pink princess."

A fire grew inside Roman, anger he'd kept buried for as long as possible. The change in Ezra's expression suggested he could see the glint in Roman's eyes, the fire threatening to return.

"It's important they know you're my pretty pink princess," Ezra said. "We wouldn't want anyone else to cover you in their cum, right?"

Roman fumed but said nothing.

"If you don't want to be my pretty pink princess, that's okay." Ezra stared down at Roman, menacing and cruel, with a smirk that revealed more teeth the longer it lasted. "I would never make you do something you don't want to do. This is a friendship. I want to show everyone how close we are. But if you don't want to be my friend, I totally understand."

Roman went to speak, went to say he would do anything for Ezra in their cell, hell even in public apparently, and he'd let him tell him what to do, but there had to be a line somewhere. He couldn't and shouldn't have to let other inmates see his face covered in Ezra's cum. The words died in Roman's sore throat, and the fire fizzled out of his eyes.

He thought about all the men eyeing him today. He thought about how boldly Jake offered to buy him. He thought about how many people he'd have to fight off and how much harder he'd have to fight now that he'd submitted to Ezra, and everyone knew he was an easy and cheap fuck.

"I'm happy to be your pretty pink princess," Roman said, swallowing all his disdain and rage.

Ezra's smile filled his entire face, and he gestured for Roman to stand.

The laughs and cutting comments ate away at Roman the entire walk back to their cellblock, but he survived it. He survived the taunting of his first day as Ezra's bitch. Ezra's friend. Ezra's pretty pink princess.

Roman got a whole two hours of rest until light's out came around, and Ezra rolled off his bed to join Roman in the bottom bunk.

He ordered Roman to assume the position and spent the night vigorously fucking his hole, calling him a pretty pink princess the entire time. He slapped Roman's ass multiple times, turning the left cheek a reddish pink, and then went to work on the other side.

"Gotta keep them even," Ezra said with a harsh smack and

brutal thrust.

Ezra eased up when he found a rhythmic pace, pounding into Roman. He wrapped a hand under Roman's jaw and turned his head, yanking him to face Ezra's cold stare. Leaning in, Ezra kissed Roman, leading with his tongue at first but soon letting Roman guide their mouths, determine the twist of lips. Roman moaned more than a few times into Ezra's mouth, breaking away from the kissing and almost unable to handle another pump of Ezra's cock into him.

Roman whimpered. "Please, finish."

"You want my cum?"

Roman muffled himself as best he could.

"Say it." Ezra railed into him. "Tell me what you want."

"Please, cum." Roman gritted his teeth. "Please, give me your cum."

Ezra eased his pace, returning to Roman's mouth with the pleasure of distracting kisses and gently caressing Roman's tired body, making him quiver in anticipation. Ezra ran his hands up and down his muscles, lips pressed to Roman, cock buried inside him.

Roman didn't know if he could do this every day. He didn't know if his body could handle the intense fucking Ezra demanded from morning to evening. His throat ached, still hoarse and pained from the violent face fucking in the afternoon. His muscles were exhausted from being a literal punching bag during training today. His cock throbbed and twitched from Ezra's powerful thrusts, and when he came, Ezra's pounding hit so much harder on Roman's insides. His ass was tender and tired and so sore, he worried if it'd recover.

When Ezra finally climaxed, he slumped over and lay on

top of Roman with his cock still inside him.

"It'll help your hole adjust," Ezra whispered, smug and satisfied. "But don't worry, I'll ease up on your ass."

"It's fine," Roman lied, willing himself to focus on the good, on the pleasure that came with this arrangement.

"I've been a little rough, but you're so fucking cute it's impossible not to pound you out." Ezra kissed Roman's shoulder, nibbling a bit too. "But I don't wanna break you. I got way too many plans for my pretty pink princess."

With that, Ezra kissed Roman on the back of the neck and went to sleep on him, in him, and Roman lay there exhausted, uncomfortable, and unable to sleep.

As Ezra rested, Roman backed up into him, enough to feel the throb and enough to carefully stroke himself to completion. He was supposed to focus on Ezra, on Ezra's needs, which he'd done and continued to do even now. The man hardened inside Roman once again, adding to the throb of Roman's own cock. Roman took the precum leaking from his dick and rubbed his palm over the head, using it to add to his silent strokes.

He desperately wanted to feel a little release for himself. Roman bounced his hips just enough to jostle Ezra, just enough to rouse the sleeping giant. He pressed into Roman again, mostly unmoving, but enough to help, enough for Roman to keep his word, enough to bite down on his wrist and stifle his climax as he held back every urge to buck and convulse in ecstasy with Ezra's cock deep inside him.

It was the best orgasm Roman had ever had. His mind flashed to the other times he'd climaxed with Ezra, but the shame didn't hit like it had those first times, which added to the pleasure as he continued milking his dick soft. The confusion didn't consume him like it had while Ezra fucked his face this afternoon and his own cock throbbed.

"That's a good pretty pink princess. Using me to feel that release. But remember, no hands." Ezra stroked Roman's hair, chuckling a bit at the reveal he hadn't dozed off entirely, and then he quietly rested again.

Roman ignored every choice that led him here and flopped down into a pool of his own cum, too exhausted with Ezra atop him and the calm release of finishing.

It wasn't much, but Roman got a peaceful night's sleep after a suffocating day.

Chapter Ten

Ezra had been true to his word. He didn't fuck Roman in the ass for the next three days, prioritizing Roman's mouth instead. He'd eased up, though, allowing Roman more opportunities for his jaw and throat to adjust. He even acquired an ointment to help with the swelling in Roman's ass. Ezra would call him over, order Roman to strip, and then tenderly apply the cream to Roman's hole.

He still paraded Roman around, but Roman learned to ignore most of the comments, and if anyone got too close, Ezra interjected. Watching his back had never been Roman's favorite thing to do in prison, but he used to have more conviction, more willingness to stand up for himself. Right now, he was learning to let go of that fire.

Ezra burned bright enough for the both of them.

Later in the afternoon, Roman tagged along for another workout until he was too tired to stand. Roman knelt on the fitness mat, winded from sparring, exhausted from Ezra testing strikes out on Roman's unguarded body, and pained from having to sit on his knees, hands rested on his hips, shoulders raised, back arched, and toes turned ever so. Ezra liked the stance, liked how Roman popped his butt out and showed off the definition of his full body, so Roman would remain statue-esque for the last thirty minutes of Ezra's cooldown routine. Roman didn't have a cooldown, except perhaps the sitting stance.

"You know what I was thinking?" Ezra asked, running a small towel over his sweaty face and giving Roman a soft grin.

Roman swallowed then shrugged. He didn't know what Ezra was thinking. He never knew. Not really. It was exhausting to pretend otherwise and much easier to just accept wherever Ezra's fancies flitted.

"Matching tattoos."

"Oh," Roman said, hiding his disappointment, his discomfort.

He had never gotten a tattoo. He'd counted down the days until he turned eighteen, a hundred ideas in his head. Some online personality with millions of videos convinced him the random tribal patterns he wanted down his arm would be a waste of space for the eventual perfect sleeve Roman would get.

He didn't know what that sleeve would be, but an arm was prime real estate for tattoos. After a girl in his senior class got "good" and "not not good" in Korean, which another student fluent in the language explained while also discussing how characters in Hangul worked, Roman realized he didn't want anything in a language he couldn't speak. He still thought about the bewilderment on the girl's face, the shock of learning she didn't have "good" and "evil" inked on her wrists.

Everything Roman considered never lived up to the permanence of a first tattoo. Like all firsts, Roman wanted it to be special. His senior year tattoo was postponed until college, then it was postponed until graduation, but once he got locked up, it was supposed to be postponed until his release. Unfortunately, his time with Ezra had taught him not to hold out much hope in special first times for anything, enjoying himself, or having a say in the direction of his life.

The closest Roman had ever come to getting a tattoo was at Stacy's insistence. She had almost as strong a hold over Roman as Ezra now held, and she'd come quite close to convincing Roman to get her name as his first tattoo. A bold request which she had readily wormed into his brain, even suggesting some discreet places from his butt, upper thigh, inner thigh, all the way to the low V cut of his abdomen she used to lick and tease before going down on him.

Ultimately, Roman declined and got Stacy to stop hassling him with her minxy pleading by throwing his own label out that she wasn't ready for: girlfriend. Stacy loved to roll in bed with Roman, but she also liked to keep it open for anyone else's company, finding life too short to commit to monogamy.

Roman hoped Ezra didn't plan for Roman to get his name branded on him but resigned himself to whatever fate Ezra had in store.

"What'd you have in mind?" Roman stayed seated, head raised so he could look up to Ezra. He always had to look up.

The pair headed back to their cellblock and ended up in an abandoned lounging area where a biker worked on Jake's back, adding some flames to a charred corpse. Jake's tattoos were often bright and bloody. Sometimes, Roman suspected they were also confessions. Lots of screaming women, lots of severed limbs, lots of random numbers which might've been part of some psychotic secret pattern. Roman didn't care enough to investigate. Jake smirked at Roman but didn't speak, nodding between him and Ezra, then puckered his lips and made kissy noises.

Roman ignored Jake, grateful when he left without a comment, and took his seat first. Ezra wanted it to be a surprise, so he wouldn't know how their tattoos matched until after Ezra's piece was finished. It wasn't the worst pain, but it was an unexpected burn. Roman anticipated more stabbing feelings, though there was that too whenever the needle used lost its heat from the lighter the biker used. Roman kept his neck craned for hours, letting the man work, letting the man cover the left side of his neck with something Roman would never be able to hide. It'd be permanent. It'd be the first thing people saw. Here and when he was released. If he was released. Some days, he thought he'd die behind bars.

"Looking good," Ezra announced with a gleeful expression. "Oh, I got one more small idea. You do colors, right?"

"Depends," the biker replied. "What'd you have in mind?"

Ezra spoke softly, and Roman didn't waste his time listening in. He'd learn soon enough. Without prompting, the biker grabbed Roman by the jaw and turned his head to face him. When the hot needle went straight for his right eye, Roman tried to scramble out of the chair.

"Relax." Ezra slapped his arms over Roman's shoulders.

Roman obeyed and squeezed his eyes shut until he felt the needle hit his cheek, searing again and again until the biker finished whatever second tattoo Ezra had gifted Roman.

Once he was released, Roman sat across from Ezra, waiting patiently for his piece to be completed.

"Thanks, man." Ezra shook his hand, keeping his neck turned and body positioned so Roman couldn't quite see the tattoo Ezra had gotten. "Thank him."

"Right." Roman stood. "Thank you."

"Thank you, what?" the biker asked with the same level of gloating Roman got from everyone. Even with Ezra's protection, Ezra's clout, Roman could feel the arrogance and joy others took for his situation, for his downfall.

"Thank you, sir." Roman didn't require more prompting. This wasn't the first time an inmate demanded manners from Roman; it wasn't the first time they wanted to call into question his subservience. It was just another day.

Ezra spun Roman around, walking behind him and ushering Roman through the halls. He got plenty of looks and a few comments, and some didn't seem terrible. He hoped that meant the tattoos weren't too unflattering, though he prepared for the worst.

"Take a look," Ezra demanded, prompting Roman to the mirror.

The first tattoo Roman spotted was the three hearts on his face.

"You know what that's for, right?"

Roman nodded. He didn't have to say it, having become so entuned with Ezra's thoughts, even if they felt impossible to gauge, they often screamed at Roman.

"Yeah?" Ezra pleaded, seeking more from Roman, always seeking more.

Roman placed a finger on his face and ran it down the three reddish hearts he'd gotten inked. "Pretty. Pink. Princess."

"Exactly." Ezra smiled. "Though, redder than I hoped. He said it'll settle soon, but they won't be anywhere near as light as your hair."

Roman had accepted that, his eyes lost on the tattoos covering both his and Ezra's necks.

In bold black ink, clearly legible and fancy enough to add a bit of flair, something to make the words stand out, were the matching tattoos they sported. The redness of Roman's neck made his tattoo more prominent, if possible, because of how irritated his skin had gotten.

"Best" and "Bested" were etched onto their necks, a matching set, a reminder for the rest of his life where he sat in the grand scheme of things, where he'd fallen, where he would remain.

Ezra stepped up close behind Roman, pressed against him as he slung an arm over Roman's shoulder. Roman's heart beat with unsteady anxiety until it synced to the steady rhythm of Ezra's heart. Every fiber of Roman's being seemed to kneel and obey Ezra's lead.

"Do you know why I got these for us?" Ezra asked, sliding a hand across Roman's chest and letting it rest just below the tattoo.

"So everyone knows who's in charge." Roman looked at himself, at his tattoo, at a failure who'd allowed himself to be bested in every sense of the word.

"Everyone already knows," Ezra whispered. "I got it, so you'd always know, always remember."

How could he forget? How could he ever hope to stand on his own two feet again?

"I know sometimes you consider walking away," Ezra continued. "As you should. The choice is always yours. This friendship goes both ways, and I would never expect—"

"I'm not thinking about that," Roman swiftly interjected.

His skin crawled, and his heart surged again. Yes, Ezra reminded him of his choices regularly, but they were an illusion, and Roman wouldn't fall for it. The illusion got harder to see each day, though, and Roman thought for just a fraction of a second, these little talks helped make the lies harder to spot. He wanted to believe Ezra. He wanted to believe that if he just stopped fighting, Ezra would be genuine, things would get easier.

"Now, how are you going to thank me for this awesome ink?"

"Ugh, oh, yeah," Roman said, pulling away just enough to turn and face Ezra but keeping their chests close, almost touching. "Sorry about that."

"I didn't ask for apologies, Princess." Ezra brushed a hand through Roman's pink hair. "I asked for gratitude. Show me how grateful you are."

Ezra kissed Roman, gentle and guiding. It was the type of kiss that didn't come with a rush. It helped ease Roman into the evening. It helped calm Roman's nerves. It helped elicit a bit of arousal as their bodies pressed together and soon were rubbing against each other.

Roman tugged at the strings of Ezra's pants and prepared for a long night as the bested pretty pink princess.

Chapter Eleven

Soon, Roman and Ezra had a daily routine. They'd wake up in the morning, and Ezra would either fuck Roman's mouth or ass, depending on the day of the week. They'd spar together, but anytime Roman moved a little too well, the training would turn into a solo session for Ezra to test his new moves on Roman. Basically turning Roman into a punching bag to remind him of his place.

Roman understood why he lost the first match. But he still couldn't wrap his head around the second loss, the way his footing faltered, the way one blow to the face left him so light-headed and winded. Ezra was good, better than damn near anyone here, but he had sloppy habits. Habits Roman easily spotted the night of their rematch and continued seeing more of every time they trained together. All the same,

Roman would bury those thoughts when they surfaced, and he'd continue his daily routine.

Roman's life turned into a hazy whirlwind of monotonous routine. Each day bled together, overlapping, and made it easier for Roman to lose himself to the time, to the subtle changes, to the acceptance, and what he hoped would be happiness. Roman wasn't sure what day he decided to be happy, but now, looking back on each one, he started to see more and more of the good in his situation and less of everything else.

Errands and chitchat and lunch filled their afternoon. It was perfect for Ezra to show off his pretty pink princess to the world. Roman would get his hair updated, he'd be mocked, and usually, Jake the Snake would crawl out of whatever hellhole he came from and gesture lewdly to Roman. He didn't hide the fact that he had every intention of fucking Roman, of owning him now that he'd fallen from grace, and while Roman knew he was stronger than Jake, faster, and a better overall fighter. While he knew he'd handled Jake and his men before in the arena and in back hallways when they'd tried to jump him in the past, he no longer believed in himself. That lack of belief made Roman's stomach churn and made his skin crawl whenever Jake came around.

Roman would inch closer to Ezra, waiting for his "friend" to protect him. It always ended the same; Ezra would put a hand around Roman's waist and pull him in close like he was delicate. The other men would snicker, and Jake would take the hint. Sometimes, he'd add a cutting comment before surrendering.

"One of these days, the champion is gonna get bored with you," Jake would say when in a taunting mood. "When that happens, I'll gladly offer you my undivided attention. All eight inches of it."

"I could never get tired of my pretty pink princess," Ezra would say whenever Jake didn't take a hint, then he'd kiss Roman on the neck or lick him, and on one occasion, both. "You'd be amazed at the lengths my friend goes to make sure I'm happy."

Roman would get queasy at those comments, knowing the truth of how much he let Ezra use his holes. How much he enjoyed it. How much he loathed himself for enjoying it. It was just a reaction of his body, which he could handle. It was how Ezra's calm temper, level attitude, and constant affirmations messed with Roman's head. This wasn't okay. But he was okay with it. He didn't understand or like himself, but it became more and more grueling to fight against the current.

In the afternoons, either after the adrenaline of their workouts or the excitement Ezra got when defending Roman's honor from taunting, it always resulted in a blowjob. Roman would drop to his knees in the bathroom stall or lay flat on the sparring room mat and let Ezra fuck his throat until he cried and slobbered all over the man's ten-inch cock. There was no point in staying strong or being brave. Ezra had complete control over his life now, control Roman offered, and giving in to what made Ezra happy usually made him cum faster.

Sometimes, he'd shoot his load down Roman's throat; sometimes, he'd make him walk around with the trace signs of cum on his face or in his hair. It really depended on Ezra's mood. Roman got used to it, and eventually, Ezra got bored with parading Roman's shame. That made Roman happy, made him finally think Ezra didn't only do this to make him miserable, and added to the haze of Roman's eventual acceptance.

The evenings were always the same, too. Ezra would want to cum again, which on days designated to allow Roman's ass rest, it meant he'd have an incredibly sore throat and jaw instead. When the night involved anal, however, Ezra was a beast in the sheets, demanding satisfaction as he tossed Roman about, using him like a cheap toy.

Either Ezra was bored from a lackluster day and sought entertainment in the form of fucking, or he was high off another victory in the arena and craved Roman's ass as a prize. Roman enjoyed the arena nights. He'd be left alone in the cell for hours, things would be quiet, and for a few breaths, he'd forget where he was or how far he'd fallen.

In any sense, the night came with pleasing Ezra yet again. An unyielding task. Roman had never known someone to be so horny all the time. Ezra was insatiable, and something about dropping his load into Roman made him so satisfied. His eyes never strayed, and his fascination with Roman's quivering body never tired. Often times, he'd get hard just watching Roman squirm after they'd finished, and Roman would find himself taking a fourth load for the night. He hated it when that happened. He hated it for the first month, anyway. By the second month, he expected the chance of a fourth load. By the third month, he'd help encourage it, sometimes to Ezra's protest.

"Look at you," Ezra would tease when refusing Roman his cock. "You're such a hungry cum slut, aren't you?"

Roman would blush at that, partially because it degraded him; it was humiliating. But the other part would blush because he knew it made Ezra happy, seeing Roman slightly frazzled and embarrassed and desperate to please him. It made Ezra happy, and when Ezra was happy, Roman was safe.

Late nights were when Ezra tested new kinks out. Morning blowjobs or fucks were always quick and brutal, meant to get Ezra off in five minutes or less. Afternoon blowjobs weren't much longer, but depending on how much pleasure he took in watching Roman choke on the girth of his cock they could last upwards of twenty minutes. Night was when their sex lasted the longest. Because Ezra wanted to make it last, wanted to fuck for hours, or try something new, he often spent time readying Roman's hole.

It'd been awkward the first few times, laying on his back with his legs spread and looking over at Ezra while he fingered him, but eventually, Roman learned to relax, allowing himself to indulge in the gentle prodding. Sometimes, Ezra would take extra time, lubing Roman, readying Roman, massaging Roman's hole, all so he could ensure it left Roman rock hard before the late-night intercourse. On a few occasions, he even made Roman cum, unapologetic as Roman convulsed from the climax. His hands would claw at the bed, desperate to grip his cock and stroke out the last few pearls. Instead, he remembered his place and would buck against Ezra, primal and pleading for more release. Ezra would merely smirk, waiting for Roman to finish and accept his orgasm required Ezra's touch. Once Roman had settled, Ezra would ready Roman all over again before piledriving him.

Ezra always had fun taking his time late at night, making his thrusts slow, and even so, he could pound into Roman for an hour or sometimes two, three if Roman's whimpering riled Ezra. They'd even take breaks, Roman resting with Ezra's hard cock buried inside him. Ezra never wanted the nights to be restful, so whether he used Roman's mouth or ass late at night, Roman expected it to be an exhausting and unending event.

Roman used to try and distance his mind from the sex, to think of something different, but that never truly worked. If he wanted to escape Ezra's gaze, wash away the sound of his voice, sometimes Roman would envision Levi. It was strange and not something he'd ever considered before, but somehow, it brought a bit of solace. He also found himself more willing to submit to Ezra's insatiable needs, which ultimately made Ezra happier, and Roman became content with the arrangement.

More than three months of this had nearly broken down all of Roman's walls. He'd accepted his fate and knew this was his life. Well, for the next five years, at least. That was the earliest opportunity he had at parole. What really worried him, what stressed him every time he submitted to Ezra, was how long Ezra would be here.

"Can I ask you a question?" Roman asked as he wiped spit from his mouth and licked Ezra's flaccid cock clean.

Ezra enjoyed the tongue bath, and Roman had gotten so used to the routine, he always went to lick off the slobber he'd left behind when bringing Ezra off.

"You just did, pretty pink princess." Ezra played with Roman's hair. His hands were gentle and affectionate, but his eyes were haunting and hollow. "But yeah, you can ask me anything. We're friends, right?"

"Yeah," Roman answered between licks. "I just wondered how long your sentence is."

Ezra stared at him, silently studying Roman, and likely very aware of Roman's thoughts based on how squeamish he appeared. Roman worried he wore his fear on his face.

"Hoping I'll be gone soon?" Ezra snatched Roman's hair and forced his gaze up, craning Roman's neck in an uncomfortable position. "That's not very friendly."

"No," Roman protested. "The opposite."

"Oh?" Ezra asked. No, demanded. He wanted Roman to elaborate, and his scowl demanded Roman explain himself.

"Everyone knows you're my best friend in here," Roman said, practically ready to take in Ezra's cock again for a late-night apology blowjob, anything to show his respect. "I just worry what will happen to me when you're gone. If you leave before me."

After three months of Ezra fucking him every which way and flaunting their friendship, their relationship, for all to see, Roman believed the minute he stepped outside the cell alone, if he ever dared something so foolish, he'd be snatched up by someone like Jake the Snake, and they wouldn't ask if Roman would submit. They'd make him. He knew as much as he hated Ezra's phony affection and playful touches and gentle kisses, they were far more bearable than anything someone else would do. He'd seen the hollowed-out men Jake the Snake assaulted, the vacant expression in men who were railed well beyond their breaking point and forced to serve Jake and his entire crew.

Even if this wasn't his choice, not really, he did have a say in things. Ultimately, Roman was free to walk away from

Ezra at any time—he'd said as much. During the first month, when Roman still had the occasional fire in his eyes, Ezra would remind him of that. But Ezra took care of Roman and ensured he never injured him, which was more than Roman ever expected. He didn't want to be raped by men that saw Roman as a fallen champion, an easy target.

Roman didn't want to be passed around. Roman didn't want to be broken. Roman couldn't see how broken he already was, though. He'd been torn down by every choice Ezra carved away. Bit by bit, Ezra had shredded and sliced away pieces of Roman so small and so subtle that he hadn't realized how much of himself he already lost. He actually began to believe this situation wasn't bad. He had protection. He had love. He had friendship.

In the fall from champion, Roman forgot all the things he aimed for, strived for, believed in, and now only sought to make Ezra happy, to keep him satisfied, and to enjoy the peace it afforded him.

Ezra released Roman's hair and let his head drop some, but when Roman kept his gaze on Ezra, it made the man smile. He was always so happy to see Roman's humble obedience, and more than anything, Roman wanted to ensure Ezra wouldn't go to bed angry.

"I would never let anything happen to my pretty pink princess." Ezra caressed his face. "Besides, why do you think we train every day?"

Roman shrugged. "So you're ready for the arena."

"And so you're capable if anyone is stupid enough to touch what belongs to me." He cradled Roman's face between his hands. "You're so powerful. I know I had to take away some of that pride, that fiery willpower, but it was only to strengthen our friendship."

Roman tensed, unsure how to react, how to behave. He only wanted to please Ezra, and normally, he understood the reaction his best friend sought. But right now, he struggled to recall what it meant to be confident and proud.

"Don't worry about my sentence," Ezra insisted. "I won't be leaving here anytime soon."

"It's just—"

"I know." Ezra kissed Roman's forehead. "I don't want to talk about your sentence, your past mistakes. I wanna bask in what we have right now."

Roman's brows knitted in confusion. It wasn't uncommon for someone's sentence to slip out and end up idle gossip, but Roman rarely discussed what he'd done, and fewer here knew about his crime or the guilt he carried for it. He'd called it a mistake, an accident, but manslaughter charges didn't disappear no matter how genuine the apology.

Nor should they, but Roman wondered if he'd paid enough for that mistake by now. He wondered if the soul of his dead friend found some peace in Roman's new life position. He wondered if the family who'd abandoned him here cared how he'd fought to become a champion in a corrupt system, then gone from best to bested. Roman didn't wonder if anyone cared about his predicament or how he'd been forced to learn how to serve the needs of another person above his own. Mostly, he assumed others would take some satisfaction in his plight.

"You're mine," Ezra said. No, declared. It was a statement that would rattle the earth if words could. He gripped Roman by the sleeve and pulled him to his feet. "You're my friend. I will always keep you safe."

"And I will always keep you happy," Roman answered, instinctual and desperate to see the sly smile on Ezra's face return. A smile that meant he was happy. A smile that meant Roman was safe for another night.

"That's why I love my pretty pink princess." Ezra leaned in and kissed Roman.

He'd kissed Roman a lot. In the beginning, he mostly kissed Roman's body. His neck in public, his forehead after a really good blowjob, his left ass cheek after a particularly aggressive fuck. Always the left cheek since Ezra favored his left side, given he was lefthanded. Roman found most of his bruising from slaps and smacks of sex on his left side. Even from sparring, Ezra had a lazy technique of always leaning left. In the beginning, when Ezra kissed Roman on the lips, he'd recoil or flinch or shoot Ezra a disgusted look, only occasionally playing the role properly.

Now, though, Roman returned the kiss without hesitation and saw Ezra's eyes light up with delight. They'd gone to kissing regularly. It was a different feeling, Ezra's muscular body, firm grip, and commanding demeanor. Roman went with it, leaned into the role, and found himself lost in Ezra's mouth more days than not. He wanted to keep kissing, always kissing. He'd do everything else, but sometimes they'd kiss like this until the sun came up, nothing more, nothing less, simply Ezra's lips, his touch, his tender affection. Most of the time, it served to ready them both, rubbing against each other, each feeling the hard erections, the heat of their bodies, the quiver of anticipated desire.

"I'm thrilled you've finally accepted my friendship, truly accepted it," Ezra said with a whisper.

Roman could see the pleasure it brought him, and while he hated surrendering himself, breaking off the more resilient pieces of himself, he couldn't imagine making it through his days by resisting every step of the way.

He'd done that the first month. It hollowed him out. It exhausted him. It broke him without him realizing it. After nearly four months of this, he'd learned to love Ezra.

"You know, this has kind of got me all riled up again," Ezra said, poking at Roman's sides until he giggled.

Roman forced the laughter, but he knew it made Ezra happy when he let out light and sheepish laughs, so he entertained him.

"I want you to eat my ass," Ezra said.

"What?" Roman swallowed hard, unsure how to feel, how to react.

This entire arrangement worked because he learned to obediently tend to Ezra. But that usually involved massaging his muscles, stroking his cock, sucking his cock, opening up, and letting his cock inside his hole. It never involved Roman pleasuring Ezra's hole.

"Some of the guys have been saying it's a nice feeling." Ezra shrugged. "It's got me curious, and I thought maybe you'd be willing to help me explore that curiosity."

"Okay." Roman nodded.

"Don't worry, my ass is clean." Ezra smirked. "Like you, I keep it nice and tidy. Well, not exactly like you."

He laughed, humored by the lengths Roman would go to ensure his hole was ready and able to handle Ezra's cock.

Sometimes, that involved douching beforehand. Especially if Ezra planned for a new kink that evening, something to test out, something that would stress Roman's hole and insides.

Roman only had an accident once, and he panicked so much that he thought Ezra would murder him right then and there. All Ezra did was pull out, clean off his dick, and say, "shit happens," before insisting Roman clean himself and the bed up before they finish the evening with a blowjob. Ezra's only scolding came in the form of a warning to never let it happen again. Inform him so he could offer Roman more appropriate breaks. He wanted to own Roman's hole, not abuse it. From that point on, Roman either watched what he ate, focused on more food during the rest days when his hole recovered, or went to properly clean himself out for his friend.

Friend. Roman really started to believe that after three months of only Ezra's companionship. It was difficult serving someone every day and not resenting them, but the more Roman accepted his role in their friendship, the easier he found things. Ezra would talk a little nicer on those days. One time, he even stroked Roman hard. He didn't let him cum. Roman still only achieved climax with Ezra inside him, with Ezra pumping hard behind him, with no hands and a reminder Roman's cum required Ezra's pleasure. He didn't mind, though. Seeing Ezra reach climax was enough for him because it meant Roman had earned another day of safety.

Ezra didn't just speak in Roman's defense when someone would make a particularly cutting comment; he'd also step in to defend Roman's honor in and out of the arena. Roman had accepted his place and carved out the smallest amount of happiness he could with the hand dealt to him.

"Get on the bed," Ezra instructed. "I'll straddle you."

"Okay." Roman obeyed, taking his place on the bed. He moved the pillow out of habit because Ezra didn't like it when Roman would cry or moan or yell into the pillow, demanding Roman make himself heard. But Roman had stopped trying to muffle the noises he made when Ezra fucked him after the intensity of the first month.

"Leave it," Ezra demanded.

"Okay," Roman said with a quizzical expression. "Wouldn't it be easier if I was behind you?"

"Oh, like me face down and ass up for you?" Ezra stripped off his clothes and straddled Roman's chest, putting the full, crushing weight of his body on top of Roman. "That would put you in charge, in control."

Roman remained quiet, not realizing he'd overstepped with such an innocuous question. He didn't want to upset Ezra twice in one day.

"Remember, I'm always in charge." Ezra stared down at him, a smile on his face and hate in his green eyes.

Roman never could understand how Ezra seemed so happy and disgusted all at once. It was a look only Roman ever brought out of Ezra. No matter who he talked with or argued with or fought against, Ezra always seemed content, calm, and collected. There was this calculated strategy to how he carried himself with every single person, from the inmates to the staff. His eyes never held the same menace they did when locked onto Roman.

"Sorry." Roman braced as Ezra moved further up.

"Don't be sorry. Be a friend and eat my ass." Ezra planted his ass on Roman's mouth, muffling his face with his taint and balls.

Roman went to work, lapping at Ezra's warm hole. He'd only experimented with eating ass twice in his life. Ezra's butt was not like Stacy Anderson's; however, it wasn't much different, mechanically speaking. Ezra's hole was hairy, unlike Stacy's. He shouldn't be thinking about Stacy right now, especially while lathering a man's hole with his tongue. The disrespect for her memory was almost as awkward as his current angle. All the same, he thought about Stacy's many curiosities and how she'd convinced him to try most of his sexually adventurous desires. She was actually the person who introduced Roman to anal, being a fan of the sensation herself and quite demanding that he learn how to use his dick in all the right ways. Roman enjoyed the experience, albeit finding it a bit bizarre the first few times.

She'd tried convincing Roman to let her use her fingers during oral, something Roman promptly rejected. It would've taken away from his masculinity, or so he believed at the time. As he lapped Ezra's hole, poked gently with his tongue, and licked at the ring of his ass, he realized Ezra had no problem surrendering a bit of his masculinity for the sake of pleasure, especially pleasure where he still remained in control.

Roman wondered how things would've been different if he'd let Stacy experiment all her fancies with him. She'd had a lot of toys and always wanted to experiment with butt stuff. Maybe the first few dozen times with Ezra would've been easier on Roman if he'd agreed to Stacy's curiosities. Maybe if he spent more time exploring kinks with Stacy, the pair would've been too busy to go out drinking. Maybe he would've never gotten in that fight. Maybe he would've never shoved her in a fit of fury. Maybe he would've never killed Stacy.

Her bloody, smashed body replayed in his thoughts a million times like it had far too many times over the years, and regret of his actions threatened to pull him from his current job.

Ezra thrust on top of Roman's face, moaning with pleasure the more Roman worked over Ezra's hole. Roman focused wholeheartedly on pleasing Ezra. All the wondering didn't help Roman and stole from this intimacy that he needed to prioritize. Following the curious wonders was pointless and led down several what-ifs that would never come to be. What if he hadn't drunk so much his second year of college. What if he hadn't gone out celebrating after finals. What if he hadn't gotten into a bar fight. What if…what if…what if…

When Ezra shuddered, arms stretched to grip the underside of the top bunk, Roman could feel the man ready to buckle. He worked his tongue more, licking and lapping and gently poking until Ezra was chasing Roman's mouth with desire. Even though Ezra preferred to be in charge, Roman found himself controlling the flow of their entanglements more and more.

The more Ezra trusted him, the more Ezra craved him, the more he would surrender dominance. Roman would still suck and bottom, but like now, when he worked over Ezra's ass with his mouth, Roman would dictate the pace, control the release, determine where things went next. Grabbing ahold of

Ezra's hips, Roman continued rimming the man while sliding a hand around Ezra's erect cock, and stroking him.

Roman's own dick throbbed. He wanted to stroke it, too. No, to hammer it away inside a tight hole. Ezra's hole. It was moments like this where Roman's dick twitched with excitement, and every fiber of his being wanted to fuck Ezra, to ram his cock into the man, and turn this sordid arrangement into something real. Roman didn't know what to make of that, so he continued stroking Ezra, continued serving the man.

Eventually, Ezra moved off Roman, slapping his dick against Roman's face, a look of rage and delight after having his ass eaten. He didn't ask, didn't give Roman a warning; he just shoved his dick into Roman's mouth, groaning with excitement when Roman choked and gagged at the sudden shock of taking Ezra into his mouth.

After a few minutes of erratically face fucking Roman, he slid off and snapped his fingers with a wave of his hand. Roman recognized the gesture and obediently rolled onto his stomach, arching his back and aligning his knees for Ezra's convenience. Ezra pounded Roman, and Roman did his best to hold his head up while he grunted at the swift thrusts. The pillow called to Roman after such a long and exhausting day, but he could rest after Ezra climaxed.

Chapter Twelve

Roman sat next to Ezra, who'd taken to attending the arena bouts in their entirety. Roman never wasted his time watching the preliminary shows, the casual competitions, the filler entertainment. He used that time to rest and relax, but Ezra used that time to parade his authority. Ezra never portrayed himself with an air of arrogance or authority, always relying on subtly and sly suggestions to get what he wanted as champion, something Roman still didn't fully grasp. But one thing Ezra did weigh heavily on was the claim to his throne.

It was large and made of stone, like something out of a fantasy world. There were animal skulls adorned along the top of the chair going all the way down to the butt of the seat, which would make sitting back uncomfortable. Not that Ezra did. He leaned forward for the matches, hands on his knees and legs spread wide. The armrests went unused, which again benefited Ezra since they were covered in spiked bones to add to the mystique of the throne.

Roman would've found it silly if he weren't already so conditioned to love all of Ezra's whims. Life was just easier when he learned to laugh, learned to accept the whispers and finger pointing. Especially since a few in the audience snickered at Roman, who sat on the floor beside Ezra's chair. He had a plush pillow to rest on so his knees didn't hurt in this position for so long and a clear view of the competition, but Roman realized almost immediately how unequal he and Ezra appeared. His stomach twisted in knots at the idea of how he looked like nothing more than a pet. But when Ezra played with his hair and made conversation in between rounds, Roman smiled and did his best to be grateful.

"We've got quite a lineup before the champion's chance begins," Warden Sadler announced. "Levi Pierce versus Landon Montgomery."

Roman's heart jumped a beat. What the fuck was happening? He turned to Ezra, whose expression had barely shifted. He was seemingly aware of this match, which made no sense to Roman. Levi was soft and sweet and too sensitive for the arena. Everything Roman did after escaping The Pit was to ensure Levi's safety. Yes, his own well-being mattered, but he'd long since accepted his fate. He sat up, searching the crowd of inmates in attendance, even the authority of spectators above, but didn't see his friend anywhere.

"What's happening?" Roman frantically turned to Ezra, poorly hiding his concern. "I thought you had Levi under your protection."

Ezra smiled at Roman. "I do."

"Then why's he being dragged into the arena?" Roman's heart surged.

"What people choose to do on their own time is up to them," Ezra said dismissively. "I can only do so much, Princess. I have to allow folks to make their own choices."

No one came down here by choice unless they relished the violence. Only desperate fools willing to accept a beating for a chance at some extra cash ventured down here. Had Levi become one of the fodder inmates? Someone chosen purely for an easy beatdown so the audience could have a laugh with their blood sport? Usually, only the junkies did that. They were often the only ones desperate enough to fight actual fighters with zero experience.

When Levi finally revealed himself, he seemed so much bigger than the last time Roman had seen him. He'd also shaved his chestnut brown hair short, barely longer than a buzzcut, which would make grabbing all the more difficult. Their paths didn't cross much, with so much of Roman's time spent at Ezra's side. Levi had always been big, but Roman learned early on that Levi was only muscle pretty, not muscle strong. The fitness training at the gym was for his aesthetic, not for combat. He'd removed his glasses, which was good since Landon was probably about to break poor Levi's face. Still, there was something hard in Levi's eyes as he squared up across from Landon.

Roman watched the fight unfold and immediately recoiled when Landon leaned in for a quick jab. To his surprise, Levi evaded the strike, pivoted around, and clocked Landon in the jaw. Roman's head tilted in curiosity and surprise at Levi's move sets. These were things Roman had attempted and failed to teach Levi countless times over the years. There were other techniques Roman was familiar with but didn't apply to his own style. It was almost as if Levi had pulled and adapted to other fighter styles from all his observations on the sidelines. Unfortunately, making himself a Jack of all Trades only went so far, and Roman noted how sloppy Levi's overall form was. His stamina still outlasted Landon, and eventually, Levi cleared the round with a victory.

The warden announced the win and showed a tally of Levi's current stats. He'd won seven rounds and only lost four.

Roman didn't know what to say, what to think, how to feel. He was so damn proud and perplexed. Mostly, he was worried. If Levi chose this life, Roman was happy he'd finally found himself growing out from under Roman's shadow, but if he was somehow forced into this because Ezra's protection wasn't enough, then Roman feared the lengths he'd have to go to ensure Levi's safety.

"He's really okay?" Roman finally asked, looking up at Ezra with sad eyes.

"Yes, he's fine." Ezra smiled. "People grow and change. Take a look at yourself."

Roman didn't consider his change growth. He felt like he'd shrunk and crumbled the last six months. He was a weak flower withering away in the harsh bester.

Levi looked at Roman only once. His cold blue eyes turned glossy for a moment when he locked onto Roman, but then he blinked away the sadness, and Levi's eyes turned stoic again before he vanished into the thicket of the crowd.

Roman sat quietly, burying his concerns for Levi, and barely focused on the rest of the arena battles. That was until they called for the champion.

Ezra stood tall, taking in the roar of the crowd, then turned to Roman, who remained knelt on his pillow. Brushing aside ruffled pink bangs, Ezra kissed Roman on the forehead, much to his shame. It wouldn't have been half as humiliating if the crowd hadn't ooooed and snickered.

Since Ezra invited Roman to join him at the arena moving forward, it proved difficult in every way. This was his former stomping grounds. This was a place he held in check for a year. This was a place where people from across the world gathered to watch him fight. Now, the elite clientele who watched from the balcony in animal masks held no regard for Roman. Worse, some of them held pity or pleasure in his circumstances.

Ignoring the feelings and everything else that consumed him, Roman did what he did best in life, what he was made for in life: he cheered on Ezra. He hoped for the best and gave words of encouragement in between rounds. Ezra's happiness was Roman's happiness, and when an opponent got a lucky shot in and cracked Ezra's ribs, Roman trembled.

Ezra treated Roman well, Roman learned to behave, and life had gotten so much better. But when the crowd turned against Ezra, when someone taunted him just right, Ezra would sometimes be swept with rage that lasted the entire night. Roman didn't enjoy himself on those nights, and he tried his best to make Ezra forget the slights, the insults, the injuries. It only occasionally worked in his favor.

Thankfully, it didn't take long for Ezra to turn the match around and win back the crowd. He pummeled his way through the next set of opponents, and when the Challenger's Chance rounds started up, Ezra unleashed all his fury on those foolish enough to come for his crown.

Roman breathed easy at that, grateful the anger had subsided.

After the final challenger had lost and no one else was left to fight, Ezra basked in the roar of the crowd, walking the arena and circling close to the crowd of inmates in attendance. Roman spotted Levi a second time for the night, standing close to a guy with a furrowed brow and a hateful expression. It looked like Levi was trying to talk the guy down; Roman recalled how Levi often brought levity to difficult situations, deflecting conflict with humor. But it wasn't working with this guy. Levi slipped away in the crowd again, and the angry man leapt forward when Ezra crossed his path.

From out of nowhere, he swung a knife, slashing Ezra's face. Blood splattered. Red filled Roman's vision. The crowd went silent. Rage and hatred consumed Ezra's expression. Roman trembled. He didn't know what to do or how to help. He watched Ezra leap back, evading the erratic swipes of a knife. An actual knife. This wasn't some shiv. This man somehow got ahold of a fucking eight-inch kitchen knife. The crowd went wild. The authority above disappeared into darkness. Guards funneled inside. Chaos controlled the inmates, and they blocked a path, drawn to random violence over any type of civility. Ezra was on his own, dodging the knife, and clearly a bit too winded from so many rounds throughout the night.

Finally, Ezra managed to knock the knife from the man's hand, but before he could drop him, the outraged inmate reached for a second blade, this one a short shiv, which would still prove difficult for Ezra. Roman saw it on his face, the annoyance over the concern, but Ezra raised his fists and prepared to knock away the second weapon.

Only he didn't have to. Order hadn't been restored, but someone swept in close behind the deranged inmate and stabbed him in the chest with his kitchen knife. Whoever it was took their tattooed hand and squeezed the shiv out of the inmate's other hand before forcing him to grab the knife and knocking him to the ground. By the time the guards broke a line through the crowd, it appeared as if the man had fallen onto his knife.

Roman's eyes went wide when he saw Jake standing over the corpse, a smile on his face and a hand on Ezra's shoulder.

The friendly words of gratitude Ezra gave Jake were all Roman heard before the noise of the crowd flooded his hearing.

Chapter Thirteen

"I'm gonna be chilling with Finnegan and his crew today," Ezra said as he adjusted his pants.

Roman wiped the spit from his mouth and stretched his jaw loose for a moment. He took in the scar on Ezra's face; it'd changed his appearance but not his personality. The deep cut didn't sour Ezra's mood. A long slash above his right eye that reached down to his sharp jawline. There was no bitterness or shame, at least none that Ezra directed toward Roman, and he considered himself fortunate that Ezra's spirits remained high.

"You got business with them?" Roman asked, cautious but curious. It was important he tread both when talking with Ezra. Ezra liked his interest in his work as the new reigning champion, but Roman also had to remember his place and how Ezra couldn't disclose everything to him.

"No business, just hanging."

"Hanging out with Jake the Snake for fun." Roman recoiled at the idea, finding Jake a literal stain on the world.

"The snake." Ezra rolled his eyes. "His pecker's not that impressive."

Ezra's gaze dropped to his own massive dick tucked away in his pants and made a flirty face. Roman realized he was alluding to the fact Ezra was the only one with a real snake in their pants. Without prompting, Roman laughed, which made Ezra smile.

"I know he helped you, but Jake's a snake for more reasons than his own hyped press on his dick," Roman said, noticing Ezra had been lending an ear to Jake more often since his assistance at the arena where an inmate almost gutted the champion.

"Sometimes folks have a bad rep." Ezra shrugged. "Look, I know he annoys you, so I'm not making you come."

"Thank you."

"But you still need to get out." Ezra brushed aside Roman's damp pink bangs and kissed his forehead. "If you're not at my side, you're just locking yourself in the room all day."

"I prefer the quiet."

"And I prefer you get a little sunlight, stretch your legs, go do something."

Roman skittishly looked at the door, the one he almost never stepped through without trailing Ezra from place to place. Being paraded around used to be a punishment, but now it ensured his safety.

"I got eyes everywhere," Ezra said, gripping Roman's chin and pulling his gaze up to meet Ezra's. "You'll be fine.

Wherever you go, someone will follow. They won't bother you. You won't notice them. Just have fun, okay? As much fun as you can have in a cellblock."

"I'll do that."

"That's my good boy." Ezra pulled Roman up until he stood to meet him and then gave him a kiss.

It was hot and heavy and came with hands running under Roman's clothes. He half expected to get undressed to satisfy Ezra one more time before he left, but without prompting, he pushed Roman off and left to go hang out with his new friend, Jake.

Roman lingered in the cell for a while, considering a nap, but since Ezra had eyes everywhere and he wanted Roman to go exploring, he reluctantly decided to make a day of it. His first stop was the gym. Roman hesitated at first, knowing this was their thing, something they did together, but everything was really their thing. Roman focused on cardio and glutes, then left without a second thought. He spent some time in the library, flipping through a few books, but didn't have the energy to read. He pretended until the seat got too uncomfortable and made his way to the cafeteria for lunch.

With three stops accomplished, Roman figured it'd be safe to return to the cell and wait out the rest of the day.

Roman went to the usual table he and Ezra claimed. When he noticed a few inmates already there, he turned to walk away, but their eyes met him, met something behind him, and without prompting, all ten got up and left without a word.

As he took his seat, Roman turned to see who or what frightened them off, but he only saw a crowd of inmates. The threat could've come from any of them. Ezra had friends everywhere, after all.

Roman enjoyed the peace of eating by himself, really doing his best to savor this time. No one would disturb him. No one expected anything of him. It was actually a decent afternoon.

"What he's doing to you," Levi said through gritted teeth. "It's not okay."

Levi's immediate anger and curt comment perplexed Roman. They hadn't spoken, really spoken, in months, and this was the first thing he said. It didn't stop Levi from tossing his tray across from Roman and inviting himself to the table. His gaze cut to something—someone—behind them, then Levi scowled dismissively and turned his attention back to Roman.

"What are you talking about?"

"Ezra." Levi glared. "You shouldn't let him do this to you."

"I'm fine," Roman replied. "It's more of a show for other people, but he's really nice when we're alone."

"Why not make the show about treating you well?" Levi asked. "Use his sway as champion to make people back the fuck off. Then, treat you how you deserve to be treated, which, if it's not clear, is nothing like how you're currently being treated."

Levi gestured to Roman's pink hair, Roman's tattoos, Roman's bruised body. The bruises Levi could see. There were so many more. But that wasn't an act of cruelty. That was sparring, that was helping Ezra train. It wasn't what Levi suspected. It wasn't what anyone assumed.

"You don't have to put up with this," Levi said. "You're Roman Grayson."

Roman didn't have an answer. He didn't know how to pivot, how to explain this was the best he deserved, how to explain Ezra really was being nice considering he could just as well abandon Roman.

"Champion doesn't work like that," Roman said unconvincingly. "There's so much to account for."

"It did when you were champion," Levi said flatly, eyes locked onto Roman. "You looked out for me every day; you kept people off me, too. You didn't parade me around. You didn't bitch me out. You didn't mistreat me. I was your friend. I still am your friend."

Levi went on to mention Roman's many futile accolades as champion, the others he helped, the subtle reforms he pushed for, the bullshit he wouldn't tolerate. None of that mattered to Roman anymore. It never really mattered. Nothing Roman did mattered except for ensuring Ezra was happy.

"Ezra's my friend, too," Roman snapped. "He looks out for me, too."

Levi tsked. "Yeah, while making you debase yourself."

"He doesn't make me do anything." Roman felt the heat in his chest, the anger that Levi would look down on him, turn this into something it wasn't, and after everything he'd done to help him. "I have a choice. I make this choice. I like my life."

"You like your life?" Levi asked. "You like the way Ezra has turned you out, treated you? Changed you."

"Yes," Roman said. "I'm fine with the arrangement. I wouldn't change it, and I wouldn't go back and change it."

Even Roman didn't believe those words, but he'd be damned if he was going to take pity from Levi.

"You only think that because he's fucked with your head," Levi insisted. "You can't see from where you're at, but it's like he's taken every layer of you, of Roman Grayson, and warped them into this obedient puppy that will do anything he says. He's forced you—"

"He doesn't force me to do anything," Roman hissed, his chest feeling like it might erupt with a rage he'd long since learned to bury underneath his contentment. "You're the one who can't see. You don't know. You don't understand."

"I understand he makes you serve him, makes you think you're a part of it, makes you think you—"

"Ezra has never forced me into anything," Roman clarified quite adamantly. "From day one, before day one, I always had a choice. Me. This right here is my choice. Everything in this arrangement is my choice."

"Oh, you suddenly just choose to be gay?" Levi asked, batting his eyes with a sarcastic flirty edge that held more anger than humor. "It doesn't work that way. I know a lot of guys in here would have folks believing otherwise, but you either feel a certain way or you don't."

"I enjoy what we do," Roman said flatly, honestly. Because he did get off on it more and more, especially the more he willed himself to accept the arrangement. "It *feels* good."

"Just because your body enjoys a situation doesn't mean you do. So, again, doesn't mean a thing." Levi shrugged. "I've tugged a load out of my fair share of straight cock."

"It's not like that," Roman clarified. "I've always been a little curious."

It was a reality he hadn't been able to accept for a long time. The brutal introduction to his curiosity didn't help matters. He'd never pondered submission. He had wondered about men. Few and far between, brief thoughts that were always washed away when he could quickly fantasize about a woman too. He couldn't be *gay* gay, and since he didn't like the idea of all the gay things, he wouldn't have considered himself bi either. There were gay positions or acts he didn't want to ever try until Ezra came along.

Now, he liked them. He reminded himself that he liked them. So, when his mind would drift from the fantasy of switching positions to actually being sucked off for a change, he finally let his thoughts focus on men. Not on Ezra. He could never imagine him being submissive. It was too dangerous a thought. Usually, his mind would drift to Levi, which was an equally dangerous thought. It pissed Roman off how Levi ruined his fantasies with an asinine attitude and aggressive assumptions.

Ultimately, Roman wasn't sure if he was gay or bi or somewhere in between, but he didn't need the answers.

"Now, he tells me." Levi dramatically gestured while flaunting just a bit.

Roman chuckled, actually chuckled. It surprised him, the genuine joy that swept through him so suddenly. It'd been so long since he smiled or laughed just for the sake of it and not for Ezra's benefit. It was also a reminder of how Levi and Roman could switch gears in their friendship, go from the heat of an argument to idle nonsense without missing a beat.

"If I'd known, I would've flirted a hell of a lot harder," Levi continued as if he hadn't been quite convincing the few times he'd hinted to Roman.

It was something Roman would go back and change. He'd never accepted Levi's advances, shutting them down and pretending he hadn't caught the suggestions, but now he let his mind wander. Levi hadn't been subtle about offering to suck Roman off.

Roman still remembered Levi's pouty face and the way he sat on the floor, organizing something. "Hands are great and all, but let's be real: the lube in this place is scarce."

The only reason Roman never made a move was because he didn't want it to be some desperate "only for the stay" kind of reason. And he didn't want it to be a powerplay. Roman firmly believed if he started making Levi suck his dick, then it would ruin their bond, their friendship. Friends didn't force themselves onto one another, didn't abuse their authority to take advantage, but he'd also learned from Ezra that friends liked to help each other out. Roman liked helping Ezra, liked proving he was a good friend.

"You said you have a choice," Levi said, quite seriously, with a hand pressed close to Roman's.

Roman almost retreated, worried Levi would overstep, worried Levi would touch him. No one touched Roman except for Ezra.

"I do have a choice," Roman lied, believing it less and less every time Ezra reminded him, though that had also become less and less now that Roman had accepted his fate.

"Then choose me," Levi said. "Choose to room with me. Not for some fucked up 'you do what I say or else' kind of arrangement. But as friends. Like we were before all of this."

"I can't." Roman's face contorted, confused and frightened. "Do you know how many people hate me? What would happen without Ezra's protection? He's the only reason I'm safe, the only reason you're safe."

"He's not," Levi spoke with bared teeth like he might tear out someone's throat. "I can protect you. I'm not the person I was."

"You've won a few fights; you've walked with your head held up because no one is trying to push it down," Roman said, shoving his tray away. "Do you know why no one is knocking you to your knees? Because Ezra protects you. Do you know why you're getting a little tougher? Because Ezra allows it."

"Whether he does or he doesn't, I will fight to keep you safe, to let you be yourself again."

"I am myself." Roman scowled.

"Roman, I can't keep watching you make yourself smaller and smaller." Levi let all the anger in his expression wash away, and he gave Roman an expression he hadn't recognized. It wasn't pity, but there was sadness in his eyes. Hope—almost empathy, maybe. Roman didn't recognize or understand what empathy was anymore.

"I'm fine." Roman stretched his fingers, which sat flat on the table. He let his pinky touch Levi's, he let his thoughts wander just a bit more than usual, he let himself ignore how mad Levi made him, and he focused on the play-pretend possibilities that he'd never have.

"You're not fine, and you won't be fine if you keep this up."

Roman frowned and stormed away from the table, unable to listen a second longer. Roman returned to his cell and fixated on his conversation with Levi. Not a conversation. An argument. It pissed him off. The way Levi could just warp things, pretend everything would be okay, pretend he understood a goddamn thing about Roman's situation. He didn't. He never would. And that was because of what Roman sacrificed. Not a sacrifice. He was happy, mostly. He'd learned to be happy. It was Levi's unnecessary comments that tried ruining the only good thing Roman had going for him.

Later that night, Ezra stepped into the room, a smile on his face and a light laugh escaping his lips as he bid his farewells to Jake and his crew. Thankfully, none of them stepped inside. Roman sat up.

"Heard you got an offer to walk away," Ezra said so matter-of-factly that it sent an icy jolt of fear through Roman.

"W-what?"

"I always have eyes to keep you safe."

Roman recalled the conversation earlier. The way Ezra said protection would be close, but he'd be unbothered. He hadn't noticed anyone watching him, but he supposed that was the point of their job. Go unseen unless required to step in.

"I didn't suggest or ask anything," Roman tried to clarify, tried to downplay, tried to hope Ezra would believe him.

"Shush." Ezra stepped toward him, hands wrapped around the back of Roman's neck. "I know. I know you chose to stay. I know you will always choose me. Just like I will always choose you."

"We're friends," Roman said, dwelling on the fact he was also friends with Levi, confused by what the word really meant anymore.

"I know." Ezra brushed a hand over Roman's "Bested" neck tattoo. "Why don't you show me what a good friend you are? It's been a long day, and I could use some relief."

Roman obediently slipped off the bed and dropped to his knees, then he fished Ezra's cock out of his pants and went to work. He was still so furious with Levi, so goddamn mad at how he looked down on him, it filled Roman's thoughts with the same resentment, the same fire he had when he first started submitting to Ezra. He'd learned long ago to accept and enjoy what their arrangement brought, but tonight, as he sucked Ezra off, he held onto that spark of rage, and he found himself thinking about Levi, picturing him as he bobbed his head up and down Ezra's shaft.

Chapter Fourteen

Roman trained exceptionally hard during his gym routine over the course of the next several days, biting back his rage during the sparring bouts with Ezra. Despite avoiding Levi since their last conversation, Roman hadn't lost the spark of anger Levi's protective judgment brought out.

Roman ran faster on the treadmill, and he did extra reps on his glute's routine, his leg routine, and the core workout meant to tighten his waist to Ezra's liking instead of bulk up to Roman's preference.

When the time came to go to the back training room and get a little private sparring in, Roman took deep breaths to let go of his anger. It'd do him no good here. As Ezra and Roman stretched in preparation, they found someone breaking their privacy.

"Whoa, so this is the champion's setup?" Levi waltzed inside like he owned the place, which he very much did not.

This space belonged to Ezra. Everything belonged to Ezra.

"Do you mind?" Roman asked, accusatory and not seeking an answer.

"Not at all." Levi shrugged. "I came here to train, but I guess I can watch you guys work."

"It's private," Roman snapped, instinctive and not remotely hiding his annoyance for Levi. "You can't be in here."

"I assumed this was open to everyone, like the rest of the champion's things." Levi pointed to the surroundings of the private gym currently in use but eyed Roman.

That pissed Roman off. Was Levi insinuating he was a thing?

"It's not," Roman snapped.

"Now, now." Ezra slapped a hand to Roman's chest. "I do try to share when I can. It keeps the people happy."

"I do like to be a happy person." Levi grinned at both men. "I can think of a few things that'd make me happy."

"Well, the list better be limited to what we can do on the mat," Roman interjected, desperate for Levi not to bring up what he had in the cafeteria, which Ezra was already aware of.

"I can think of a lot of things to do on these mats." Levi wiggled his toes and pressed his feet into the cushioned flooring.

"I'd love to see what you're capable of, Levi." Ezra locked eyes with him. "Fighting wise, of course."

"Of course." Levi smiled. "I'll gladly show you."

Levi stripped off his shirt, revealing his flawless skin. Not a bragging point for a fighter. While Levi might've stepped into the arena and had a few successful bouts, none had proven a struggle, and his unblemished skin was proof of that. It didn't mean Levi was just that skilled; no, Roman declared in his thoughts, it was merely a sign of Levi's weakness, of the fact he hadn't gotten dirty enough. An omen he'd only scratched the surface of the brutality in the underground arena.

Still, Roman couldn't help but steal glances at Levi's muscular abdomen. He'd always been bigger than Roman, more fit, but Roman had only now started to realize just how firm and strong his body was. Levi's arms and chest were so broad it would take Ezra and Roman combined to reach those measurements.

The tight joggers Levi wore clung to his thick thighs and strong calves, a gift from a patron of the Lawless Authority, no doubt, sponsoring Levi's meager successes in the fighting arena. Roman suspected as much because the gray left little to the imagination, and the fabric accentuated the curve of Levi's thick ass. No way would Levi acquire something so striking without help from the audience on the balcony.

Roman buried the thoughts, the curiosity, but he couldn't hide the heat on his face as he eyed Levi.

"So, you ready to spar?" Ezra asked, eyeing Levi, then looking at Roman, who tried to hide his reddened face by turning his shirt into a fan.

He hoped he could feign exhaustion from the cardio earlier.

"I'd love to go a few rounds," Levi replied but smiled at Roman, all his attention fixated on the man he claimed he wanted to help.

Roman didn't need his help. Maybe this little sparring lesson would give Levi an insight into his foolishness.

It didn't take long for Ezra and Levi to size each other up with feints and light jabs. Soon, they'd moved into more aggressive styles. Surprisingly, Levi moved with a lot more grace than Roman expected. Given his size and lack of experience, Roman predicted Ezra would run laps around Levi. But Levi didn't falter, didn't leave himself exposed for long, and managed to keep distance between them while he struggled to catch his breath.

That was the real problem here. Levi might've been more of a natural than Roman gave him credit for, but Levi still lacked the stamina for a real fighter. The fodder battles in the arena meant nothing when faced with someone with real experience.

"What's the matter?" Levi taunted, shocking Roman and Ezra when he managed to slip behind him and lock Ezra in a chokehold. "Figured you'd love this move."

Roman stopped breathing. He couldn't believe what Levi was doing; he couldn't believe Levi had locked Ezra up with this move. He couldn't believe he'd missed it by blinking away for a moment, a silly little moment where he hoped they'd wrap up things soon.

And they would, but Roman figured—no, knew—Ezra would grow bored and end things. He would win. He always won.

"Levi, stop." Roman stepped forward, bitter fright in his voice, chilled at what would happen to them both if Levi asserted some pointless dominance in a sparring match.

Levi smirked, an expression suggesting he had so much more planned, but that joy dropped away when his feet hovered off the ground. Ezra had done what Roman lacked the strength for during their first fight. Ezra lifted Levi's feet off the ground a second time, wrapping a hand under Levi's arm and giving himself a bit of breathing room as he worked to flip Levi off him and wriggle out of the chokehold.

It only took a few tries, and then Ezra flipped Levi over his head and slammed the man hard onto the mat. Ezra panted, gathering his stolen breaths, then reeled back a fist as he dropped to the ground and prepared to smash in Levi's face.

Ezra stopped short of striking Levi; his knuckles grazed against the man's cheek. Levi hadn't flinched, fully prepared to take a bone-breaking punch. It surprised Roman, surprised him to see how much Levi had grown and continued to change since their divide.

"I think that's the match." Ezra smiled, offering his hand to help Levi up. "I wouldn't wanna break that pretty face of yours. It wasn't all that long ago I wanted to fuck that pretty little face."

Roman's body warmed, angry at the idea, reminded of the pressure Ezra had put on Levi and the way he used him to get Roman.

"But now I get to fuck the prettiest face in here." Ezra winked at Roman, who blushed, then turned his gaze back to Levi. "Guess I never properly thanked you for that, did I?"

Levi glared, an icy stare strong enough to kill. Roman knew Levi blamed himself. Knew Levi desperately wanted to avoid this fate and had inadvertently set Roman on the path to handing himself to Ezra. But Roman didn't blame Levi. He never could.

"How about you show him some real moves, Princess?" Ezra poorly broke the tension with Levi by playfully calling Roman over.

Not that it helped lessen the mood, though Roman suspected this wasn't about that. This was meant to show Levi what Ezra really could do. Roman went along, bracing himself for brutal punches that Ezra used to knock out the fury in Levi's eyes. Now, he watched with concern, the same concern he expressed to Roman in the cafeteria, the same worry, the same desire to help. That pissed Roman off, and he played his role a bit too well, fighting back and knocking Ezra away.

Roman knew he lashed out too hard, too fast, too aggressively, but that shouting warning paled in comparison to the part of him that wanted to put Levi in check. He pelted Ezra, then slipped around and jabbed him in the ribs. Roman only saw red. Roman only saw the chance to prove to Levi he was still strong.

The cathartic freedom that came from landing successful chained strikes washed away months of shame. Roman was still in there, truly himself buried underneath all the submission he offered, beneath the guilt of failure he harbored, beneath the broken boy meant only to please Ezra's needs.

Fuck!

Roman stopped, slowed himself, and took in what he'd done, how he'd fought back. This was not what Roman was supposed to do when they trained. Roman was made to serve, nothing more.

The fury in Ezra's eyes had turned his expression sour. No anger there. It was so much worse. Roman could see the disgust, felt it radiating in the air between them, and it made him shiver.

If Roman surrendered outright, Ezra would take offense. The audacity that Roman thought Ezra needed him to submit would lead to trouble for Roman, so he let his next moves hit slower and miss closely but still present themselves as actual efforts. Ezra moved in more brutally, pummeling Roman over and over until his body throbbed from the fresh bruises that would take hold soon enough. After a convincing loss, Roman gestured pleadingly for submission.

Once Roman disengaged, it didn't take Ezra long to knock him back, change the flow of the fight, and flip Roman over his head and onto the mat like a ragdoll. Ezra pinned Roman on his back and took full advantage of Roman's surrender, not easing up simply because his opponent had faltered. Roman braced himself for any beating, understanding these trainings were a privilege, an opportunity to help Ezra, not a place for Roman to vent his rage or show off.

"That was so good." Ezra smiled, much to Roman's surprise, and kissed him on the lips. A quick, fleeting peck that fueled a longing in Roman. And an idea. "Who knew there was so much fight in you?"

"I'm just full of surprises," Roman answered Ezra, but his eyes drifted to Levi.

Ezra nuzzled Roman's neck, tempting him, hungry for him. Roman felt it in the buck of his hips, the aggressive squeeze of his arms, the gentle lick of his tongue coupled with the rough bite of his teeth.

"Sorry," he growled. "I know there's an audience. Just can't help myself with you."

"The only audience I'm concerned about is you." Roman turned Ezra's head, locked eyes with him, and kissed the man with a fiery passion.

Heat and rage he'd surrendered months ago, but somehow Levi managed to ignite the spark, the fury. It created a carnal desire, an all-consuming hunger of lust and want and need. Roman thrust against Ezra, lifting himself, adjusting himself, and offering himself, and it didn't take long for Ezra to catch the hint.

Ezra yanked down Roman's sweats and then his own. Roman wriggled loose of his pants, spreading his legs and wrapping them around Ezra's hips for easy access. Ezra spat on his hand and stroked himself until he'd poorly lubed his cock, and then he shoved into Roman with such rough force, he screamed, dragging his nails across Ezra's back and pulling the man into a tight hug. Ezra was too big, too rough with his strokes, to go in unlubed, but all the same, Roman called out for more.

"Fuck me," he moaned with hazy vision.

Roman allowed Ezra to bury himself in him, caressing Ezra's back, gripping Ezra's hips, encouraging Ezra to rest his face in the crook of Roman's neck. Each time Ezra plowed into Roman, they grunted in unison. It didn't take long for Roman's grunts to turn into desperate panting. Roman barely held back his furious tears, taking the entirety of Ezra. All the while, he let his head fall backward, staring upside down at Levi, who watched Roman get fucked.

Levi's anger built as his breathing hastened. Roman didn't blink, didn't look away. He studied every inch of

Levi's sweaty body, the slight bulge of his crotch, and the rage in Levi's striking blue eyes. Roman held onto his own rage as Ezra pounded into him faster and harder and meaner. Roman imagined Levi with each new thrust; he envisioned their bodies entwined from messy combat; he wondered how much anger Levi could bury in him, how merciless he could be with Roman, how much he'd like to use Roman.

Roman begged for more, giving Ezra permission to ruin him, wreck him, and leave him a broken mess on the mat, all while glimpsing Levi in his thoughts. It was a dirty secret he couldn't divulge, a craving he couldn't satiate.

Levi's angry expression finally cracked and fell apart, leaving a somber man whose blue eyes held a yearning for Roman. Not to fuck him—no, Roman didn't believe that. Levi merely wanted more for Roman, more than this path. But there was nothing left of Roman to be salvaged, and he wanted to show Levi that, show him he would be okay all the same, show him that even in the primal lust of submission, Ezra did care for him.

"Roll over." Ezra slipped off Roman and grabbed him by the hips before spinning him over.

Roman's face slapped against the mat, and he rested his arms in front of his head, then raised his ass to meet Ezra. He groaned when Ezra reinserted himself forcefully.

"Fuck, fuck, fuck." Roman gritted his teeth.

"Too much for you?" Ezra asked, hand pressed to the nape of Roman's neck as he pinned him in place and plowed.

Roman eyed Levi one more time. "It's never too much."

And with that, Levi took his leave, and Ezra railed Roman until he cried and begged for Ezra to finish.

"Please cum," Roman whimpered.

Ezra snatched Roman by the jaw, craning his neck to face him as he banged into him from behind. With a fierce kiss, Ezra climaxed, bucking desperately into Roman's sore hole. Roman kissed back, muffling his cries into Ezra, who growled with a bit more assertive strength the weaker Roman became.

"You're so fucking perfect." Ezra kissed Roman with heavy panting breaths, stealing the air from his lungs. "I think it's time you take a bigger role in things."

"How much bigger we talking?" Roman jested, helping slip Ezra's softened cock out of him. "I don't think I can handle much bigger."

"You can handle anything, so long as I want it, right?" Ezra's green eyes were fixed on Roman, the pleasure on his face didn't mask the malice in his gaze. This was less a question and more a demand, an understanding between them, and Roman sheepishly nodded.

"What do you need from me?"

"I'd like you to join me during a meeting," Ezra said. "I'd like for you to see the full extent of the champion's responsibilities, to see the power of this title."

Power Ezra held. Power meant to remind Roman that, despite everything he did to stay on top, he'd never fully grasped what his role in life was. Now, he'd never be on top again, and Ezra helped Roman understand that a little more each day.

Chapter Fifteen

Roman held his head high—but not too high, nothing an onlooker would notice, but enough to lift Roman's spirits—when he followed Ezra through the hallway past the library and to the adjoined rec room between cellblocks C, D, and E. Given its close proximity to the library and the overlap in inmate use, those not technically supposed to be in the rec room often went unnoticed.

Roman suspected few guards would comment on those in attendance, though. Ezra stopped a few feet from a poker table, a friendly game with no sanctioned gambling—not that anyone bet on cards when the fights in the basement arena held the real cash flow.

"Stay close, stay quiet, stay stoic." Ezra smirked, giving Roman a light pat. Nothing to fawn over him or show him off. Roman understood this wasn't that type of meeting, and he wanted to impress Ezra.

He'd hoped for something a bit less intimidating than a meeting with the crime syndicates that ran Marlow Penitentiary. Well, the gang leaders who ran pieces of territory Warden Sadler permitted since Roman knew he was the most corrupt person in this prison.

"Welcome." Daniel Sullivan shook Ezra's hand. Daniel handled all the imported tech in and out of the prison, so if anyone so much as slipped a cell phone inside without his permission, they either handed it over or offered him a piece of the profit.

Paying for unmonitored texts and calls went a long way for convicts.

Ezra took the seat beside Daniel, and Roman stood behind and slightly to Ezra's left side like the other men who watched over their leader. It was such a moment of pride, being tasked with the responsibility and purpose of defending Ezra. Not that he needed it, not that Ezra couldn't handle every single person here singlehandedly. Still, it lifted Roman's spirits, gave him encouragement, and made him a bit queasy. It'd been so long since he'd found himself feeling genuinely good that the foreign thoughts made him skeptical, even slightly paranoid, but like all things with Ezra, Roman did his best to bury the bad thoughts and focus on their friendship like he'd told Roman from day one.

Roman paid close attention to each of the men rounding the tables and their lieutenants at their sides. None of the faces had changed from what Roman recalled, not that the vacuum in power shifted much. Well, except for things like champion title.

As the current reigning champion of the arena, Ezra had earned a voice during negotiations. The champion had a hand in organizing the fights, something Roman had never cared about, something Roman saw more as a chore than a tool of power, but Ezra recognized the authority that came with having the warden's ear and realized how to orchestrate matches to benefit the gangs.

It was so much more than rigging a few fights and cashing out on insider bets. There were ways for groups to work out their grievances in arranged fights, there were chances for payback against unsuspecting offenders, and so many other aspects Roman barely wrapped his head around. Ezra had a calculating mind, which he used to steer the other members at the table.

Roman clenched a fist, noting he never stood a chance against Ezra. It was here where Roman silently observed Ezra sweet talk other members, delicately drop intel, push and persuade negotiations here or there that Roman realized how simple it must've been to puppeteer him. Roman must've looked like a pathetic fool, an easy mark. Unfortunately, it was a fleeting thought, an ugly blip that Roman quelled quickly.

He'd learned months ago that holding onto his resentment for Ezra only made his days more grueling. Instead, he focused on how impressive Ezra's display was. He released his balled fist and almost openly smiled at how proud Ezra must've been of him. Parading him around was one thing, but bringing him to a meeting like this, letting him witness conversations on how to run the prison and divide up territory… Roman believed it meant Ezra was starting to see more in him, and maybe… No. Roman didn't want to daydream. If he started to daydream, he might actually smile.

"What's so funny, sweetheart?" Jake Finnegan rocked back in his chair, kicking it onto two feet and wobbling momentarily.

To steady his grip, he grabbed ahold of Roman's waist and let his hand slide lower than Roman liked.

Jake the Snake controlled the drugs in and out of Marlow Penitentiary, which made him one of the biggest players here. He had the strongest voice and was part of the reason Roman never bothered attending these meetings as champion. Jake's desires were clear the first day Roman entered his cellblock. Roman hoped the day he knocked Jake out of the arena as champion, the psycho would take the hint, but that only made him want Roman more. In fact, Jake had only recently lessened his pursuit since Ezra claimed Roman.

"Huh?" Roman tried to shake away from Jake's grip, but when he did, Jake dramatically wobbled and made it appear as if Roman's ass was the only thing holding him upright.

"The smile." Jake nodded to Roman's face, to the smile plastered there he didn't even realize. "Care to tell me what's got you feeling so good? I'd love to know how to make you feel good."

Roman wanted to shove Jake off, wanted to remind him that they would never happen, that just because he was with Ezra now, he had no intention of debasing himself with someone as sadistic as Jake the Snake. But Ezra made it clear that Roman couldn't become a distraction and needed to stand beside his chair the same as any lieutenant would. Roman desperately wanted to believe Ezra acknowledged him as a lieutenant, hoped maybe this was the first step of Ezra's to make the gangs see Roman that way, too.

That thought, that little whisper of a fantasy, made Roman smile. A smile that caught Jake's eye and now had him curbing attention so he didn't distract from the meeting.

"Let me help." Ezra grabbed Jake's thigh and knocked him forward, so he sat firmly in his chair. "Wouldn't want you to fall."

Jake kept his gaze locked on Roman. "I don't mind falling if it's for the right reasons."

Between Jake's deranged smile and Ezra's aggravated frown, Roman found himself wanting to collapse. He hated the idea of failing Ezra, and seeing that expression with his angry green eyes filled him with dread.

"Can we continue?" Daniel scowled at Jake, then turned his gaze to Roman and sneered.

He despised Jake's need to screw men, the way he'd flaunt his affections, and chase young men who didn't stand a chance against his advances. But more than that, he found Roman's willingness to subject himself to such depravity outright disgusting. Roman knew this because men like Daniel didn't hide their hate. Roman was worse than Jake. Jake was an animal of a man, a perverted one in Daniel's eyes, but still a man. Roman was trash; that single glance told him that much and so much more.

It also reminded Roman why he hated the heads of Marlow Penitentiary.

After the meeting ended, Ezra casually made his way around the cellblocks, keeping Roman a bit more distant than usual and ignoring him in favor of sparking up conversation with others. Roman didn't like the slack, the extra steps of freedom. It didn't feel like trust or a reward. It felt like a punishment; it made his skin crawl when he thought of how Ezra might be mad and what he might do if he was mad.

Despite the way Jake behaved during the meeting, Ezra still pulled him aside and shared in idle chitchat. Since Jake had interfered with the knife attack during an arena match, Ezra had considered him less of a tolerable ally and more of a budding friend. Roman couldn't determine whether Ezra kept his distance during their conversation as a way to protect Roman from more of Jake's lewd behavior or as a note on how Roman had already screwed up once today. Roman rarely believed in the positive what-ifs. No, his mind raced with how he could fix things, how he should apologize to Ezra.

"Relax." Ezra's mood completely changed when they returned to the champion's suite.

He closed the odd distance he'd kept between himself and Roman. He smiled when the last thing Roman had seen was a frown of disappointment. He even lightly kissed Roman before tousling his ruffled pink hair.

"I'm not mad," Ezra said. "Disappointed, maybe. But I still think your first meeting went well. Who knows? Maybe we can try again in the future. Maybe."

Roman clung to those maybes. But he clung more to the disappointment.

"How about you get prepped?" Ezra wrapped his hands around Roman's waist and eyed a drawer where they kept douches. "I'm feeling kind of feisty tonight, and I know usually we focus on oral so you can—"

"No, totally fine," Roman quickly interrupted. If this would make Ezra happy, he'd get ready. If Ezra was happy, then he'd forget he was disappointed, and Roman believed it would make everything better.

Ezra rested while Roman gathered his things and headed off to the showers. He figured he might as well get fully cleaned up. The perfumy body washes used to irritate his skin, but Ezra liked the smell, and honestly, so did Roman. He preferred the fruity ones, but it wasn't easy buying top-shelf hygiene products.

When Roman arrived at the showers, he waited for it to empty out. Nothing quite like douching in front of an audience. Once he had a modicum of privacy, Roman got to work and lay on his side, semi tilted to wait out the rinse cycle so to speak. After he'd cleaned up and doublechecked himself, he went right to the showers and hopped in. The cold hit hard, but he didn't want to keep Ezra waiting any longer than necessary.

Drying off as quickly as possible, Roman wrapped the damp towel around his waist and went to the sink to freshen up. He primped himself a bit, styling his ruffled pink hair so it'd dry exactly how Ezra liked.

"Look at you, pretty as a picture." Jake the Snake strutted into the bathroom, a man on either side of him and a hungry expression on his face. "Getting all dolled up for date night?"

Roman ignored him and finished brushing his teeth.

"Good, you can really get it far back there, can't you?" Jake invaded Roman's space, watching him brush. "No gag reflex anymore?"

Roman choked from the question, then spit the last of the paste from his mouth and rinsed.

"Ah, so just when you're handling something big at the right angles?" Jake nodded. "I can help train that outta you."

"Pass," Roman finally said, collecting his things and preparing to leave.

"Wasn't a request." Jake grabbed Roman's arm.

"Get off." Roman shrugged loose, and Jake dramatically stepped back, playing as if he'd somehow been miraculously undone.

One of the men who'd stepped into the showers with Jake moved forward, and Roman fought back every instinct engrained in his head. Ezra had taught him to pause, to fall back, to listen to him, but Roman knew from too many years of fighting to never back down. He'd always known how to defend himself. He wouldn't let this happen. Couldn't.

Roman knocked the second man back into the third, then used the weight of both men's collision to drop them to the floor. When Jake swept in, sneaky as always, Roman was prepared as he'd been every single time Jake made a move on him.

Without a second of hesitation, Roman punched Jake square in the nose, then pulled back and used the open palm of his other hand to fucking break it apart.

Jake roared. Blood gushed everywhere. The other men scrambled to their feet to assist. They couldn't do anything—Roman knew that much.

Roman lifted his fists, fighting every shaky impulse back. He was twelve again, standing up to his father for the first time after training for months on how to snap back and finally put an end to everything. Unlike then, Roman wouldn't back down. He'd actually tasted combat now. He'd fought off Jake and his crew in and out of the arena. He could do this. He didn't need Ezra.

"Take another step, and you're facing the champion." Roman tried so hard to be assertive, to send his fear to his opponents, to make them quake.

"You're no fucking champion," Jake spat, blood gushing down his face.

"I'm the champion's friend," Roman said, needing Ezra more than he realized. "You don't wanna piss him off."

"You're his bitch, nothing more." Jake spit a bloody loogie onto the floor. "You're just his favorite slut to break in."

Roman shook at this.

"But I had eyes for that ass first." Jake pushed himself up off the floor. "He broke you in, sure. But I'm gonna break you so much harder."

Roman steadied his stance, shifting his gaze between Jake and his men, while he backed away to the door.

"When I'm done showing you your place, and you're bloody and bruised and broken in every way you can fathom and so many more you've yet to experience, you'll ask me, nay beg me, to fuck you a little bit harder the next time."

Roman paused at the doorway.

"Toodaloo, sweetness." Jake waved his fingers in a farewell and puckered his lips. "Be seeing you real soon, best believe it."

Chapter Sixteen

Roman took a few heavy breaths before he walked back into his cell. His towel show from the showers back to his room definitely caught more attention than he expected, but he hoped to smooth things over before going into the details. Ditching his clothes wasn't exactly the plan.

After catching his breath, Roman stepped inside with a red-faced smile and a playful strut he hoped would be enough to turn the conversation. Ezra quirked a brow, studying Roman from his chair.

"And where are your clothes?"

"I'm just really excited," Roman said, forcing a smile.

He knew he needed to explain, needed to tell Ezra about the altercation, but he'd already caused a minor scene at the syndicate meeting today and would basically be ruining Ezra's friendship or alliance or whatever with Jake. Roman wanted to ease Ezra into the news. He wanted to help him relax, remind him why he liked Roman to begin with.

"So, you ran here in just a towel?"

Roman stepped closer to Ezra's chair and dropped his towel.

"What can I say? You really get me worked up."

"Yeah, and you really get everyone else worked up." Ezra's expression fell flat; only the anger in his eyes remained. "You think I didn't hear about that scuffle?"

How? Roman had literally just left the showers, escaped Jake. How had Ezra already heard about the near incident? An incident, but Roman couldn't call it that. Nothing happened. Nothing.

"I have eyes everywhere." Ezra spun a hand around, gesturing. "You were gonna let Finnegan treat you that way and say nothing?"

"No, I was." Roman paused, embarrassed, ashamed, regretting his silence. "I just didn't wanna make a big deal out of it. I didn't wanna ruin your night."

"Embarrassing me was better?"

"What? No. Never." Roman shook his head. "I was fine. I handled it."

"Oh, you handled it. Did he apologize? Did he regret his choices?" Ezra stomped toward the door. "I'm finding him and handling this."

"Wait—"

"Stay here until I'm back."

Roman stood alone and naked, awaiting Ezra's return.

Dinner time had come and gone, and lights out would follow in another two hours. Roman had redressed while he waited. His stomach gurgled, and he rifled through the desk drawers, grabbing a couple snack goods. He considered all the prep work he put into getting himself ready for a passionate evening with Ezra and figured that was probably off the table.

Part of him anxiously awaited Ezra's return, worried what Jake might do, what his crew would do. Another part of him buried that concern with sweets and the knowledge that Ezra was no fool. He didn't do reckless; he didn't do foolish. Everything about Ezra was calculating. The problem was that so was everything about Jake "the Snake" Finnegan.

"Well, well, well, if it isn't my favorite boy in the whole wide world." Jake breezed into the cell, whistling as he took in Roman.

He dropped his snack, eyed up Jake, and tried to prepare for the worst.

Jake's eyes were swollen, dark rings from the bruising that spread across his face like a blotchy painting. Roman didn't see any rage in his eyes, any aggravation at the massive bandage that covered Jake's nose. The man appeared as carefree and dangerous as he always did.

"Here I thought I was your favorite boy in the whole wide world." Ezra slapped a hand on Jake's back as he trudged on in after.

What the hell was happening? They were smiling, laughing, acting buddy-buddy like nothing had happened between them.

"Favorite man," Jake corrected, turning to wink at Roman to ensure he caught the distinct difference. He did.

"What's going on?"

"We worked out our differences," Ezra said, arm flung over Jake's shoulder. "Come here."

Roman anxiously obeyed.

"We realized it was just a big misunderstanding."

Misunderstanding? Roman nearly boiled over at that, but when Ezra swung an arm around Roman too, he worked to settle his emotions for Ezra's sake. Roman couldn't stand this hold Jake had over Ezra. Since saving his life during an arena event, Ezra continued giving this psychopath the benefit of the doubt. Jake had attempted to assault Roman, and all Ezra could manage was that it was a misunderstanding.

"Can I talk to you?"

"Absolutely." Ezra smiled, tightening his hold around Jake's neck.

"Alone."

"Well, we can't talk and be alone because then you'd be alone and unable to talk to me," Ezra stated with a perplexed expression. "Unless by talk, you really mean communicate, in which case you could most certainly communicate alone in the form of a letter and then pass it along to me when you are no longer alone."

"Can I talk to you without Jake here?" Roman snapped, a bit more aggressive than he intended, a bit more aggressive than Ezra liked. Taking a calming breath, Roman let the rage fizzle away because he wasn't mad at Ezra.

Jake raised his arms in surrender and stepped away until he reached the door where he stood watch, clearly not offering real privacy.

Not that anyone expected it in Marlow Penitentiary.

"What happened to taking care of things?" Roman asked in a not-so-hushed whisper as his glare fell on Jake.

Jake, who'd gone to playing with the door and shooting the men a minxy grin, much like a devilish cat about to pounce.

"I did take care of things," Ezra insisted, stealing Roman's attention.

"By bringing him back here?"

"By smoothing things over." Ezra brushed Roman's face, gentle but controlling. "It's important not to make enemies of everyone for any little reason."

Roman scoffed, drowning in his thoughts, his resentments, his *little reasons* for not wanting to be around Jake Finnegan.

"I'm uncomfortable around him," Roman said as nicely as he could possibly fathom when, in reality, he wanted to finish what he'd started in the showers.

It was a level of fury Roman had long since learned to bury, and despite the discomfort of Jake's proximity, Roman did secretly relish the feelings of anger. It wasn't quite palpable but the closest to finding himself in a long time. He wanted to punch Jake again and again until he broke every bone in his body; he wanted to punch Jake for every bottled-up resentment he held over the last several months; he wanted to punch Jake for everything wrong in the world. And then he wanted to punch Jake a few more times for good measure.

"I know he's not your favorite person," Ezra said with a yawn. "But I think you just need to relax a little. He's actually not too terrible."

"And how are you suddenly so relaxed?" Roman asked since the last time he spoke to Ezra, he wanted to slaughter Jake too. "Are you okay?"

"High," Ezra said.

"Hello?"

"No," Ezra said with a laugh that he buried in Roman's neck, kissing and licking and giggling the entire time. "I'm high."

Roman raised his brows in concern and confusion. At least that explained the bizarre behavior. "And why are you high exactly?"

"It was to help discuss matters," Ezra said as he wrapped a hand around Roman's neck, waving Jake back over to them.

"Did you really need to discuss things high?" Roman asked, giving Ezra a pleading expression.

"I find it's the best way to smooth out an argument," Jake said.

"You know what I think the best solution to smooth out problems is?" Ezra asked.

"Don't attack people in the showers, maybe?" Roman shrugged as if stating the simplest of details to a life of proper etiquette.

"Easier said than done when you're strutting around all cute and kissable." Jake winked, much to Roman's disgust.

"I think we should all just kiss and make up," Ezra professed, quite loudly and clearly lost on his high. "It's the best way to resolve a resolution. Solve a solution. Revolve a solve?"

Roman glared at Jake's grinning face.

Ezra gave Jake a peck. Ezra gave Roman a peck. "Come on now."

Roman rolled his eyes and gave Jake a peck.

"I don't feel like we really made up," Jake said, phony disappointment in his tone.

Ezra kissed Jake again, a bit more fire in his touch, a bit more primal, even growling a bit as he turned back to Roman and kissed his lips with a passionate force and just a touch of a bite.

"Now, that is how you mend fences." Jake laughed.

"*Fuck it,*" Roman thought, snatching Jake by the back of his hair and locking his gaze.

"Look at you, all aggressive and such." Jake chomped at the air. "Rawr. I like it."

"Just don't have any more misunderstandings," Roman said firmly.

"Oh, definitely." Ezra waved a finger. "I don't fuck around about choices, Jake. Don't mess with him again without making sure he's okay with it, or I'll have to kill you."

As if Roman would ever be okay with Jake's advances.

"Defending your little princess' honor?" Jake batted his eyes.

Ezra glared, green eyes furious before he blinked away the rage in a way he often did around Roman. "It'll just be such a hassle to have to find someone else with your connections, Jakie Jake."

"All righty." Jake held up his hand like taking an oath. "No more funny stuff."

Roman rolled his eyes, over this whole thing and hoping when Ezra's high wore off, so would his patience for Jake.

Jake leaned in, gently kissing Roman and parting his lips with his tongue. Roman nearly retched, but his tongue slipped out as quickly as it slipped in, and Jake backed off.

"Kiss over. Total gentleman."

Roman almost felt relieved until the chalky grain of a small pill moved along his tongue. Roman went to spit the pill, but Jake slapped a hand over his mouth.

"Relax," Jake hissed. "It's my way of saying sorry, saying all's well that ends well."

Roman fumed, nostrils flaring. He looked at Ezra, who smiled.

"Come on," Jake insisted, bandaged face on full display. "Don't offend me twice in one day."

"We could roll together," Ezra insisted, nuzzling his head against Roman's. "It's such a mellow rush."

"It's nothing serious." Jake smiled. "Cross my heart and hope to fly."

This wasn't the first time Roman had taken a pill without a name. Though he generally trusted the person who handed him a party favor at the frat house. Roman didn't trust Jake, but he absolutely trusted Ezra. If Ezra could handle himself with a little happy pill, then so could Roman. He reluctantly swallowed.

"See, you're good. I'm good. We're all good." Jake stared Roman down before skirting around him and over to the bottom bunk. He sprawled out and took a seat. "Now that we're flying high for a few, let's talk business."

"No," Ezra said, ushering Roman to follow him as he circled the room. "Now is the worst time to talk business."

"I find I have my best ideas with a little help from big pharma."

Ezra led Roman all the way back around until they stopped at his bed. The pair sat down, and Roman ended up sandwiched between Ezra and Jake.

"The only business I wanna discuss is minimizing Sullivan's hold," Ezra said plainly.

"You fucking hate him, too." Jake leaned forward excitedly. "Oh, I've wanted that prick dead for years. Say the word, friend, and I can increase our territory by…oh, fucking math. By a lot."

"And provoke a war with his guys, no thanks." Ezra placed a hand on Roman's thigh, gently rubbing it. "I don't kill what I can use. Sullivan has authority he no longer requires but skills and connections that could be beneficial."

"What'd you have in mind?" Jake waved his fingers around, adding the tiniest flickers of light between them that caught Roman's eye.

"Just thinking of ways to humble Sullivan." Ezra squeezed Roman's thigh, reminding him of how Ezra had humbled him, how he'd found a use for Roman but taught him some lessons along the way.

He doubted Ezra had the same intentions for one of the five men running this facility, but with Ezra, Roman had no clue.

"Someone's feeling it, feeling it, feeling it." Jake shook Roman, waking him from the fog that had struck. He wasn't sure if Jake was repeating himself a lot or if the echo was part of the high. It could be either. Jake was fucked up, too.

When Roman looked to Ezra, he seemed completely steady, talking more firmly about business with each passing minute. In fact, the more confused Roman felt, the more stable Ezra seemed.

"Riding that wave." Jake leaned over and slapped Roman's chest, startling him with the rush it sent.

His body was the wave, and his skin rippled in every direction, giving him the most euphoric sensation.

"Now you know why I'm always such a chipper person." Jake kissed Roman again, the taste chalky and a little fruity, too.

Roman laughed, lost on himself more than anything else at this point.

"I'd love to keep this party going," Jake said, running his hand through Roman's hair. "But it's gonna be lights out soon."

"I have a bit of finesse," Ezra said.

"Oh, yeah?" Jake perked up, smiling at Roman, who smiled back. He was lost in Jake's eyes, like he was a reflection of himself. "You up for a little partying?"

"Huh?" Roman leaned into the head scratches, finding they reached his brain. Jake's touch made the room pop with colors Roman had forgotten about in this bland prison.

"Maybe bring a few friends." Jake looked at Ezra expectingly.

"You know the kind of clout it takes to swing an after-hours cell party?"

"We'll be super quiet." Jake pressed a finger to Roman's

lips, shushing him.

Roman playfully shushed himself, uncertain what was happening.

"Fuck it." Ezra shrugged. "I'll see what I can do."

Roman turned his attention to Ezra, who seemed levelheaded at this point. It eased the tension in the back of Roman's mind, whispers of worries he didn't need to concern himself with. Those concerns died out quickly when the next wave of his high hit. This feeling was fantastic but fleeting. He'd be steady in a few minutes. He'd be as calm as Ezra looked.

"What do you think?" Ezra asked. "It's your choice."

That was a comforting reminder. Roman never had to worry, to truly worry with Ezra. He always had a choice in things; even if he'd finally accepted his gilded cage, it was always left open for him to fly away whenever he wanted.

"Flapping your wings?" Jake asked, noting the sway of Roman's hands. "If you wanna fly, all you gotta do is say pretty, pretty please."

Everything faded away, and Roman didn't want to surrender the high just yet. For the first time in years, he felt free, truly free, lost in a fuzzy world of possibility.

"I'm up for whatever." Roman smiled at Ezra before collapsing back onto the bed.

"That was the plan, sweetness." Jake continued running his hands through Roman's hair, whispering sweet nothings he couldn't follow, but Roman laughed when Jake laughed, and he smiled when Jake smiled, and he kissed Jake back when chalk hit his lips, and even when the kiss was just a kiss. It was a surprise Roman hadn't expected.

Chapter Seventeen

Rustling in the room startled Roman awake. His entire body ached. His head felt like he'd been hit with a hammer several times over. The light stung his eyes when Ezra moved from serving as a buffer shadow rifling at the desk to crossing over to the doorframe.

"You heading to breakfast?" Roman's throat still throbbed from last night. "I'll join you."

He performed for hours, he serviced, and remembered… He remembered more than he realized as he squeezed his head in a futile effort to fight off the pulsing pain.

Ezra stared with a raised brow, questioning Roman, confused by something Roman had done. He couldn't quite place it yet.

"You already missed lunch," he said, edge in his voice. "Just sleep away the day, I don't give a fuck."

Roman stared, completely dumbfounded. How had he lost so much time?

After Ezra left, Roman lay in bed, trying to piece together last night. He knew what had happened. He recalled so much with ease but desperately held down the memories beneath the floorboards of his mind. He needed pieces, bits at a time, not the eruption of ecstasy turned sour. Mostly, Roman wanted to see if he'd missed something with Ezra's mood.

"Swallow," Jake had said. He'd said it a lot and for a lot of different reasons.

Ezra hadn't looked mad, not like he did now. Not like he did when storming out of the room, leaving Roman alone, so Roman tried to figure out if he'd done something to upset Ezra. His mouth was so dry now that his tongue ran along the inside of his cheeks with a scaly texture. Not a drop of moisture left.

"Oh, he likes it," Jake had whispered. "Don't you, you fucker?"

He seemed to slither from one end of the room to the other, following Roman as he made his way through partners. More of the crew had shown up than expected. Not at first. It was Roman and Ezra and Jake. Roman was happy they were happy. Then it was Roman and Jake and two men. He remembered Jake insisting on another kiss. Remembered chanting. Encouragement. Roman shook away the thoughts.

Jake wanted to have fun. Jake wanted Roman to be fun. Roman wanted Ezra to have fun. Ezra kept insisting Roman could help everyone have fun. But whenever Roman looked at Ezra, in the flashes of sweat and kisses and grunting and sex and everything else, Roman couldn't recall once finding

Ezra happy. His eyes were angry. They were trained on Roman, and he kept trying to make him happy. Kept listening to his suggestions. Jake's suggestions. The room spun. Everyone laughed. Roman laughed. Maybe.

If he did, that might explain why his teeth ached so much. Not the same as his throat, which had been reamed raw, or his jaw, which had been stretched wide for what must've been forever.

Roman lay in bed, ignoring the loud flashes of memories that clawed at his head, the same way hands clawed at his flesh. He couldn't get the images of hands raking over his skin, slapping him, squeezing him, caressing him. He didn't want to remember everything he'd done, everything he'd agreed to, everything he craved while the room swirled and Roman's mind danced free.

When Roman finally had the energy to stand, he made it to the other side of the room and saw his mortifying reflection. Bloodshot eyes. Red marks on his face. A permanent marker had been used to fill in around his eyes to make Roman look like a raccoon. He recalled that moment. Not specifically with his eyes but the marker itself. Someone had written something somewhere else; he wasn't sure where now. He'd laughed it off, though, and playfully told them to stop.

Roman huffed, exhausted at the idea of how long it'd take to wash off.

He supposed the marker was better than the bruises on his neck. At one point, Jake had wrapped an arm around his throat, holding him close, pinning Roman in place as he bucked behind him, both panting in union with the rough thrusts. When Roman whimpered, Jake only rutted harder into him, strengthening his chokehold. But Roman didn't think the grip was that tight. He'd been in worse headlocks during actual fights. Hell, he'd lost his title thanks to a chokehold. No, opening his unbuttoned shirt revealed the source and reason for the bruising.

"Bruise me/Use me Daddy" was written across his chest in marker and served as a welcome invitation last night. It wasn't the only thing scrawled across his abdomen. Words written in various handwriting covered him everywhere his eyes flitted, and he knew there was so much more written on the parts of his body not exposed in front of the mirror.

'Cum Slut.' 'Cheap Toy.' 'Hole For Rent.' 'Good Boy.' And so much more he ignored after he read 'bitch' written below his 'Bested' tattoo as if to cement where he'd ended up full circle, much in the way Jake always promised.

"Take it, take it all," Jake had panted, breath eating away at the back of Roman's ear, the hot heat of his breath on Roman's face, the loud command from across the room as Roman worked. Everywhere he went, Jake commanded him.

The worst part was Roman had said yes. He held onto that stretched truth, ignoring the twine of reality quickly unraveling. He allowed this. It only happened because he allowed it. That was what this was, what he repeated, so he didn't choke on his own breath.

"Fuck," Roman groaned as the night's events surfaced one unwanted fragment at a time.

He couldn't stay here. His skin was clammy, his body was sore, his insides burned, and he was a complete and utter wreck. Roman grabbed his things and headed to the showers, hoping no one would be using them at this time of day.

As he undressed in the showers, he got a closer look at his body and his fun night. Welts, bruises, and more phrases trailed in every direction of his torso, arms, and legs. Roman's ribs hurt when he lifted his arms to adjust the shower nozzle. It was like he'd been punched in his sides. A lot.

The cold water was too much, so he waited for the warm to finally run through. He rinsed and washed and scrubbed and did it all again and again, taking his body one layer at a time. He must've scrubbed his face ten times over before moving to his chest, before tackling his arms one by one. Nothing felt clean enough. He didn't even want to work his way past his waist. He knew what waited for him. He knew what he'd done.

Carefully, he rubbed his butt and winced when his hand went over a fresh sore. Not a sore. He craned his neck and caught a faint glimpse at his new tattoo.

A tattoo of tally marks ran across the right upper cheek of Roman's butt, and his chest nearly fell through the floor. It came back in waves. With each flash, the sharp sting.

"It'll be fun, sweetness," Jake had insisted. "Gotta ink you up. Way to remember the party."

One for every guy. Roman held his breath. He touched the tender skin and bit his lip from the hot pain radiating off the tattoo. They were black tallies, seven in total, and pooled with as much dried blood as they were with ink.

The last tally was further off. He remembered adding the seventh for Ezra. Even though Ezra wasn't in the mood to celebrate, wasn't in the mood for fun, he'd had fun with Roman many times before. They all had. They all would. Jake kept telling Roman about how much fun they were all having.

Roman agreed. Roman kissed Jake again and again to inhale more fun.

Each tally was more jagged than straight; somehow, they'd added the ink while still moving around, still using Roman, still having fun. Roman remembered the tattoo started on the bed. At some point, he was standing and complaining about it. Then Roman was bent over Ezra's chair, face buried in the cushions, finishing the tattoo, only Ezra wasn't there anymore. He'd come and gone, from what Roman recalled, or maybe he'd just moved around the room. It was so crowded inside, and Jake seemed to take up all the space, standing everywhere and nowhere all at once.

Every time a memory of sex surfaced, every time he remembered a new voice, a new order, a new encouraging request, Roman's stomach twisted into tighter knots. He wanted to hurl. Wanted to throw up everything left over from last night, throw up what remnants of the pills bubbling in his stomach remained. He raced out of the shower and over to the sink, but when he started dry heaving, the memories of puking up his guts last night returned.

Roman had said yes to Jake. All he thought was how it'd make Ezra happy. Roman had agreed to two of Jake's friends. Because what was the big deal of having fun with a few friends? Ezra always wanted Roman to treat his friends well. Somewhere along the way, though, somehow Roman had accepted more.

More fun.

More men.

More sex.

He'd tried everything with everyone, and the flash of Jake's kisses came crawling back to him. The pills he'd passed, the little song he'd hummed about swallowing a drop of fun before swallowing a lot of loads. Roman couldn't remember how many men he'd blown. He hoped the number didn't fair much higher than what they'd tattooed on his ass.

"It's a party," Jake hissed, kissed, missed Roman's lips more times than not. "You having fun, sweetness?"

Roman didn't say yes. It hurt to speak; his throat was as sore then as now. Most of the time, when someone asked, he couldn't exactly answer that given second, occupied, busy, helping someone get off.

"Jesus fucking Christ, Roman." Levi's voice hit like a battering ram, bulldozing through the last shreds of stability Roman had left.

He wobbled, gripping the sink, and almost certain he'd fall face-first into it.

"What the fuck happened to you?"

"Nothing," Roman could barely force the word out.

"Who did this?" Levi approached. "Was it Ezra? That sick fuck has gone too far."

"No, it wasn't." Roman tried to swallow the words. He couldn't explain it to Levi, couldn't explain he did this to himself, that he'd allowed it to happen. Levi wouldn't understand.

"Who did this to you?" Levi stared, silently waiting for a reply.

Roman couldn't answer. He wouldn't answer. He was tired and ashamed and guilty of letting things get a little too fun.

Levi didn't wait silently much longer. He continued badgering Roman with questions he didn't have answers to. It kept stirring up memories, kept knocking Roman's thoughts around in all the wrong ways, kept making the room spin, until finally, Roman couldn't stand anymore.

He didn't remember Levi catching him, but he'd fallen so much last night the pain was a familiar one. Someone had caught him, carried him, called out to him. But Roman was too tired to look, to answer.

When he'd finally rested enough, he woke up inside the infirmary with a nurse standing beside him and Levi sitting far off, eyes locked on Roman with this unblinking stare.

"Tox screen came back," she said, and Roman couldn't tell if she looked annoyed or offended or something else altogether. "Had quite a lot…"

As she trailed off, he couldn't grasp the number of drugs he'd done. He remembered Jake's kiss. He remembered the chalky pills he shared. He remembered Jake insisting he swallow. That might've been another memory, though. He didn't remember any other drugs. Any other party favors. Just more kisses.

Levi's puppy-dog blue eyes at the opposite end of the room hurt more than anything last night. More than any fight in the arena. More than any trauma Roman had long since buried. He felt like he'd betrayed Levi, partying it up and nearly overdosing after everything Levi had done to get clean, to fix his life. And Roman shouldn't feel guilty when he didn't even remember taking half of the drugs in his system, accepting them, but the nurse's glower and warning lecture about overdosing made Roman believe he might actually have a problem.

"You're pretty banged up. We did our best treating the cuts and scrapes." She paused for a long minute, the longest minute of Roman's life, as she looked down at him, on him. Both. "And tended to the tattoo."

"Thank you," Roman forced out.

"We'd also like to run…"

When the word of kits came up, internal injuries, bleeding, Roman shook his head in protest before clawing his way out of the bed. The nurse didn't argue with him on the matter, didn't ask again, didn't fight a battle she'd probably been told 'no' to a million times before. And Roman didn't need anything. Nothing had happened. He'd tried to have fun. He'd had too much fun. That was it.

Levi cut Roman off as he grabbed his things and got dressed.

"What are you doing?" he asked.

"Going back to my room," Roman said. "I'm fucking exhausted."

"You are not going back there," Levi said with such demand in his voice Roman had to lower his head, sheepish and shaky, in order to respond.

"I don't have a choice."

"You always have a choice."

That fucking hit hard. It knocked the wind right out of Roman. Nearly dropped him to the floor. This all came back to the fact Roman had choices. Choices that led him here. Choices he had to live with. But he couldn't remember the last time in his life he had a real choice. Every choice offered felt like a trap, another prison, a deceit waiting to watch him fall and beat him down harder than even last night. Roman hated his so-called choices. Hated his options. Hated his life.

"You have choices," Roman snarled, resenting how free and healthy and strong and capable Levi had become. Roman kept wilting and withering, and Levi continued improving.

Roman wondered if he was the obstacle in his friend's life, the thing holding Levi back. Maybe it had nothing to do with Ezra giving him a bit of protection, nothing to do with Roman's sacrifice. Maybe Levi was just meant to do well, and Roman was destined to fail.

Burying the thoughts, Roman bolted ahead and made his way into the hallway, away from ears and watchful eyes.

"We can get your room changed," Levi insisted, following Roman out of the infirmary. "Get you sent to my cellblock, room with me. My cellmate hates me. Old guy. Hates everyone. He's funny, though."

"Yeah, the warden's definitely gonna sign off on a room change," Roman said with a bit more sarcasm than he believed he had left in him. "And what happens if I move?"

Roman didn't want to say it. Didn't want to point out how last night would just happen again and again, only it'd be worse. It wouldn't be fun. Christ, how he clung to last night being fun gone a bit too far. It was the only thing that held the band to his sanity. If what he thought had happened actually happened, happened under Ezra's protection, happened after so many months of service, of loyalty, of commitment—no! Ezra wouldn't have allowed it. Ezra protected Roman, and Roman served Ezra. It was a balance. It kept Roman safe. It was the only thing that kept Roman safe now. What happened last night was Roman's idea. Roman encouraged it, suggested it, said yes to it. Roman caused this.

"It was just a little partying too hard," Roman said, shoving past Levi. "Some of us can actually have fun without ODing."

Regret stabbed Roman the second the words left his lips, the second he twisted his own pain into something that'd hurt Levi.

"I didn't mean that," Roman said, unable to look at Levi's face. "I just got a little too wild is all."

"You got too wild, or that piece of shit made you?"

"I did this," Roman insisted. "I said yes. I wanted this."

Levi grabbed ahold of Roman and pulled him close. The tight grip made his wrists throb.

"This is what you wanted?" Levi showed Roman his bruised arms, and then he touched his neck ever so gently, turning Roman's head. "And that? You said yes to getting choked out?"

He hadn't said yes to everything. But he hadn't said no. He never said no. But he knew he had a choice. Ezra always gave him a choice. Roman clung to that almost as hard as Levi clung to Roman's wrist.

Roman shook his head and pulled away from Levi. He was confusing things, confusing Roman.

"Sup, pretty pink princess." Jake breezed down the empty hallway, practically materializing from nowhere.

Roman knew this wasn't random. He'd fucked Jake last night—well, been fucked by him—and now he'd shown up to the infirmary. This was a warning many men got if they thought something happened that hadn't happened.

"I had so much fun last night," Jake said with a swagger. "I've spent years dreaming of what we could do together; I had no idea it'd be this fun."

Fun.

Roman hunched, quelling Jake's voice, silencing the memories his happiness carried. The light lilt in his voice, the joy in his raspy whisper, it carried a tidal wave of memories Roman didn't want to piece together.

"Show me what a good bitch you are," Jake's venomous voice rang loudly in Roman's thoughts. "Show me how much you like it."

Heavy, sweaty bodies one after another in such a haze the only thing Roman could truly track was the sound of slapping skin and his muffled whimpers. Then came the gentle smacks. Lips pressed to his. Lips pressed to his neck. Lips whispering in his ear.

"The things you've learned with the champion," Jake had said. "The things I can still teach you."

"Get. The fuck. Away from him." The bass in Levi's voice dropped to absolute gravel as he growled out each word slowly and threateningly.

"Oh, bestie boyfriend has a temper." Jake took the attitude the same way he took everything, as an open invitation to taunt and provoke. "I remember you used to be so nice and quiet."

"Not anymore." Levi snarled, fists clenched and body an instant from attacking. "Back. The fuck. Away."

"And if I don't?" Jake tilted his head, enticed by Levi.

Levi didn't respond, merely fumed with each breath, chest and biceps flexed, ready for a confrontation.

Curiously, Jake poked Roman's face. Before he could even attempt something else, Levi snatched Jake by the wrist and throat and slammed him against the wall. When Jake resisted, Levi headbutted him, sending a splash of fresh red to the bandages over Jake's nose, and twisted his arm further back. It was only when Jake gurgled and gasped and his legs gave out to the fight that Levi released him.

With a helping shove, Levi pushed Jake to the ground and pressed his foot over one of Jake's hands. Roman hadn't noticed at first, but Jake was reaching for something pocketed, a blade most likely, and Levi put a quick and painful stop to it.

"Don't ever go near Roman again," Levi said. "Don't look at him. Don't talk to him. Don't even breathe the same fucking air as him."

"But we were breathing the same fucking air while I fucked him for hours," Jake said with a laugh. "Can't expect me to give up on that pretty pink princess after he let me wreck that pretty pink hole."

Levi pressed his foot further until Roman could hear Jake's hand crack. He shouted and raged, but all Levi did was lean forward and punch Jake until he silenced his own outbursts.

"You're feistier than I remember." Jake pointed a finger with his free hand. "I considered bending you over once upon a time. I like 'em big and dumb, but meek boys bore me. You didn't have any fight in you, and railing the fight outta a guy is half the fun. Just ask sweetness over there."

Levi looked down on Jake, still crushing his hand, still debating whether to attack him. Roman could see it in his eyes, so furious and unlike Levi. Roman hated himself for letting Levi sink this low, throw away all his kind thoughts and turn violent. Especially for someone like Roman.

"Might have to revisit this romance." Jake gestured to himself and Levi as if they were having a moment instead of mutual threats. "I wonder if you'll cry as much as your boyfriend."

Roman froze when Jake's eyes turned to him, a viper's stare, a gaze so venomous it nearly made Roman collapse.

"I spent so much effort trying to get you, and to my surprise, you just handed that ass right over," Jake said with a laugh. "I'm gonna treat you well, though. Especially since the champion's bored with you. Don't you worry, I'll never get bored with you, sweetness. Got a whole lotta guys who'll never get bored with you either."

"Shut up," Levi commanded.

"Seriously," Jake said, looking up at Levi. "This fire is hot. I can't wait till the champion revokes his protection on you, too. The both of ya can be tally butt buddies." Jake turned to Roman, feeding off the shame that oozed from Roman. "Gonna show your little boyfriend here your new art?"

With that, Levi had enough and punched Jake in the face.

"Stop laughing," he demanded, furious fists hitting Jake again and again.

Jake didn't stop laughing. It was a haunting reminder of last night. Roman couldn't take it. Couldn't believe what Jake had said about Ezra. He couldn't believe any of it.

"Wait," Levi shouted, chasing after Roman and abandoning a cackling Jake.

Roman didn't stop; he couldn't stop. He had to find Ezra. He had to fix this.

When Roman reached the champion's suite, he waited outside, trying to catch his breath. Ezra rustled with things inside, and Roman wasn't ready to face him.

He replayed Jake's words, Jake's kisses, everything else Jake did with him.

"There a reason you're just standing there?" The edge in Ezra's voice hadn't lessened.

Roman shook his head and slowly made his way inside.

"If you're gonna party hard, maybe don't go running to the infirmary because you can't hold your what-ever-the-fucks you were popping," Ezra said it so annoyed, so matter-of-factly as if he'd watched the events unfold and saw a completely different night, as if he hadn't taken and encouraged the pills to begin with, like all this was some inconvenience brought down on Ezra.

Roman hadn't been partying for the sake of it. It was for Ezra, right? It was to patch things up. He hadn't said no to the kisses and candy that came with it because… Roman didn't know anymore.

"I didn't wanna upset you," Roman said. "That's why I hung out with Jake. I'd messed things up with you two, so I thought—"

"I told you to make things right," Ezra interrupted. "Told you to be nice. I didn't tell you to fuck him. Didn't tell you to fuck his whole crew. That was all you."

It wasn't. He hadn't. Roman remembered Ezra's voice, his encouragement. No. Now the night didn't make sense.

"I didn't fuck everyone." Roman sank in the shame of clarifying that fact.

"Might as well have," Ezra scoffed. "Look, if that's what you're into, whatever. You do you."

"What?" Roman trembled. "No… I don't… I'm not... That's not what I want."

"Maybe Jake's right." Ezra shrugged, making his way to the door. "Maybe you two have more in common than I realize. Maybe this whole forcing your friendship is a waste of my time, your time. Maybe you'd be happy with Jake."

"No." Roman rushed over to the door. "It's not a waste. It's not forced. You're the best person I know."

Roman didn't understand what was happening, what he'd done wrong. Ezra was mad at him for something he suggested; he always had a say in Roman's choices. He helped Roman make the right choices.

"I gotta think, Roman," Ezra said, taking his leave and abandoning Roman in the cell.

He'd called him by his name, which he never did. He always used a pet name. Roman sat alone for hours dwelling on that fact, dwelling on how Ezra would likely stay gone until light's out.

Getting ready for bed, Roman changed his clothes, tended to the new tattoo, and tried to wipe away what remained of the permanent marker drawn on him. When he caught sight of letters written on his lower back, Roman turned more to the mirror and almost broke out into tears at what he read.

"Property of Jake the Snake Finnegan and Crew, Inc."

It was spelled out like Roman was some type of fucking product. A fuckable product. One that Jake would pass around to anyone and everyone. One that he'd already enjoyed passing around. One Ezra had grown sick of because Roman never did anything right.

Roman had offended Ezra, and he didn't know how to fix this situation. He didn't know how to undo this mess, a mess he'd caused.

Roman fell to the floor and cried. He cried in a way he never allowed himself to cry. He cried like he had before his father beat it out of him. He cried like he had after murdering Stacy. He cried like he had when they brought down his sentence, and the rest of his life ended.

It hadn't dawned on him how awful it'd be. His incarceration. How exhausting and painful and grueling every second would be. It hadn't been awful, not like now, not while he kept his head above water. But he floundered once, just once, and now he just kept sinking, kept drowning, kept falling deeper and deeper, losing pieces of himself along the way. Those parts of Roman floated up, lost to the current like the air bubbles he'd never get back.

Roman sobbed, alone in his cell with no answers to the problems he faced, no way out, no way to fix them.

Chapter Eighteen

Alarms rang from out of nowhere, and without a word, the entire prison was locked down. Even the guards were stuck in the cellblocks where they were posted until SWAT retrieved them one small group at a time. It was chaos. They had to usher inmates out halfway through the mandated lockdown. People kept demanding the prisoners remain in their cells while other instructions came down, insisting the buildings had to be evacuated.

Pure fucking chaos.

Roman didn't know what to make of it; he didn't have the energy to care. Every day since his incident…since his fun. He held that word close, praying for it to become reality. Every day since he looked back on the fun he had, it became more excruciating than the next. Nothing Roman did managed to piece together the events properly. Oh, he recalled everything vividly, even when he lied to himself and said most had faded away to a haze of shame. No, the only part he couldn't recall was where he messed up, where he'd offended Ezra. Memories kept screaming that Ezra wanted this, that he wanted Roman to do this, that he pressured it. Not pressured. Encouraged. Roman always needed encouragement.

Now, he remained close to Ezra even if the man continued acting cold toward him in the days since his fun with Jake. Roman held onto that word, held onto the misunderstanding as just that. The minute he let his walls down, the moment he actually considered it something more. Acknowledged what he already knew, he'd break into a billion pieces of shame.

When firetrucks arrived, Roman figured out why they prioritized evacuation. He also surmised they wanted a lockdown to determine who set it. Well, he guessed at that. As he and Ezra ended up stuck in the clustered crowd, he did his best to stay within a few feet per their arrangement. Not that Roman thought Ezra cared much about that anymore. Jake's words continued to haunt him, horrify him, and he tried to think of how he could make Ezra happy again. How they could be happy together again. Roman blamed himself. He didn't show enough respect to Ezra. He spent too much time resisting this arrangement. He wasn't good enough.

"I'll do better," he said in a low hush, too afraid to raise his voice, too frightened to be heard until he had a real apology to provide Ezra.

"They fucking killed him," someone said.

Ezra and Roman searched the crowd, conversations and speculation spreading almost as quickly as the fire that hit the prison.

It didn't take long for Roman to piece together the news. Cellblock D had been hit by the fire; their rec room had been burned down. Roman scanned the area, searching for Levi. He lived in that wing of the building. His heart surged at the idea the last time they saw each other, the last time they ever encountered one another, was much to Roman's shame. He couldn't fathom how he'd ever face Levi again, but the idea of never seeing him again sent more startling fear through him.

"Let's go," Ezra demanded, which Roman appreciated.

Their current spot offered him no real vantage point, and Roman desperately wanted to continue searching the crowd for Levi. He couldn't tell Ezra that, with the champion already annoyed by him, already bored of him.

When Roman bumped into one of Jake's pets, he flinched. The man was wispy and frail, eyes wide with exhaustion and bloodshot from whatever high coursed through him to make it another day. Roman trembled, staring into his future, seeing how much further he could fall and how terrible the collision would be.

"He's dead, you know," another person said.

The rumors of death had swept back around, this time carrying more intel alongside the gossip.

"They're all dead."

"Heard the fire was just to cover up the bodies."

"Stabbed him like fifty times."

Roman's breathing hitched as he continued listening, continued searching, continued worrying about everything all at once until finally, a familiar face offered him the smallest relief in this sea of chaos.

Opposite the crowd over by the firetrucks and ambulances, Levi sat with some EMTs being tended to with a small group of inmates covered in ash. He didn't appear burned or injured, but he looked completely devoid, like all his energy had been sapped.

Roman didn't care who'd been caught in the flames, how this had happened, or even what would befall him in the days to come. He took a bit of solace in Levi's safety and remained close to Ezra.

After hours of waiting, standing outside, and missing dinner, they finally allowed everyone back inside but relocated a bunch of inmates thanks to the loss of a cellblock. Levi ended up near Roman, and every part of him wanted to walk over, but shame and guilt held him back. Shame for what Levi knew about Roman's fun night, guilt for how he continued to upset Ezra.

As the night swept in and lights out came close, news finally came in some tangible form. Ezra had a guard provide him and a small group of his friends with the news. Roman was hesitant to stand among them, expecting the friends he'd already serviced to be among them, but Jake and his crew were nowhere in sight.

"They're all fucking dead," the C.O. said, her voice low and harsh and nervous.

Roman blinked, completely bewildered as the information unfolded. The fire had been intentional and possibly a cover. Someone lured and locked most of Jake Finnegan's crew inside the rec room and then set it on fire. They suffocated from the smoke, but a few were found with fatal cuts, too. They weren't the only ones.

Jake himself wasn't in the rec room, either lucky or unlucky enough to escape the trap. The few members of his crew who followed him out of the rec room ended up with their throats slashed in a nearby hallway. As for Jake, he'd been stabbed multiple times in the groin and left to bleed out.

"Forty-eight times?" Ezra scoffed, unconvinced.

"Look," the C.O. said with her hands up in disgust. "I know where I work and who I interact with, but some of you fuckers are downright disturbed."

"Did they find any evidence?"

"You mean aside from the bodies?" the guard asked with a roll of her eyes.

"No," Ezra snapped. "I mean, witnesses, footage, DNA. Something they can use to pin on a person."

She got really quiet and shook her head. Ezra seemed especially concerned from that point on.

Roman couldn't believe what he'd heard. Jake's entire crew had been killed. He wanted to smile, but then he recalled the violent brutality of Jake's death, and his stomach twisted with queasy confliction. There was absolutely no way Roman would mourn the death of Jake "the Snake" Finnegan, but he'd also never wish that type of carnage onto someone. Onto anyone.

The amount of rage it'd take to stab a person, to stab any living being, forty-eight times and in the groin. There was a severe degree of malice involved, someone who hated Jake and certainly hated his snake. Roman thought back to the pet he encountered, the guy who'd likely endured enough pain to certainly carry the rage necessary.

He shook away the thought. The guy he saw was too frail, too broken, too strung out. No, the person responsible had to be someone like Jake, a rival gang member perhaps. Roman continued studying Ezra's concerned expression as he questioned again and again about evidence until he was absolutely certain they didn't have any.

Roman's eyes widened. Ezra would absolutely have the strength for something like that. And he had left Roman alone in the cell before the fire was announced, barely returning before the lockdown started. But even Ezra couldn't attack his entire crew. He wouldn't have to, though. Ezra had built his own silent army of men during his stint as champion; he had the favor of the rest of the syndicate at Marlow Penitentiary.

Would he have the rage, though? Roman had seen the hidden undertones of fury behind Ezra's green eyes, but he thought only he provoked it. Maybe Ezra hadn't grown bored with Roman. Maybe he was mad that Roman offered himself over. Roman struggled to figure out Ezra's tests, what would make him happy, and he thought servicing Jake, patching things up with the crew, was what Ezra wanted in the bliss of a delirious high. Maybe Ezra didn't like the idea. Maybe he removed Jake.

After everyone settled in their cells, Roman stepped over to Ezra, who stood at their open doorway, staring out of the suite to the barred cells.

"Did you…" Roman paused, unsure if he wanted to know the answer. "I just want you to know if you… Well, if you had to do something…"

"For Christ's sake, just fucking speak," Ezra said through ground teeth.

"Did you get rid of Jake?"

Ezra's face fell flat.

"I'd understand, I just—"

"Why would you think that?"

"Because of what he said to me. Did to me. With me." Roman swallowed hard, quickly correcting more for his sake, his sanity, than anyone else's. "Because maybe you didn't like how he treated me."

Ezra smiled, chuckling a bit to himself as he reached out to caress Roman's face.

"You really are so fucking pathetic and stupid that you'd build up a fantasy like that in your head."

Roman's stomach dropped.

"You think I'd do something so outlandish for you? You? Roman fucking-pathetic Grayson." Ezra squeezed Roman's cheek, nails stabbing his skin. "You think you're worth that type of effort? No."

He shoved Roman back a step.

"I was actually hoping Jake would take your cheap ass off my hands."

"I'm sorry," Roman said, pressed against the wall and staring out at the cells, hoping no one saw this argument, hoping no one knew how he'd upset Ezra.

"Apologies from worthless whores mean nothing." Ezra spit. "I'm tired of you, tired of the headache your presence brings me. I'm just gonna hand you off to the next person who wants you. Let you be their problem. Hell, maybe we can have an auction, huh? I'll give you to the lowest bidder because you're not worth a goddamn thing."

Roman's eyes teared up, and it took everything not to break down and cry.

"And when you're passed around from one gang to the next," Ezra said, cupping his hands around Roman's face again. "I'll laugh at your agony. I'll smile at your defeat. I'll relish every day that you suffer."

"Why?" Roman finally began to cry, trying to understand how he'd ruined this friendship, where he'd failed to behave, how he'd let Ezra down.

"Because you broke me first, and it's about time you fucking understood why I've always hated you." Ezra released Roman and turned to go to sleep.

Roman stood silently at the open door in complete confusion by Ezra's comment, by the day's events, by what would happen to him soon enough.

Standing on the first floor with his arms wrapped around the bar cells was Levi. Levi pulled out a lighter and sparked a cigarette. It was against the rules, but inmates regularly smoked inside, same as the guards. The bizarre part was seeing Levi with a cigarette at all. He hated them and anything else that reminded him of the addictions he'd put down after being locked up.

Still, Levi took a deep drag and showed he'd watched the conversation unfold, then gave Roman a quiet, empathetic expression. Roman wanted to say something, to apologize for always falling apart in front of Levi, but he didn't have the strength to form any more words tonight.

Chapter Nineteen

Ezra ignored Roman in the days that followed. He didn't say a single word inside their shared cell. He didn't acknowledge Roman's presence at all. Still, Roman tiptoed around the room, worried one misstep would offend Ezra, and he'd suffer his wrath. Wrath to a rage Roman had seen stirring in him for months.

Roman left the room and went to the library so he could hide and cry and process everything. He sat on the floor in the furthest aisle. It wasn't his favorite place in the world, but it didn't get many visitors. When Levi found him, he hid his face with as much shame as he had when Levi caught him with Jake.

"You okay?"

"I'm fine." Roman wiped away the tears.

"Obvious lie." Levi stepped closer, cautious and careful. He saw how frail Roman had become, but while he seemed concerned, Roman didn't see any pity in Levi's expression.

"Ezra's mad at me," Roman said, his throat sore. "I don't know what I did. I have an idea, but it doesn't add up."

"You didn't do anything. He's a fucking piece of—"

"No," Roman protested, so engrained to sweep in and defend Ezra's nonexistent faults. "I did something, and I have to fix it."

"No, you don't." Levi braced his back on the wall and slid down beside Roman.

"Yes, I do." Roman swallowed the lump in his throat. It was too awful to say how Ezra was done with him, how he planned to pass him off, how Roman had somehow messed up their arrangement.

"No, you really don't."

"You don't understand, Levi." Roman thought maybe Levi heard enough of the argument last night, but he clearly hadn't. "If I don't fix this, I won't be safe. You won't be safe either."

"I don't need you to protect me," Levi said, grabbing ahold of Roman's hand. "I'm sorry it took me so long to find my strength. I'm sorry you had to surrender so much of yourself to give me that opportunity to get stronger. I'm sorry I distanced myself because it hurt to see you lose yourself piece by piece. I'm sorry for being a terrible friend."

It'd been so long since Roman had heard genuine sincerity that it left him awestruck. He was baffled, confused, and consumed with guilt that he'd somehow made Levi feel this way.

"I'm the one who needs to apologize—"

"No," Levi said, voice firm but not angry.

It made Roman shake, but he wasn't frightened. It was the first time in a long time he'd heard the edge of anger without fearing what it'd result in.

"You will never have to apologize for anything ever again," Levi said. "I'll make sure of it."

Oh, how Roman desperately wished those words were true. There was a certainty in Levi's expression, in his grip on Roman's hand, in the soft gaze of his blue eyes. Roman wondered, perhaps fantasized, if Ezra would consider giving Roman to Levi. He could find a way to make this friendship work. He'd learned how to be a good friend, a loyal friend, an obedient friend. He pushed the thought away. Ezra would never agree to something like that because he wanted Roman to suffer. And Levi would never want someone so damaged and worthless, someone who made an enemy out of the champion of the arena.

"I want you to know I'm making a move for power," Levi said almost casually.

Roman blinked in response, perplexed and like he'd somehow missed an entire conversation.

"I've changed," Levi continued. "I've finally learned to be strong, finally started to understand the way things are run here."

"I've seen you fight," Roman said softly, but he didn't have the heart to say it wouldn't be enough, that it wouldn't change the field here.

"You've seen a few, and only what I want people to see." Levi shot Roman a dark look and a curious smile.

"Sometimes, you want people to see your successes; sometimes, you want people to predict your movements, your techniques, and that helps walk them right into a trap."

Roman didn't know what to say, didn't understand the turn of this conversation.

"I will set you free from Ezra, from everyone who's ever touched you," Levi said. "You won't have to serve anyone, you won't have to make yourself smaller anymore, you won't have to accept your fate. I will carve a path out of anyone who dims your smile."

That actually made Roman smile, which resulted in Levi brushing his fingertips against Roman's cheek, happy to see his happiness. But as much as Roman liked the daydream, he needed to explain to Levi how things really operated here. It was more than just taking the title of champion.

"I've been building alliances," Levi said, almost like he'd read Roman's mind. "Ezra's not nearly as beloved or feared as he wants folks to think. Soon enough, I'm going to take him out. I'm gonna lift you back up, too."

Roman shook his head, dismissing the impossibility of him ever becoming more than where he'd fallen.

"You'll be my equal, and people around here will respect that."

"You can't make people forget what I've done, what I've allowed to be done to me," Roman said shamefully.

"I don't care if they remember, but they will show you respect; they will treat you how you deserve," Levi said. "Or I'll get rid of them, too."

Roman snickered at that. "Gonna get rid of everyone who wrongs me? Might be a long list."

"You'd be surprised how creative I can get." Levi stared at Roman. "If I'd known about Jake sooner, about his intentions, or that Ezra would fucking allow that, I would've ended him sooner."

Shock spiraled through Roman's thoughts. Levi couldn't have… Jake's crew was over twenty men… Jake himself was a fierce fighter, ruthless, and psychotic… And how he died… Levi could never.

"Wait…did you?" Roman lost the will to speak as he found himself quite lightheaded.

"I would do anything for you, Roman." Levi placed a hand on Roman's shoulder, steadying him. "I would quite literally burn the world down to protect you. I'm only sorry it took me this long to get here."

Roman looked at Levi in awe. There was something humbling and frightening about the man Levi had grown into since they were divided. While Roman shrank and crumbled, Levi had grown into someone ferocious.

He didn't know if he could trust it, trust Levi. Every part of him desperately wanted to, but he trusted Ezra. He had willed himself to trust and love and accept Ezra in every way, and now he would be swept aside like the trash he was. How could someone like Levi ever care for Roman? How could someone who did something so brutally violent care about anyone?

"Did you really stab him forty-eight times?" Roman trembled, speaking in a low whisper.

"He laughed about what he'd done to you," Levi said, his cold blue eyes staring off at nothing. "He laughed about what he had planned; he just couldn't stop making jokes."

Roman stared at Levi, wordless yet accepting. He didn't know how to express it, if Levi understood the look, but he couldn't fault his friend.

"Eventually, though, he stopped laughing."

Roman didn't know right from wrong anymore. He didn't know what justified anything and where the line really fell. And truthfully, he didn't care. There was a warmth that filled his chest over Levi's protective actions. He worried Levi would tarnish his good soul, his kind heart, and over someone as expendable as Roman, but he wanted to believe in his friend. He wanted to believe in Levi's plan. He wanted to believe he could really be happy again.

Roman leaned over, pressing his head on Levi's shoulder, and the two sat in silence together. Levi's calm breaths became rhythmic for Roman, and he relaxed in the gentle ebb and flow of Levi's body. It'd been a long time since Roman felt comfortable with the quiet.

Chapter Twenty

In the days that followed Levi's confession, his promise, Roman did his best to sort his feelings on the matter. Too much of his bandwidth stretched to worry for Levi and Ezra in equal measure. Even as Ezra continued being cold to him since the night Roman spent with Jake…with Jake and the other men. Roman twisted in his bed, ignoring the faint smell of sex that still lingered in the cell. Not sex with Ezra, no, he'd tired of Roman by this point. Roman could smell Jake, the other men, and himself. The perfume of lust and deceit made each breath excruciating.

Roman couldn't outrun his memories of what he'd done, his thoughts of Levi's promise, or his concerns for what would happen to Ezra. Worse, what would happen to Levi if he lost?

Roman snapped open his eyes. Was that worse? Was his worry for Levi stronger than Ezra's? That gnawed and clawed at Roman's insides. He buried the thoughts, the hope and desire he held for Levi, the happiness it filled him with, the curiosity that bubbled every time Levi approached. Roman wasn't allowed to think such things. It wasn't good for him, it wouldn't be condoned by Ezra, and it wasn't fair to Levi.

"Hey," Ezra said, slipping off his top bunk and finally breaking the silence.

Roman sat up, eagerly awaiting more words, desperate to fill the silence from Ezra's pause but worried he'd overstep and end the conversation prematurely. Roman didn't want to overstep.

"Come suck my dick." Ezra fished his cock out of his pants, expectingly.

"Sure." Roman slipped off the bed quickly and crawled over on his knees to where Ezra stood.

It'd been so long since Roman and Ezra had been intimate. Intimate. That was a word Roman clung to about the arrangement. It helped sort his feelings, helped him accept his situation, and helped him come to terms with his sexuality.

There had been harsh words, ugly words, and Roman thought he'd lost their connection, their friendship, but as he went to work stroking and sucking Ezra hard, he believed this bond could be salvaged.

Roman would do better. He'd try harder. He'd make Ezra happy again. Everything would be okay.

As Roman's head bobbed, Ezra got a firm grip and rammed his cock down Roman's throat.

"You think you'll choke on Levi's dick this much?" Ezra looked down at Roman, watching him struggle, watching Roman desperately swallow and hold all of Ezra.

He'd done this to Roman a hundred times over. He could handle it, could resist the gag reflex and let the tears roll down his cheeks. But Roman couldn't handle the accusation, the question that hit harder than Ezra's entire shaft down his throat.

"I didn't realize there was any fight left in ya." Ezra bucked his hips, choking Roman with his cock, demanding Roman take every inch, not with words but the rough thrust again and again. Ezra hadn't been this brutal in a long time. He wanted to break Roman down all over again, it seemed, shatter his willpower, and remind him of his place in life. But Roman already knew his place and accepted Ezra for everything he craved. Roman would give the man anything and more if possible. He just needed to understand why Ezra was angry, why Ezra suddenly rejected him, why Ezra allowed—no, arranged—the night with Jake Finnegan and his crew.

As Roman gagged, Ezra spit onto his face, holding Roman to the base of his dick and rocking his head forward. Roman worked to keep up, to fix this.

Roman didn't know what to say, didn't know how to react. What did Ezra know? This was some new trick. Ezra always managed to trick Roman, but he could never see the trap until after the fact.

"Bet you thought you were pretty clever, huh?" Ezra controlled the motion, as he often did, moving Roman's head, making him obediently compliant to servicing the man.

Ezra's dick became easier to hold in Roman's mouth as his erection lessened. It seemed Ezra struggled with this information almost as much as Roman.

"I can't even keep it up—that's how much you make me sick." Ezra tucked his slick dick into his pants and shot Roman a look of absolute disgust. "Bet you're just dreaming of the day Levi becomes champion. Bet you're hoping that'll save your cheap ass, keep you from getting passed around."

Roman trembled.

"But he'll get bored with you just like I got bored with you, just like everyone who takes a turn on you gets bored." Ezra ran his hands through Roman's ruffled pink hair and dragged him to his feet.

"Levi's not going to do anything," Roman said weakly, regretting the lie the second it left his mouth.

"You really think anything happens in this place without my knowledge?" Ezra leaned in close, invading Roman's space in a way he'd grown so accustomed to, yet for the first time in a long time, it sent a shiver through Roman's body. "Your little no-nothing friend thinks he can make a move for my power. He thinks he can step up to the rank of champion because he got lucky against a few nobodies."

"No." Roman held his head low, unable to look into Ezra's angry green eyes.

"For too long, I've dragged out this slow death of yours." Ezra slapped his hands on Roman's face, forcing him to meet his gaze. "You know I hate you, right. You know I've hated you. I've hated you since the first day I saw you."

These weren't questions; they were facts, truths that Roman had learned to ignore over the long, brutal months. He gave way to Ezra's carnal desires as a way of mutual pleasure, not subservient torment. He focused on Ezra's charming smile, not his hateful eyes. He accepted his feelings would always need to be second in order for them both to be happy.

"In the arena…" Roman hadn't seen Ezra's hatred during their first match, but he'd seen it nearly every day since. When Ezra talked to him, laughed with him, kissed him, fucked him, Roman always saw the hate and malice and rage in Ezra's eyes, but he tried so very hard to focus on the smiles and kind words.

"Not the arena." Ezra shook Roman's head with a no. "I've hated you so much longer than that."

"W-what?" Roman looked at him pleadingly. "Why?"

"The name Stacy Anderson mean anything to you?"

Hearing Stacy's name come from Ezra's mouth hit Roman like a fucking sledgehammer. If there were any shreds of calm, collected stability left inside his psyche, it'd surely been shattered at this point.

Roman stared wide-eyed and bewildered.

"I loved her with everything I had," Ezra spoke calmly but was unable to hide the hate in his glare. "You took her away and then had the audacity to live your life."

Roman withered a bit with each word, listening intently to Ezra, though his confession struck harder than any fist.

"When you got locked up, I tried to move on, tried to see the justice in you losing a few years of your life after you took all of Stacy's years away. Everything." Ezra's words held a venomous heat that hit Roman's cheek with breathy rage. "But then I found out you were just living it up! When I heard you were some hotshot champion, swinging your dick around and acting like you owned this place, it made my skin seethe."

Roman never considered himself that lucky as the champion. It always felt one misstep away from falling apart. And it had. Ezra had ensured that much, taken it from Roman. He didn't need a further explanation. He'd pieced it together. Ezra wanted Roman to suffer, so he took away his title.

"Stripping you of your title, that took so much training and preparation," Ezra said. "And I really just wanted your ranking so I could make you a target, make your death quick and easy and satisfying."

Roman listened obediently, having months of training to not flinch at Ezra's words, Ezra's actions, Ezra's wants and needs and desires. Roman let Ezra satisfy himself with a confession meant to cut Roman down—if there was anything left in the man to break.

"When I first arrived, I wanted you dead," Ezra said plainly, no hidden malice, just a fact of life. A fact Roman accepted. "After what you did, you thought you could live your best life, riding on top of the world as some fucking wasteland champion to a tiny prison that you carved into your image."

That made sense. Roman didn't deserve to keep his head above water, to swim against the brutal currents. No, Ezra had arrived so he could shove Roman's head underwater and let the undertow drag him to the depths where he belonged.

"But then I realized with what you did to Stacy, you deserved so much worse," Ezra continued. "I wanted to break you the same way you broke me. You hollowed out my soul and left me with nothing. A vacuum of a man. I decided to hollow you out, break you, own you, make your every waking thought a service to me."

Roman hated looking back on the night Stacy died. The blood that covered Roman's fists. The man gasping on the ground. The way one angry shove knocked Stacy into traffic. The way one moment, one action, had changed the entire course of Roman's life.

There were so many things Roman hated to look back on. He hated thinking about the night he spent with Jake and his crew. He hated thinking about all the ways he willingly insisted on Ezra debasing him, encouraging it even. He hated thinking about all the looks he got from everyone in Marlow Penitentiary. More than anything, Roman hated himself and wished to forget all the ways he deserved this.

But maybe he did deserve this, mind flitting to Stacy's broken body. Corpse. Flesh barely held together in the wake of a semi-truck. Maybe Roman could finally accept his place, his punishment. This was why the universe let him fall; this was why the universe laughed as he plummeted, as he crashed, as he shattered into a million pieces of desperation and insecurity. Roman finally accepted his fate.

"So, all of this…" Roman gestured to the cell, the champion's suite, the life he now lived under Ezra's thumb. "This was because of what happened to Stacy."

"Because of what you did to Stacy," Ezra corrected.

"I'm s-s-sorry." Roman shivered, the word colder than any blizzard and a useless waste based on the scowl that burned through Roman's flesh.

He didn't want to apologize. He wanted to fall back to his knees. He wanted to tell Ezra he understood that he'd accept this. Part of him wondered if that would finally free him from the guilt he harbored, from the resistance of secretly wanting more in life. Roman never deserved more from life. And he certainly didn't after taking a life.

"I don't need or want your apologies." Ezra playfully smirked. "I just need you to suffer, which you have and will continue to do. It was so easy to make you compliant, like you knew you deserved this."

Maybe Roman did know that on some level, some warped perception of guilt for his actions. But did he really deserve all of this? Did his cruelty truly warrant complete and utter destruction? How much suffering would he need to continue enduring until the scales were balanced?

"Once I decided I could break down your mind and ego, make you serve me completely, make you love me, need me, I knew I could lead you where you belonged."

"Belonged?"

"You don't think Jake was a mistake, do you?" Ezra laughed. "It took some time to get you there, to make it your choice, always making it your choice."

Ezra had arranged it. He'd sent Roman to the showers knowing Jake would fake an attack, knowing Roman would run to Ezra, knowing Ezra would then bring Jake back and make things right, and Roman—being the desperate, broken man he was—did whatever he could to see Ezra smile, even if he died a little inside every time Jake or one of his men raked their hands over Roman's body, every time he served them, every time they broke him in a little more.

"The long-term goal was always to send you to Jake and his crew, let you choose it even." Ezra wrapped his hands over Roman's face, still smiling, still laughing. "I was so excited to watch them slowly decimate what I'd already shattered."

Roman trembled in Ezra's grasp, trying to free himself from the hands slapped on the sides of his face, but he was too reserved, too well-trained to properly defy the unwanted grip.

"Then Jake the psychotic Snake went and got himself killed in some gang feud bullshit," Ezra spat the words more annoyed than angry.

Ezra hadn't pieced together what Levi had done. He didn't know Levi's involvement in Jake's death, in burning down his crew.

"No matter. Plans change." Ezra smacked Roman's face, then released his hold on him. "You took away the most important person in my life. You killed my best friend. Maybe when I kill yours, you'll understand how I feel."

Ezra left the room. Roman collapsed to the floor, each breath a wispy struggle as the walls spun and his thoughts twisted into gnarled nightmares. Everything that had happened. Everything that would happen. It was his fault. Ezra had come to destroy him. Ezra had warped his understanding of friendship. Broken Roman until he could no longer recognize himself. Now, Levi would die. The last person who actually seemed to give a damn about what happened to Roman. He didn't deserve someone so kind, so caring, so brave. And Levi certainly didn't deserve to die for someone as weak, as lost, and as useless as Roman.

He crumbled into himself, crying over the last year of his life, the lengths he'd gone to live just one more day. To survive. This no longer felt like surviving. It was a chore, a waste, and Roman didn't know what to do.

Chapter Twenty-One

The lead-up to the next Challenger's Chance haunted Roman. He couldn't move, he couldn't think, he couldn't even probably feel past the guilt he carried for causing this. Every part of him secretly thought back to how much he deserved his fate, how karma had finally come for him after what he'd done to Stacy, but to learn Ezra came in karma's stead. To know that Ezra made it his mission to take Roman and break him, make him love the servitude, expect the pain, and show gratitude for everything he'd been forced to endure for months.

He thought about how Ezra warped his understanding of friendship, how he used friendship to punish Roman, and now would take the only friend Roman had left in the world and kill him.

Roman swallowed hard as he followed a small crowd being escorted to the fighting arena. Would Ezra honestly murder Levi? The warden didn't tolerate competitors getting slick and pressing their luck by killing a fellow inmate. There was no profit in casual murder, and the warden was a businessman, after all. But accidents happened, and this was a rough, no-rules arena where every fighter came with their own shady background of breaking the law.

Ezra could easily make it look like an accident. Hell, maybe it had nothing to do with their fight at all. Roman scoured the crowd, searching for threats. Ezra might have someone in the audience ready to gut Levi, just like the inmate who'd come for Ezra with a knife all those months back.

Roman dwelled on that moment, that incident that cemented Ezra's friendship with Jake. Had it been real? A real altercation Ezra merely capitalized on, or a ruse meant to justify his fake friendship with Jake? Roman didn't know the truth, didn't know if he wanted to know. Ezra had said he'd always planned to break Roman and pass him off to Jake. Had he really been planning it from day one? Roman's mind was lost in the layers of manipulation, the web of lies, the fog of deceit. He couldn't see through any of it, not truly, and he worried he never would.

"Welcome to another evening of the most riveting competitions you'll ever experience," Warden Sadler came on the mics and livened up the crowd. "Normally, we warm you all up with a few preliminary battles, but tonight, we have something mighty special. A Challenger's Chance made by Levi Pierce and graciously accepted by Ezra Delgado, our strongest champion."

The crowd booed Levi's approach, offering no support, but the stoic expression he wore didn't falter for a second.

Ezra stood from his gaudy throne chair, raised fists to fuel the crowds' cheers for a moment, and then quickly took his place. Neither man had come tonight with the intention of putting on a show. All they wanted was to strike down the other.

Warden Sadler sounded off the match, and both fighters moved in to attack each other. Ezra came in fast and hard, not bothering to conserve his strength because this was the only fight that mattered to him. Roman could see it in his hateful green eyes; he could see it in every brutal punch, in the swift kicks, in the dangerous fake-outs. Ezra moved with deadly force.

Levi kept up, though, unsurprising to Roman since he'd seen Levi hold his own against Ezra—at least for a little while. But he also knew Levi fought with an air of deceit for the last several months. Everything he did steered him to this match-up without actually giving away his true talent. That power revealed itself in every heavy punch he landed, in the solid counters he led Ezra into, in the godly speed he wielded. Roman's eyes darted to keep up with Levi, shocked to see a man so bulky move with more speed than Ezra.

It panicked Ezra, too. The way Levi bulldozed his way from one end of the arena to the other. He already had height and weight and muscle on Ezra, but now he revealed he had the speed, too. Not only that, but his secret training shone through in every move set. Ezra continued making sloppy strikes, continued falling short of evading blows, and looked so exhausted Roman could almost breathe easy.

Almost.

Every cell of his body told him he'd never be free of Ezra, that he belonged to him. His stomach even twisted in knots, filled with guilt and remorse at the idea of cheering for Levi's success. His own body turned against him, shaming him for yearning for Ezra's defeat.

It didn't matter, though. Levi continued winning ground, leaving Ezra more and more vulnerable. He might really win this, become the next champion, and free Roman.

The thought was shameful, to see how far he'd fallen, to feel this pitiful and desperate, but Roman didn't know any other way.

The crowd roared with excitement when Ezra landed an uppercut. It wouldn't win the fight, but it forced Levi back, forced him to pause and breathe and collect himself while Ezra did the same.

Levi backed up, gathering his bearings, but too close to the crowd for Roman's liking. The crowd was never a safe place to breathe. When a man low to the ground swept in between others at the front line, Roman panicked.

"Levi, move!" Roman screamed.

Not soon enough. The glint of the blade shimmered under the lights, red flashed across the concrete, and Levi shouted.

The surge of pain dropped him to one knee, buckling under the weight of pain that tore into the heel of his ankle. It only took seconds for Levi's face to go from winded to washed out and exhausted, but Roman moved through the crowd, furious and worried and unthinking.

Ezra didn't waste the fortune of his staged interference. He rushed at Levi and punched him across the face. Again. Again. Again. Each hit was more brutal than the last. Roman shouted almost as loud as the cracks against Levi's face.

"Stop it!" He shoved Ezra off, consequences be damned.

Roman lay beside a bloody and beaten Levi, unwilling to let him die here for something as pitiful and pathetic as Roman himself.

"You're okay." He cradled Levi's head on his thighs, keeping his bloody face away from the pool of blood still pouring from his ankle. "You're okay, now."

"I don't think it's a win yet," Ezra said, encouraging the crowd to rage with him. "He might be faking it. I better finish this."

"Stay away from him," Roman said with an angry edge of a growl. "Stay the fuck away from him!"

"Mouthy." Ezra chuckled. "Thought I'd fucked that outta ya by now."

Roman glared, every fiber of his being burned with rage.

"Guess I can endure a few more rounds with you," Ezra said with smug hatred. "Before passing you along, of course."

"Interference with the competition has seemed to bring this match-up to a halt," Warden Sadler chimed in, ready to smooth things over with the authority above, the elite clientele, who probably cared more for the drama unfolding than the declaration of a winner.

"You can take him," Levi wheezed.

"I could never." Roman shook his head, carefully looking up to Ezra. It was already too bold, too reckless to interfere with this much. But Roman couldn't watch Levi die. "He's already beaten me twice."

And a hundred times since then. Every time they trained, Ezra won. Yes, Roman held back, but only because he knew his place. Ezra beat him at everything. He had thoroughly fucked Roman into compliant submission. It was all Roman knew now. Fighting for victory or valor, they seemed like faint dreams of a past life, another man, someone surely stronger than Roman ever was.

"He only beat you because of underhanded tricks." Levi spat blood as he spoke.

"The chokehold was tricky, but I still should've been prepared," Roman said dismissively, not even noting his other pitiful three-hit loss during their rematch.

"Maybe," Levi wheezed. "But he only beat you the second time because he drugged you."

"What?" Roman's eyes went wide, memory searching back to when it happened, how it happened. So much had happened over the course of this year that he hardly recalled anything outside the sex, violence, and servitude of his days. Was Levi speaking the truth? Impossible. "You can't know that."

"Jake's a chatty snake when he screams…" And with that, Levi passed out.

Roman had so many other questions, but it became apparent either Ezra planned to drug Roman from the start with Jake's assistance or shared that detail after the fact while preparing to pass Roman off as a used car.

"Let's finish this," Ezra said while taking careful breaths.

"Lets." Something inside Roman snapped at Levi's announcement.

Roman waged Levi probably never wanted to share it because Roman was so delicate and broken. He wondered if Levi would tiptoe around him like this forever; he wondered how he even wondered about a life after Ezra. But he did. He could see it clearly now and craved it more than he'd been trained to crave Ezra himself. After every grueling effort made to break Roman's spirits and teach him to behave, he finally snapped out of it.

After all, what was the worst Ezra could do? Roman sought death more days than not. Roman lived only to endure pain. Roman had been fucked and used in so many ways his brain couldn't very well keep track of how much abuse his holes had endured for the pleasure of sadists.

There was nothing left to take from Roman at this point. Except maybe Levi. But if he didn't act now, Roman would surely lose him.

"If you take one more step, you'll have to go through me."

Ezra laughed. He laughed so hard, he had to brace a hand against his aching ribs. "You? Go through the bitch I've broken in in every way conceivable? Honey, there's nothing left to go through. You're broken and cheap and just plain pitiful trying to look tough."

"If you take a step forward, it's me you'll face." Roman's jaw clenched as he spoke slowly and enraged. "I won't go easy on you for the sake of your ego. This isn't a workout, after all."

Ezra glared, making no effort to bring up his actual victories against Roman, his two wins that cemented his reign as champion. Roman considered this the closest thing to a confession he'd ever received from Ezra about the deceit.

"Fine, fine, fine." Ezra shrugged. "But two on one isn't very fair."

"You're the champion. Thought you could handle anything."

"Come on, Roman. I'm not you." Ezra smiled. "I can't just take everything thrown at me, in me, on me."

Ezra mouthed "slut" and Roman didn't flinch. It was a tiny victory, but it helped Roman straighten his shoulders and stand taller. For the first time in a long time, he didn't look up at Ezra.

Roman rolled his eyes at Ezra's blatant posturing, then looked to the unconscious Levi, who served as the second fighter of the competition.

"Fuck it. Tag a friend." Roman squared his shoulders and lifted his arms. "I'll take both of you."

Ezra snorted. "The number of times you said that to Jake and his crew."

It should've unnerved Roman, should've filled him with shame and guilt well past his limit. He wasn't truly ready to face what had happened to him that night, what Jake and the others had done, but for this fraction of a second, he didn't blame himself for what they had done to him. And he thought of the worst thing ever.

"Well, hell, I needed someone who could fuck me right." Roman smiled, daring himself to be ugly with his words. "I'm guessing that's why Stacy screwed every person she could get her hands on, too."

Ezra cut his gaze at Roman and shot him a look that, under any normal circumstances, would've made Roman collapse to the ground and beg for forgiveness. Now, though, it fueled him.

"Maxwell." Ezra snapped his fingers. "Put this little bitch back in his place."

The towering man who'd nearly bested Roman every time they crossed paths stepped through the crowd. Roman had barely beaten Maxwell King when at his best. He couldn't fathom fighting this titan when he could barely stand on his own two feet.

"When I'm done with you," Maxwell said, cutting his gaze to Levi, "I'm gonna finish him, too."

With that, the world fell away, and Roman unleashed months of pent-up fury. He didn't see his movements, didn't feel them. Something in his body snapped, and he ignored it in favor of the thread of rage that led him forth.

Blood. Screaming. Pain.

None of it made Roman falter. He continued until his mind became his own again, and he stood over Maxwell's crumbled, whimpering body. It made no sense. Roman couldn't figure out what he'd done, even in a primal, blacked-out state, but he hoped someone might explain it later. Might explain it after he finally bested Ezra.

Ezra, who stood in shock and anger, was probably more insulted by Maxwell shaming him with such a loss than by Roman daring to speak up. The crowd had backed away a few steps, offering Roman and Ezra more space, their expressions wary perhaps for Roman's actions or Ezra's anger. Roman didn't know for certain if he could still strike fear in others.

"Say the thing that'll piss them the fuck off," Stacy's words came to him like a vision. "Once you got them by the emotional balls, you own that fucker."

The memory was faded and random and weird. It didn't make any sense at the time, her encouraging him to provoke someone over something petty. But now her words hit with purpose, with drive, like maybe she'd always known Roman would land here faced with Ezra in a dark basement surrounded by criminals.

"Seriously, I get that you were in love, but are you as bad at finding the G spot as you are at hitting my prostate?" Roman chuckled, forced and ridiculously loud, but it drew silence from the crowd. "Imagine swinging a dick that big and still lacking when it comes to hammering in a good fucking time."

"Shut your whore mouth!"

"Ooooh, guess I hit a nerve there." Roman quivered with dramatic flair, almost smiling at how much it pissed off Ezra. "Said every guy, gal, and nonbinary pal when they fucked Stacy, and she actually came."

Not his best attempt at slut shaming Stacy, but he wanted to really drum in the fact that she fucked around with everybody who caught her eye. It was actually what Roman loved about her, admired even, craved when she granted him time at her side or in her bed without the distraction of another partner. He'd known who she was from the first day their paths crossed. She was honest and uninhibited and never submitted to norms that didn't fit her way of life. It made him a little sick, bad-mouthing her as she lay dead in the ground— because of him—but the posturing hurt Ezra more, which fueled Roman.

He could almost hear Stacy whispering words of encouragement, ways to cut down her memory. She'd never liked bullies, and if Ezra had acted like this when she was alive, she would've never tolerated it.

"I almost feel a little better about offing the bitch, knowing she doesn't have to endure your cheap ass version of what love is." Roman slapped his fist into his open palm and made a splattering noise.

He let his fingers mime Stacy's corpse dancing in the air the same way he recalled it a billion times before when drowning in his regrets. Only this time, there wasn't shock on her face before the truck slammed into her. No, she smiled in Roman's memory, blew him a kiss even, and reminded him that no one ever deserved to suffer.

Stacy loved love and believed in joy and pleasure above everything else. Wallowing in pity for his actions would be admirable to a different soul, but chances were, Stacy shook her head at Roman for not living his life and moving on. She was too fucking wise for him, which was why he never convinced her to really date him. Ezra never convinced her either, hence why she fucked Roman and so many other partners up until the day she died.

"I gotta ask, are you trying to break me for revenge, or are you hoping I'll be as easy as your dead not-a-girlfriend?" Roman gave a minxy grin, doing his best to imitate Ezra. It probably didn't work, probably looked silly on Roman, but he stayed strong the same way he had during every gala and event and pretentious party he'd attended with Stacy.

"And if you're a good boy, maybe I'll reward your efforts," she would whisper when dragging Roman somewhere outside his world of possibilities. "Just fake it until you make it, baby."

She kept calling out to him, reminding him how true strength looked. He repeated the mantra to himself silently until Ezra bolted toward him and walked right into an easily avoidable strike. Roman knocked him away with a punch to the face and a trip of his leg.

Roman could win this. He saw it now.

They continued clashing, and Roman thought back to every sparring match he held back, every time he intentionally faltered, every time he stood silent and listened to Ezra's lectures on things he already understood. Roman pummeled him, outmaneuvered him, and bested him in every way conceivable. There were techniques Roman had long since forgotten, but his body reminded him through pure instinct, instinct he'd trained himself to quiet. Now, he let his body rage, let himself shine, let himself be the best he could possibly be.

Roman stayed close to Ezra's right side, almost feeling guilty at how easily exposed he kept himself. But Roman had warned Ezra a thousand times over, and he never heeded the advice. Why would he? He was champion, and Roman was just some cheap hole meant to serve. Now, though, Roman put away all the shame he carried and hit Ezra harder each time.

A flash of Stacy's corpse struck his mind when he hit Ezra in the jaw, and he glimpsed Levi in the corner of his eye. The silent dread of failure sparked for a moment. Just a moment. But that was all it took. Roman had been down this path of failure too many times before.

"Got you, bitch." Ezra wrapped an arm around Roman's throat and prepared to beat him the same way he had the first time they met.

Roman didn't hesitate. He defended himself and blocked Ezra's arm before he stole Roman's breath. Once he'd secured himself, he shifted his position ever so slightly and shoved Ezra away.

And then the impossible happened. Ezra stumbled and tumbled on nothing in particular. It was as if Roman's defense carried more force than anticipated, or some ghost in another realm knocked Ezra's footing off. Roman didn't believe in ghosts, but he also forgot to believe in himself and his strength. It was easier to think a ghost had rescued him than that he'd rescued himself.

Ezra's head hit the arm of his throne chair with a powerful crack and a heavy thud as his body slammed onto the floor. His neck had twisted too far before landing on the ground. Blood streamed too much.

It was over. It was really over. Just like that. A careless misstep with a push harder than expected to stop a trick that'd ruined his life once before. Roman had defeated Ezra and left him bloody, broken, and unconscious on the ground.

Chapter Twenty-Two

Roman sat inside the champion's suite alone, unsure what to do with his restored title. It wouldn't last. It couldn't. Sure, the crowd cheered for Ezra's downfall, but they'd soon want to see Roman's defeat once again. He wasn't the man he was before, and too many inmates believed he wasn't worthy of such a title, such respect.

It didn't bother him as much as it should've. Things like this, watching his back and fearing for inevitable outcomes, used to haunt his every waking moment. Now, Roman felt like he could breathe again. Ezra was gone. Gone for good.

Roman lay down in his bed and closed his eyes without worry for the first time in a long time. The next few days were a blur of events. Roman found himself lost in sleep most days, finally getting restorative rest instead of the bare minimum to simply survive. When his energy did return, he used it to wash away the pink in his hair, to work out the muscles he'd neglected for far too long, and to dream about the possibility of maybe better days ahead.

Levi had been released from the infirmary and announced they were once again bunking together. He walked into the cell, bruised and face covered in bandages, but he smiled the entire time, unwilling to let what happened take away his joy. Roman winced at the limp Levi had, worried it wouldn't heal properly, especially not here.

"Oh, you're cool with me being on top?" Levi joked, nodding to the empty bunk.

Roman rolled his eyes. Then he smiled just a tiny bit. It was crass and absurd, and if anyone else had made the joke, Roman would've recoiled, reminded of everything he didn't want to dwell on. But having Levi give him a carefree grin set Roman at ease. They wouldn't be who they were before, but Roman couldn't wait to explore their friendship, find out their new dynamic, and survive together.

No. More than survive. Roman wouldn't settle for that any longer. He wanted to be happy, to be truly happy. To live and look forward to life.

"See, I knew my jokes were comedian-level gold." Levi waggled his finger at Roman's smiling face.

Without a second of hesitation or a chance to regret it, Roman swooped in close and kissed Levi. It wasn't incredibly intimate, and even though part of him wanted to run his hands over Levi's broad chest, he settled for the taste of Levi's lips. Brief and fleeting and enough to make Roman happy.

"What was that?"

"Nothing," Roman said, unsure what he really wanted. "I don't know what we are. What we'll be. What I want."

"That's okay."

"I don't want that." Roman gestured to Levi's body, to his everything. "But maybe. Maybe later. A lot later. I don't know, and I do know it's not fair to make you figure it out with me—"

"I am completely fine with waiting and wondering," Levi said, tilting his head but not leaning in, not invading Roman's space, and that was a comfort he'd completely forgotten about. "I am fine following this journey wherever it goes. If it was just one little kiss, that's cool. I'm pretty damn kissable, so really, everyone has to try my lips out at least once."

"I've been told the same." Roman snorted. "Well, not for my kisses."

Levi's entire face went rigid like the words Roman had spoken tore a hole in the floor. Then, without missing a beat, he burst into laughter and mimed himself handing over his comedy crown.

"Seriously, dude. Trauma jokes are all yours."

The pair turned the champion's suite into something livable again. Roman couldn't forget all the horrible things he'd done, everything he'd survived in this space, but he also remembered all the silly things he and Levi would do to pass the long hours. And he cherished the new memories Levi helped him build each day, helping wash away the unwanted thoughts and the nightmares piece by tiny piece.

After Ezra's defeat, the arena was closed while the warden dealt with the incident. Ezra hadn't died, but he hadn't woken up either. Roman hated himself a little bit, but he hoped Ezra never woke up. He didn't think he could face him again and wasn't sure how long this spark of courage and strength would last.

Levi made it bearable standing on his own two feet again, always acting as a buffer when they left their cell, always ready to provide a carefree distraction, always there to shake away the nightmares that would hit Roman at any given moment for any given reason.

When the time came to return to the arena, Roman wouldn't. He could. He could force himself to fight down there the same way he'd forced himself to submit to Ezra, the same way he'd forced himself to do everything he'd done since the day he arrived at Marlow Penitentiary. But he didn't want to swallow his nerves and do what had to be done to survive.

Levi accepted that and never brought it up again. There was only one match-up after Roman surrendered his title unceremoniously by refusing to show. Unfortunately, a fire broke out on the balcony above, taking out several members of the Lawless Authority, and the underground arena had been exposed to the world.

Marlow Penitentiary had the nation's eyes locked onto their facility when the news got out, and the warden had far too many questions to deal with that he never had the chance to taunt or scold or threaten Roman for refusing to return.

The champion was done. The title burned to ash. The arena left barren.

"Did you…" Roman quirked a brow, never officially asking Levi the question, but certain of the answer.

Levi had a cigarette the evening the arena caught fire. For a man who didn't care for cigarettes or vices of any kind since beating his own addictions, Roman had seen him with a smoke twice in his life. Both times after Marlow Penitentiary caught fire.

Warden Sadler didn't last long as the head of this prison. Too many questions. Too many scandals. Too many deaths. He was put on administrative leave and given a chance to fade away without his pension. Warden Sadler returned to Marlow Penitentiary one time and went to retrieve his things, twenty-seven years of service summed up in a few trophies and one box, but the news of his final farewell spread almost as quickly as the fires Levi may or may not have set.

After a tumble down a flight of stairs, Warden Sadler was rushed to the hospital but declared dead by the time EMTs got him out of the parking lot. It wasn't the fall that'd done him in, but the way he fell onto one of the trophies. The sharp glass edge impaled his neck during the fall.

"Did you, you know?" Roman mimed stabbing himself in the neck multiple times until Levi caught the not-so-subtle hint.

"Seriously?"

"What?" Roman shrugged. "It wouldn't be the first time."

"You stab one person one time—"

"Forty-eight times," Roman corrected.

"One person in one instance, and suddenly every mishap with gravity is blamed on you." Levi dramatically threw his hands up in defeat and then slapped his thighs.

Roman squinted, a playfully suspicious expression that he finally broke with a tiny smile. One that grew so much bigger when Levi tickled him. Levi didn't often engage contact first, but when he did, it never went further than a handhold, a pinky touch, a tickle above the waist and outside the clothing, and that made Roman crave those tiny embraces a little more each day.

He didn't know if Levi really had done something to Warden Sadler—how could he pull it off to begin with—or if it really was just a terrible accident. More importantly, Roman wasn't sure which he wanted it to be. If Levi would go to such lengths for Roman and Roman fantasized about the possibilities, what did that say about him? What did it say about either of them?

Roman mostly ignored those thoughts and focused on Levi's sweet smiles, his carefree nature, and his genuine kindness. Even if there was darkness in Levi, it wasn't the same as Ezra's. Roman never once saw hate or malice or disgust in Levi's eyes. Not for him and not for anyone they crossed paths with, and Roman paid very close attention. He'd learned to study every shift in the person who he trusted most. Ezra had taught him that lesson along with so many more he hoped would fade over time.

Inmates started being transferred from Marlow Penitentiary until the alleged allegations of corruption could be investigated. Roman panicked. He didn't care about starting over, about the new obstacles, the new dangers. He'd done all that before and suspected he'd continue facing challenges for the rest of his life. But he couldn't imagine being transferred somewhere without Levi. Not yet, anyway. He still needed his friend, still needed the light and hope and happiness he brought into Roman's life. The gentle patience and unyielding willingness to settle for just a friendly hug or touch when the rare occasion hit Roman.

Thankfully, Roman and Levi were shipped further upstate together, along with a few dozen other familiar faces. It was a real opportunity for change. Unfortunately, some inmates still remembered Roman's very public fall from grace and the things he subjected himself to just to survive. It wouldn't take long for the men at Kleinfield Prison Complex to see how easy and breakable Roman would be there.

After two chatty inmates had very bloody accidents, everyone else who knew Roman during his stay at Marlow Penitentiary suddenly had difficulty recalling what and how they knew him. This made it easier for Roman and Levi to slip by unnoticed. Kleinfield Prison Complex didn't carry nearly as much animosity between their inmates, and Roman actually managed to carve out a bit of his old self during his time there.

He didn't feel sane, and he wasn't sure he ever would again, but he did feel safe. It'd taken years of quiet recovery and talking with the therapists at Kleinfield—occasionally talking. There was so much Roman never wanted to unpack, and he still found himself wary about trusting staff. No matter how polite and sincere, Roman spent several years waiting for the secret horrors of Kleinfield Prison Complex to be revealed. There were none. The facility was far from great, and there were some definite scumbags on the payroll, but overall, this place didn't make every waking moment miserable.

With Levi's parole fast approaching, Roman didn't worry about the year-and-a-half time difference; he didn't dread the days he'd have to stand alone. Levi had been preparing Roman for this since their last days at Marlow before the fire. Only Roman hadn't noticed it then. He'd only actually noticed it a few days ago if he were being true with himself. And he was. He'd learned to be honest with himself and his feelings and his thoughts and his desires.

Most of all, he wanted to be honest about those things with Levi.

"Hey, hey," Levi said when Roman returned to their room. "I made a schedule for when would be good for visits, but like, then I realized that only took meetings with my PO into account. I forgot I actually have to work and stuff. I'm thinking we need more calls set up just in case."

Roman plopped onto the bed next to Levi with such force, Levi bounced a little. When Levi gained his bearings, his glasses were askew just a hair. Roman leaned in to adjust them and went a bit further for a kiss. Levi didn't speak, he didn't move, he just savored the taste of Roman's lips while Roman worked his tongue into Levi's mouth.

"I think someone is gonna miss me and the cuddles." Levi rocked away and then shoulder-bumped Roman.

It was something the pair had fallen into naturally over the years, something Roman wanted to be absolutely certain about before pursuing, something he desperately wanted to take a step further before Levi left.

"I'm ready," Roman said, which left Levi slack-jawed.

Roman knew Levi never expected those words. After everything that happened, after how Roman kept shutting down, after how Roman would advance and make moves and then ignore Levi for weeks at a time. Roman didn't expect

Levi to believe him, to understand, but Roman had to try.

"Are you absolutely sure?"

"Yes." Roman kissed Levi. It was passionate and beautiful, and Roman straddled Levi in the process, letting the two become entwined by their lips, tongues, and bodies. Roman wanted to feel all of Levi.

"It's just…you need to know I'm not pressuring you for something," Levi interrupted the kissing, trying to speak as Roman continued planting his lips over Levi. "And like, maybe you think, 'Levi's leaving, I better hop on his dick,' but, like, so not the case."

Roman slapped his hands over the sides of Levi's face and locked their eyes on each other. "You talk way too much."

"I just don't want you regretting choices or making choices or choosing to—"

Before Levi could speak more, before he could politely protest since he'd experienced Roman teeter at this stage before, Roman slipped off the bed. He jerked Levi's pants down to his knees as he moved. By the time Roman had positioned himself on the floor, Levi's dick had flopped out, fully erect, and he froze at the sight.

"You don't have to do anything," Levi wheezed, biting back his arousal. Roman could taste the heat of his desire. "I'm fine. Kissing is fucking epic. Or cuddling. Or just chilling. Literally zero expecta—"

"Shut the fuck up, dude." Roman mashed his lips against Levi's, stealing his voice and some of the fiery desire in his lungs.

Roman hadn't meant to pause so long, to stall, but Levi was bigger than he realized and ready to go almost immediately. Not as long as Ezra but thicker and closer to Roman's length. He just needed a few seconds to collect himself. He just needed a few more kisses to get there. He just needed to know he really, really wanted this.

And when a wispy moan of excitement escaped Levi's lips as Roman's leg brushed Levi's cock, Roman knew he needed this. He knew he wanted Levi in every way possible.

Without second-guessing, Roman kissed a trail down Levi's chest and wrapped his lips around the head of Levi's cock. With a hand to stroke and lube and help Roman adjust, he bobbed up and down until he swallowed the length of Levi.

It'd been so long since Roman had held another man's cock in his mouth, he'd forgotten the work involved, the strain on his jaw, the difficulty it took to breathe in, but when Levi noticed the struggle in Roman's efforts and went to pull Roman back, it only further encouraged him. Roman wrapped his hands over Levi's and leveraged the grip to instruct his partner to push down. Levi obeyed, and Roman took in the entirety of Levi, holding him in his mouth while his hands caressed Levi's abdomen.

Levi bucked, and Roman steadied himself, bracing and encouraging a faster pace. He wanted this. He wanted Levi. Every groan and growl satisfied Roman. Every time Levi begged without words, it drove Roman further. Every time Levi held himself back, stifling a primal need that consumed Roman in equal measure, it made Roman work harder at pleasing Levi.

Finally, unable to stop himself, Roman sprang up and kissed Levi again, pulling his own pants down off his hips and sitting on Levi's cock.

"Wait, wait, wait." Levi tried to push Roman off him while simultaneously trying to push into him.

"I want this." Roman could barely breathe between kisses, trying to adjust Levi's cock, and take it into him. "I want you. I want us. I—"

"I want lube." Levi snickered between kisses, rolling on his side and dropping Roman on the bed before scrambling through his bags to find the small packets he'd gotten when visiting the clinic in what Roman thought seemed a million years ago.

By the time Levi had returned, Roman had properly stripped off his clothes and went to work fully undressing Levi before shoving him back onto the bed in an attempt to straddle him.

"Not so fast." Levi grabbed Roman's waist, lifting him off like a small doll and dropping him beside him. "Roll over."

Roman gulped. He wanted this. He wanted every part of this. But he didn't want to be beneath Levi, didn't want the weight of his body, the complete surrender. Roman worried he'd never be ready for such things, but he didn't want to stop because of misplaced anxiety, so he obediently rolled onto his stomach and hoped the nervous flutter stopped.

"Before we do anything involving penetration, I wanna get you comfortable." Levi gently kissed the small of Roman's back, again and again, as he palmed Roman's cheeks. "Is that okay with you?"

Roman nodded.

"Is it okay with you, Roman?"

"Yes," he whispered.

Levi continued working soft kisses along Roman's ass as he squeezed and spread his cheeks. He licked the length of Roman's crack, which sent a tingle of arousal coursing through him, but when Levi's mouth moved closer to Roman's hole, he quivered. Levi continued teasing Roman while also preparing him for what came next. When Levi's tongue reached out and licked him, Roman almost melted into the stiff mattress. He'd never felt something so intoxicating, never been the one to be rimmed. Levi's tongue moved with sophisticated purpose, gentle and tame, which elicited a warmth of pleasure throughout Roman's body, then rapid and lethal, only in the best sort of way, the way that made Roman moan and lose himself in the sensation of Levi's mouth.

When Levi stuck a lubed finger into Roman, he hadn't even noticed. It'd only been the nip of Levi's teeth on Roman's ass that alerted him. His mouth wasn't done working over Roman's hole, though. He returned, giving Roman a tongue bath which simply erased everything. Roman floated in his cell, unaware of his bed, unaware of his body, unaware of anything except for the way Levi lapped at Roman with his tongue.

"Fuck," Roman gasped, delirious on the ecstasy.

The more Levi used his fingers, the more he poked his tongue deeper inside Roman, the more Roman craved to take this carnal satisfaction to the next stage.

"Stop." Roman barely had time to turn over before he noticed Levi scoot to the opposite end of the bed.

There was no friction in his expression, no frustration at being called off, or confusion on why they'd suddenly stopped. Levi didn't need clarification. Roman knew that

Levi only needed one thing from Roman: his comfort.

Roman's look of arousal did spark curiosity in Levi, body ready to move, but Roman could see Levi hold himself in check, awaiting consent.

"Get over here."

As Levi returned, prepared to continue eating Roman's ass, he found himself pushed back onto the bed and pinned by Roman. It was an adorable look of shock, which Roman savored as he quickly straddled Levi's hips, allowing the man to lube his dick before gently applying some more to Roman's hole.

"You're sure?" Levi's arms held Roman's waist.

"Yes," Roman growled, leaning forward and biting Levi's neck with a kiss and a pull and a hunger.

When Levi thrusted into Roman, he froze. It took a bit to get used to; it took a second to remember he wanted this; it took a few deep breaths to remind himself he was okay. But then Levi paused, and Roman kissed him again.

"Keep going."

And so Levi did, thrusting upward into Roman as he leaned back and gripped the underside of the top bunk. He closed his eyes and braced himself for each stroke Levi took. He focused on the pleasure he felt, on Levi's erratic and excited breathing, on how Levi gently caressed Roman's body with each stroke, on all the ways he'd reclaimed pieces of himself, and how he'd reclaim this piece too.

Roman pulled Levi closer to him, doing more of the work so Levi could sit up and leverage himself onto Roman. Levi wrapped his arms around Roman's body, softest of touches until Roman squeezed Levi's shoulders. Levi followed the unspoken instruction, the guidance, the permission to tighten his hold as he bucked upward. Roman muffled his shouts into Levi's mouth, kissing him with enough force to nearly knock the man onto his back again, but they clung to each other, bodies entwined and lips linked. Roman moved faster, throbbing.

"Fuck." Roman gripped Levi's broad shoulders, shoving him back onto the mattress and riding him.

It didn't take long for Levi to shudder, to try to slow down, to ask Roman to wait, but Roman wanted to feel Levi finish, wanted to achieve this with him, wanted to—

"Uhhhhh," Levi groaned before going still. "I'm sorry. I'm sorry. Sorry. Fuck, that was intense. Told you I needed to slow down. Damn. Fucking hell, I haven't cum in a while, and fucking A, your A is amazing."

Roman giggled, still hard as a rock and somehow so happy to see Levi happy.

"It's all good." Roman slid off him. "I did sort of surprise you with this. Spring it on you."

"You literally jumped on my dick." Levi laughed.

"Yeah." Roman stood and stroked himself a few times, reimagining what he'd just experienced with Levi, replaying Levi's expressions, rewinding the intimacy so he could properly time their shared climax. He wanted to cum with Levi, so at least he could imagine that much.

"What are you doing?" Levi broke his concentration. "Get that dick over here, boyfriend."

"Didn't realize we were on relationship terms."

"If I let a dude fuck my ass, he's definitely gotta be a boyfriend."

Roman paused, watching Levi lube himself.

"What?" Levi gave the most nonchalant shrug in the world.

"It's just…you've never…" Roman scrunched his face, knowing Levi's preferred position. "And I don't wanna make you do something you're uncomfortable with. I'm fine just jerking."

"I told you I haven't done more, not that I wasn't open to more," Levi corrected. "I've made it very clear that for the right person, I'm definitely open to be opened."

Roman chuckled. "Yeah, me too. Um, it's just I haven't done this. I mean, I've done this. I have fucked people. Women. Mostly. Um, men, too, but I wasn't the one doing the…yeah. But I have done anal. Like a few times. Um, I just, um…it's been a while. Like before prison, which is ironic, right?"

"Well, it's been sort of nonexistent for me...you know." Levi wiggled his eyebrows. "Wanna help change that?"

Roman had willed himself to stop craving such things. So much of his sexual desires had been lost and forgotten and surrendered in order to ensure he always pleased his partner.

"Let's give it a whirl." Levi tossed a lube packet at Roman.

"Yeah." Roman swallowed hard and approached the bed. "I'll go easy."

Roman steadied himself between Levi's spread legs, readying himself, and slowly moved closer until the head of his cock brushed up against the crack of Levi's hole.

"I trust you." Levi leaned forward as much as he could, waiting for Roman to fill the space.

Roman did. He leaned forward, pressing his head against Levi's and swallowing the sound of his moan as he thrust into him. Each push sent waves of euphoric pleasure through Roman's entire body. He couldn't remember ever feeling like this in his entire life. He wondered if this was what love felt like, what trust felt like, what happiness felt like. Real happiness. God, he couldn't fathom ever surrendering such a feeling.

Each time he slammed himself against Levi, he studied his friend's breathing, he listened to the sounds of Levi's grunts, he stroked Levi while he fucked him, hoping to get him off a second time.

"Whew, whew, whew." Levi breathed heavily, struggling to take in all of Roman, so he did his best to ease up.

It helped him last longer, but it didn't feel half as good as when he'd pushed all the way to the base inside Levi. Still, he focused on stroking Levi more, helping him find the pleasure of getting fucked, and limiting the pain to the best of his ability.

Roman wanted this to be a wonderful experience for Levi. He wanted his first time to be special, something Levi wouldn't be ashamed to think back on, even if it was just with Roman in a dirty cell, on a cheap bed.

"You know I love you, right?" Levi looked up at him like he could read Roman's mind, like there wasn't a thing in the world Roman could hide, and that Levi would accept him for anything and everything.

Roman thrusted hard, allowing Levi to steady his quickly rhythmic strokes with a well-placed hand. Levi held a hand at Roman's stomach, off to the side, and another pressed to

Roman's shoulder. It guided him, held his pace from overexerting inside Levi, and it allowed Roman to sink into Levi and let himself be consumed by the love Levi held for him.

"I love you, too." Roman kissed Levi, staring into his glossy eyes, his questioning eyes. "I mean it. You're the only person for me. You're my everything. You saved me more than I could ever explain."

Levi wrapped his hands at Roman's hips and pulled him in tight with so much force and pleasure he erupted. Roman groaned, lost and delirious as Levi swept him into passionate kisses, swallowing the sound of Roman's orgasm. He bucked a few times, unwilling to surrender the sensation of cumming in Levi. He collapsed atop Levi, both men sweaty and pleased and happy to have each other.

Roman hoped Levi would remember him when he got out. He hoped to relive this joy when released. He hoped more than anything to make a life for himself and Levi.

Roman had finally found his way back to himself and found someone to be himself with, and that made him wake up every day a little more excited than the last.

Epilogue

Levi Pierce had been released for two weeks now, and finding ways around his parole schedule turned into a grueling jigsaw puzzle of overly complicated bullshit. Thankfully, he had a nest egg of cash he'd set aside for the fees that came with freedom. Partial freedom. It'd be three years before he was truly free of oversight. It'd be seventeen months and two weeks until he was reunited with Roman. Really reunited. Not phone calls. Not glass panel visits. Not letters. No, he'd have to wait for what felt like an eternity before he could truly touch Roman again, before they could embrace, but it'd be worth it. He'd wait a million years for Roman.

On the walk to the hospital, Levi walked with a bit of a limp, an injury he still carried from when he had his ankle slashed. But he found himself ignoring the pain and lost in the bliss of being inside Roman, of having Roman inside him, of being united and together and in love. He never wanted those feelings to end. He'd worked so hard for so many years to bring it to fruition. But if he wanted to keep the happy ever after he'd carved out of blood and bone and the lives of cruel men unworthy of even breathing the same air as Roman, then he needed to handle one more loose end.

He checked in at the hospital, a bit surprised and disappointed no one asked to see his ID. He'd pissed nearly four hundred dollars on a solid forgery, ensuring no one knew he'd come to this hospital. He even wore sunglasses and a cap and the plainest muted colors to an outfit he'd never wear again. All the same, he suspected no one would care much about what he had planned, but that didn't mean he needed to get sloppy now.

Levi waltzed into Ezra Delgado's room on the fourth floor to a wing few staff checked and even fewer during shift changes Levi had studied. After Ezra's accident, his blood-soaked defeat at the hands of Roman restoring his honor, the state released Ezra and shipped him off to a hospital. Levi wasn't sure who footed the medical bill now, and he didn't care.

Ezra was a loose end Levi needed to tie. Few things frightened Levi Pierce, but the idea of losing Roman sent chills through his body. The things Ezra knew, the power he had at his fingertips. No, no, no. Levi couldn't allow that.

"I hope you can feel this," Levi said, running his hands over Ezra's unkempt beard. "I hope every day has been a prison of your own making."

Levi didn't believe in hope, finding it arbitrary and useless, but after so much time watching Roman from afar and waiting for just the right opportunity, he'd learned to lean into the concept. After all, he'd done a lot of hoping the day Ezra was shipped out of the Marlow Penitentiary infirmary.

He'd hoped Ezra wouldn't wake up.

He'd hoped Roman wouldn't learn the truth.

He'd hoped he could make Ezra and the only thread of knowledge to his plan disappear.

It was a cruel idea, one conceived too quickly, and one Levi now realized carried more variables than even he could calculate. But at the time, when Ezra first stepped into their lives, it seemed like the most fortuitous of events.

Levi had wanted and loved Roman since the day he met him. Not in prison. Not in the shabby halls of Marlow. No, no, no. Levi had seen Roman in the streets of the downtown mayhem, bloody and enraged. He beat a man to a pulp and glittered so pretty that Levi found his breath had hitched. When Roman shoved his friend into traffic, when he resumed beating a man half to death like nothing had happened, when he fought officers and nearly got himself killed in the process, Levi knew he'd finally understood what love was.

He had to know Roman, had to have Roman, so he learned everything there was, starting with the trial and everyone involved. That was when he first learned about Ezra, though he didn't play that hand for quite some time.

No, Levi thought it'd be enough to get himself locked up in Marlow Penitentiary too, blame it on drugs which he could just miraculously get over his addiction for while he moved in close to Roman. It hadn't been enough to cement the bond Levi wanted, the bond Levi needed. They were friends but never anything more. And Levi needed more. So much more.

He needed all of Roman, but while Roman stood tall as champion, that would never happen.

Levi turned off the machines and thought back to Ezra's arrival, about the letters he'd sent about Ezra's little girlfriend never truly getting justice, about how he couldn't do a thing about it. Ezra was an easy mind to sway. Those who knew they were smart, who believed themselves the smartest, often were the easiest to exploit.

Ezra came with a plan to kill, and it didn't take much for Levi to twist that desire into one of revenge, truly life-destroying vengeance. It was easy to play on Ezra's emotions, knowing his motives from a trial he tried to hide his presence at—always sitting in the back and out of sight, much like Levi did before Roman finally took a shitty plea deal when he could've done so much better with the right counsel.

It was harder to twist Roman's motivations at the beginning. So much of the plan hinged on Roman caring for Levi; it took finesse, delicate conversation, and planting the seeds of the bet. Levi knew he'd made the right decision, even if difficult to bear at times. When Roman allowed himself to be dragged to The Pit instead of fulfilling his deal, it nearly destroyed Levi. It took time and convincing, but he managed to make Ezra realize a quiet death in the dark wouldn't be nearly as satisfying, but the time there would likely have made Roman more malleable.

Levi had acquired a drug, something to help slow down Ezra's heart, something similar to the drug he spiked Roman's drink with the night of his rematch. It nearly killed Levi to watch Roman fall. To watch them burn his wings and let him crash and break to pieces, but Levi knew more than anything he could restore Roman.

He'd planned every step of breaking Roman in just the right ways, ways that would bond them, ways that would tie them together, ways that would allow Levi to slip pieces of himself into the mended cracks of Roman's repaired psyche. This was the only way they could be together, truly together, mended as one heart. Roman had everything Levi wanted, desired, deserved, and Levi knew he could and would be everything Roman wanted. He'd changed himself a hundred different ways to fit Roman's tastes. He would change himself a thousand more to be the man Roman required.

But he hadn't accounted for all of Ezra's malicious intentions. Yes, Levi knew and encouraged their dark romance. Ezra's malcontent obsession with warping Roman's comprehension of what a friend really was all so he could play on the irony of how Roman killed a friend. The drivel still made Levi roll his eyes. Levi had plans to fix that, to wash away Ezra's nonsense, and his time behind bars had done just that once they got transferred.

Roman never came to terms with his sexuality, and Levi suspected this would be the messy push Roman required. He'd offered himself a dozen different ways to Roman with no avail, so clearly, Roman needed a firm hand when it came to such things, someone to break him in and show him how much he could enjoy the company of another man. But then Ezra involved Jake Finnegan. The deal he'd made still disgusted Levi, making him sick to his stomach. The idea that Ezra would condone it, encourage it, manipulate something so depraved.

Somehow, Levi had dropped the drugs and found himself choking the life out of the comatose Ezra.

"I wish you could feel this." Levi let out every bitter note of hatred buried deep inside him, hatred he'd learned to keep behind a perfectly trained mask since his fourth foster home. By his fifth, he'd learned never to let loose ends live long.

Levi released his grip on Ezra and reminded himself that, ultimately, the plan worked out accordingly. Roman was a little worse for wear, but Levi had all the time in the world to heal him, help him, hold him.

"Bet you were shocked someone slashed my ankle," Levi said, wishing he could actually have the conversation he so craved with Ezra. He wanted to let that fool know he was never the puppet master he deluded himself into believing he was. He was nothing more than an easily hooked fish on a string for Levi to toy with.

Still, the limp in his walk reminded him of the errors in reckless plans. He needed to be dropped by wicked means during his fight with Ezra, though. A tactic that Ezra expectantly took full advantage of by punching him again and again, leaving him bloody and broken.

Roman needed the right motivation to step back into the role of champion, to find his voice and power again. Levi knew if he arranged for dirty tactics, Roman would have to sweep in and save him. At least Levi hoped Roman would; he hoped Roman loved him that much, and he hoped he could make Roman's life a beautiful and peaceful forever now that they'd cemented their bond.

As much as Levi wanted to drag this out, as much as he wanted Ezra to feel the crushing defeat the same way he made Jake Finnegan and Warden Sadler feel their deaths, feel what it was like to hurt what Levi loved, he knew it was a futile endeavor. Ezra wouldn't wake up, and Levi came here to ensure he never would.

"But I've got so much time to kill until Roman's release," Levi said, grabbing a pillow from behind Ezra's head. "And you've got family I could kill as recompense, so I think the scales will even themselves out eventually."

Levi smothered Ezra and left the hospital, knowing no one lived with knowledge of what he'd done to bring Roman a little closer to him.

For the next several months, Levi did everything he could to build the life Roman dreamed about. He wanted his first day back on the outside to be perfect. He wanted their lives to be perfect. They would be. Levi would see to it.

Roman walked out with a bag slung over his shoulder, and his beautiful brown eyes bulged at the sight of Levi's car. He tugged at his ruffled brown hair, nearly undoing the effort he'd put into making it roll-out-of-bed perfect, something Levi suspected was for his benefit. But alas, the bright yellow Porsche Cayman had Roman captivated. Levi had only gotten it because he knew Roman loved this make and model. He had actually gotten two and planned on surprising Roman with the blue one soon. It matched Levi's eyes, and he knew Roman would love that.

Levi had never cared about opulent wealth or bragging for the sake of feeling significant. But he did like the opportunity money afforded him. If he didn't have money, he couldn't give Roman the life he deserved. If he didn't have the funds to bankroll his life after his release, then things wouldn't have gone according to Levi's plan.

"Damn, this is a nice ride," Roman said, eyeing the vehicle from outside for a full three minutes. "How are you so loaded?"

"Bank robberies."

Roman made a face, the face he always made when part of him itched to know if it was true, hopeful and excited, and the other part said it was wrong to feel such things. That was why Levi loved Roman. He never shied from the darkness, he stepped into it and wondered where it led, but he understood that wasn't the right reaction. It took Levi many years of diligent training to pretend to understand that fact.

"IT start-up firm with way too much money and not enough brains between their benefactors," Levi finally answered so Roman could have a bit of ease in the funds.

Levi had always liked technology. It made finding and removing people and problems so much easier. Plus, corporations paid big bucks to folks willing to skirt the rules and keep up with competitors. No one cared Levi was a felon; it practically gave him a certificate for under-the-table cash jobs.

"Wow." Roman slid inside. "There is no way I'm going to find a job anywhere near this level of…I don't even know."

"You never know," Levi said with a shrug, waiting for the right time to fan the flames of Roman's dreams.

"Hey, wait." Roman pointed at Levi, eyes wide and filled with realization. "Where are your glasses?"

"Lasik." Levi shrugged, downplaying the tiny spike of nervousness that gave him. "That firm has awesome insurance and don't require weddings to add dependents."

"Damn, there goes my excuse to propose and become a trophy wife." Roman grinned, goofy and carefree, letting the wind ruffle his shaggy brown hair. "Also, digging the stubble, dude."

Levi rubbed his chin and smirked. It was a long-term plan, something Levi still wanted time to ponder, but he hoped to share his true self completely unmasked one day, but only safely. He never wanted to scare or hurt or upset Roman. Not after everything Roman had survived. Levi would unravel facets of himself layer by layer and test the reactions.

The glasses were a tool he used to appear meek and in need of a strong friend. It helped cement Roman's hero complex. The clean shaved look made Levi appear younger, softer, weaker, and he used that to catapult Roman's alpha side. It worked on a protective notion, but not when it came to getting Roman to fuck him. That took so much more work than Levi anticipated.

The drive was quiet, and Levi appreciated how Roman could be content with silence. He never had to fill the void with hollow words like he did with everyone else. He could be himself around Roman, even if only a few layers at a time. Roman had seen his soul bared raw, seen the lengths Levi would go to remove Roman's enemies, and Roman hadn't flinched. He hadn't approved or disapproved, merely accepted Levi. That was enough. It would be enough because Levi had made it so.

When they pulled into the driveway, Roman stood awestruck at the sight of Levi's house. Modern and sleek and far enough from neighbors that no one could complain about wealthy felons and blah, blah, blah. Levi didn't need nosy neighbors upsetting Roman. It'd taken time and patience for Levi to remember he couldn't deal with all the people who upset Roman. It wasn't healthy for either of them. Roman needed to be strong, strong like he was when Levi first spotted Roman. Only now, that strength made room for Levi and allowed him inside.

They stepped through the front doors, and before Levi could start the massive tour to a house that overwhelmed Roman in all the best ways, a pair of Pitbulls ran up, wagging their tails and sniffing Roman. He fell to his knees in love the instant he saw them, and they gushed over Roman's arrival, licking and kissing the most perfect man in the world.

Levi liked dogs. They were easy to condition like people. Trusting with the proper incentive. Levi slipped a treat into their mouths as he went to pet them and hold them and show Roman how much he cared for animals, too.

"They're rescues," Levi said. "This is RJ, and this is LJ."

Roman fell into Levi at the names, letting Roman Junior and Levi Junior swarm him with kisses. Levi nearly collapsed himself when Roman crashed into him, forgetting how much he craved the gentle embrace, the perfect touch.

"You know, I actually got some interesting info from the rescue," Levi said, wrapping an arm around Roman and testing how he handled the physical contact.

Roman didn't recoil or shy away, and so Levi let his arm stay.

"Oh, yeah?"

"Yeah," Levi continued. "Might've even asked their hiring policies, volunteer policies, how they felt about particular citizens with particular situations and particular state records."

Roman stopped petting the dogs and awaited Levi's answer. Levi could see the desperation in Roman's eyes, the hunger for an answer. He'd daydreamed about opening a rescue shelter for animals one day, dreamed about fixing them and teaching them the world wasn't so bad. Roman wanted them to feel love again, to understand it. He wanted animals to know not every hand that reached out meant harm. He spent so much free time reading about studies and statistics and state policies. It'd been something he talked about for hours during their time at Kleinfield Prison Complex.

"You might have an interview that you'll definitely need to tell your PO about," Levi finally answered, basking in the smile Roman gave him.

A smile so bright Levi almost worried he'd never see it again, worried he'd taken too much sunlight out of Roman's spirit. But he hadn't. He'd changed Roman just enough so they could be perfect together.

Roman moved in closer, letting the full weight of his body rest on Levi. It was an act of trust—one Levi would live up to. Roman kissed Levi. His lips, his chin, his cheeks, his nose, his neck, his everything. Levi was in heaven. For a man who felt like he'd crawled out of Hell itself, he never knew how good paradise could feel until he met Roman.

Levi would do anything to keep this feeling, to keep Roman. Anything.

THE END

Acknowledgements

WOW! That ending, right? Between Ezra and Levi, it's no wonder Roman had such a difficult journey. I'd like to thank you with my whole heart for giving this story a chance and reaching the end. It means a lot that you chose to explore Roman's world and my words. If you wouldn't mind leaving an honest rating and/or review of your thoughts that'd make a huge difference in visibility for this story. Word of mouth remains one of the greatest assets in helping new readers find a book.

I was very anxious about this dark romance, so I ended up sending it to quite a few early readers just to gauge their thoughts. Some of the readers offered helpful critiques to strengthen the story, some just helped offer encouragement, and some helped me understand that while this story is dark it is still something worth sharing. It was actually nice sending it out to a few early readers outside of the standard beta feedback because it really allowed me to see Roman's story through the lens of avid readers. It was exactly what I needed to move forward with this story. Every detailed note and random musing gave me the confidence to put this book out into the world.

I'd really like to thank Josiah Haller, Brent Perrotti, Sofia, Elizabeth Summers, S, Jarrod Murrell, Breanna, and Love Romero for taking the time to read the early draft.

There's so much about this book that I enjoyed. From Roman's anger and impulsiveness to Levi's sweet smile and charm. I even enjoyed Ezra's snark and quick wit. Ezra was never intended to be enjoyed. He was meant to be villainous and unredeemable, but if you found yourself enthralled by his devious nature during the first half of the story, you're not the only one. Apparently, those green eyes also worked as green flags because folks seemed to really ignore the red flags he was showing.

Levi's character was obviously one of my favorites and I loved writing the epilogue through his perspective revealing everything he worked to push together. Part of me has considered continuing this journey, writing a part two and making it a duology, where we'd follow Levi's POV. Another part of me wants to let the story rest. If I picked up and continued, I know there'd be some threads I'd have to tie up and part of me wants to leave that to the reader.

You get to decide, do Roman and Levi live happily ever after with Roman in ignorant bliss or does he find out what Levi orchestrated? If I write a book two, I know where I want the story to go and where I know the story needs to go.

Hmmm. Maybe one day we'll get Levi's side. You let me know how you feel about it.

Thank you again for picking up my book and for reading to the very end—even my little rambles. If you're curious about my other work, check my author bio below and find me.

Author's Bio

MN Bennet is a high school teacher, writer, and reader. He lives in the Midwest, still adjusting to the cold after being born and raised in the South.

He enjoys writing paranormal and fantasy stories with huge worlds (sometimes too big), loveable romances (with so much angst and banter), and Happily Ever Afters (once he's dragged his characters through some emotional turmoil).

When he's not balancing classes, writing, or reading, he can be found binge watching anime or replaying Dragon Age II for the millionth time.

Author website:

https://www.mnbennet.com

Amazon page:

https://www.amazon.com/stores/MN-Bennet/author/B0BLJJK5NF

Goodreads page:

https://www.goodreads.com/author/show/23017668.M_N_B ennet

Patreon: patreon.com/MNBennet

Newsletter:

https://mailchi.mp/e2ee2caea89a/newsletter-sign-up

Find All My Stuff: https://linktr.ee/mnbennet